Daisy
and
the
Duke

ALSO BY ELIZABETH COLE

Honor & Roses

Choose the Sky

Raven's Rise

Peregrine's Call

A Heartless Design

A Reckless Soul

A Shameless Angel

The Lady Dauntless

Beneath Sleepless Stars

A Mad and Mindless Night

A Most Relentless Gentleman

Breathless in the Dark

Daisy and the Duke

ELIZABETH COLE

SkySpark Books

Philadelphia, Pennsylvania

SkySpark Books
Philadelphia, Pennsylvania
skysparkbooks.com
inquiry@skysparkbooks.com

Publisher's Note: This is a work of fiction. Names, characters,
places, and incidents are a product of the author's imagination.
Locales and public names are sometimes used for atmospheric
purposes. Any resemblance to actual people, living or dead, or to
businesses, companies, events, institutions, or locales is completely coincidental.

Ordering Information:
Quantity sales. Special discounts are available on quantity pur-
chases by corporations, associations, and others. For details,
contact the "Special Sales Department" at the address above.

DAISY AND THE DUKE / Cole, Elizabeth. – 1st ed.
ISBN-13: 978-1-942316-47-3

Prologue

❀✿❀

"…FIVE, FOUR, THREE, TWO, ONE. Ready or not, here I come!"

While counting down, Mrs. Bloomfield could hear the giggling. The five girls in her care were hiding in the garden, though *hiding* implied a sense of discretion that none of them mastered at this point, as shown by the stifled laughter and the shuffling sounds of dainty feet.

Nevertheless, she kept up the pretense of searching. "Now where could those girls have gone?" she asked loudly.

More giggling. Mrs. Bloomfield smiled and deliberately wandered away from the nearest source of the sound, allowing whoever it was to enjoy the deliciousness of pulling the wool over a grown-up's eyes for a few moments longer.

The rosebush sneezed, and then shook. *Oh, goodness,* Mrs. Bloomfield thought. *That will be Daisy*. The girl ought not to hide in the plants. She suffered terribly in the autumn, her little nose red for three weeks as she went through a dozen handkerchiefs a day. But she wanted so badly to become invisible!

Mrs. Bloomfield understood children very well, despite not having any of her own. Her marriage had been a happy one, but also very short. She'd lost her husband before they could have a child together, and she had never remarried. But she had children aplenty all around her now, for she was the owner and headmistress of the Bloomfield Academy for Young Ladies of Quality at Wildwood Hall, a boarding school that educated the daughters of the gentry.

Sometimes, that education included a healthy game of hide and seek.

"Is that Poppy's gown I spy by the willow tree?" she asked out loud, and was rewarded by a high-pitched shriek as one of the girls dashed away, the willow boughs rustling in her wake.

Mrs. Bloomfield gave chase, and soon captured a bright-eyed girl in a blue dress.

"Poppy! I've got you and I deputize you to help me find the others."

"Yes, ma'am!" Poppy cried, cheerfully switching her allegiance. "Let's go! I know where Rosalind hid in the herb garden, right behind the fountain wall…."

Poppy was undoubtably the boldest of the bunch of Mrs. Bloomfield's current crop of girls. Together they found Rosalind crouching behind the stone fountain, her head tipped to hear any approaching sound, even her friend's light footfalls.

"Oh, Poppy," Rose cried in dismay. "I know it's you. I won't ask you to help hide me if you're going to betray me like that!" Since Rosalind was blind, she relied on her cousin Poppy every day of her life. In addition to being family, the two girls were the best of friends. They giggled together as Poppy took her in her arms.

"I wanted to find you first so you can have the fun of finding the rest with us!" Poppy cried. She always had an answer at the tip of her tongue. Then she twined Rose's hand in her own, ready to guide her cousin safely, as she always did.

Next, Mrs. Bloomfield went with her girls to seek out Camellia, who was dark-haired and slender and already showing the pretty pout in her lips that heralded a personality to reckon with.

"Lia, Lia," Rose cried. "You smell like you *bathed* in lavender!"

"Well, I was hiding in it for half an hour!" the other replied, emerging from the impressive bank of lavender, growing rampant at the edge of the gardens. "That's as good as taking a bath. Who's left to find? Let's get Heather, before she leaves the parish."

But rather than running, the fourth girl, Heather, had hidden herself up a tree. She was half-wild and fearless when it came to such things. But upon discovery, she came down willingly and with a broad smile.

"I let you find me," she declared. "I kept plucking off the ash leaves and flinging them down when someone walked under. Honestly, I could have slept up there all night if I waited for you lot to notice me!"

"Now where is Daisy?" Camellia asked, looking around thoughtfully.

Mrs. Bloomfield knew, but she allowed the girls to search out potential hiding places. It was her belief as a schoolmistress that young people must be allowed to puzzle things out on their own, rather than having answers handed to them.

"Daisy!" Heather called out, far more loudly than appropriate for a well-bred daughter of the gentry. "Daisy! Oh, Lady Mar-gar-et!" She howled Daisy's title and full Christian name, which Daisy never used since she disliked it so much. But as the only child of a baron, she would be a baroness in her time, and she'd have to get used to the title as well.

Following Heather's call, they all held silent for a moment.

Another faint sneeze emanated from the rosebush.

Mrs. Bloomfield took pity. *Better to get the girl out now*, she thought, *or she'll be sneezing all night.* "Let's check the roses," she declared.

And among the pink blossoms, there was the golden-blonde head of her smallest charge.

"I was the best at hiding, ma'am!" Daisy said in wonder. "Everyone else was found before me."

"Clever girl," Mrs. Bloomfield replied, not mentioning the sneezes. "Now, it is getting to be time for tea, I think. Shall we all go in?"

"Yes, Mrs. Bloomfield!" five young voices chorused back.

They all walked back toward the school, which was housed in a gorgeous old manor called Wildwood Hall. It had been owned by her late husband, and the two had started the school together, wanting to provide a warm and happy place for the often forgotten girls of families who thought far more about their boys…until it came time to marry the daughters off. At Wildwood, the girls had no such worries, at least not for many years to come. They could simply be girls.

Following her husband's early death, she kept up the school, which he'd left to her in its entirely—an unusual decision for the time, but then, she wouldn't have married a man who didn't share her views.

Behind the gardens, the red brick of Wildwood Hall glowed deep and rosy in the afternoon light. The glass panes in the many windows glimmered, reflecting the sunlight back into the garden, beams landing on the sweet-smelling roses and bright chrysanthemums and the endless shades of green of the herbs.

What a paradise, Mrs. Bloomfield thought. *These girls will soon enter a world that is not always so beautiful or protected. I must prepare them well.*

Chapter 1

❧ ⁊ℰℴ❧

TEN YEARS LATER

Tristan could not remember a time that he had not been in pain. There had been such a time—he knew it had to be so, since his injuries dated back less than two years. But it felt as if that were another life, as if that were another man, someone who moved through the world without care.

Now everyone stared at him, and he could barely take a step without someone jumping to attention. Partly it was the injuries. The worst of the scarring and the brokenness of his body was covered by clothing, thank God. But his face couldn't be hidden. The deep, puckered, ragged line was always going to be there, running from his temple down to his neck, a memento of the battle that nearly killed him.

The person who had manufactured the shell should be pleased. He'd hurt Tristan far more than any measly bullet to the head ever could.

The scar pulled at his whole face, offering the world a perpetual squint and scowl no matter what he was really thinking. And now people seemed to care very much what he was thinking, because another unexpected result of the war was that a few other men died too—a random but very important chain of deaths—leaving Tristan an inheritance he'd never dreamed of, and frankly didn't want.

Maybe Jack could get him out of it. If Jack didn't die first.

Tristan looked over at the man riding opposite him in the carriage. He'd seen corpses in better shape. And in a way, it was all Tris's fault, because Jack had fallen ill after taking charge of Tristan when he returned to London. Just when Tristan started to need fewer doctors, Jack suddenly needed more.

"Should I have the coach pull off the road for a while?" he asked, preparing to knock on the wall nearest the coachman.

"No, no, no. Honestly, Tris, you're worse than a mother hen. I'm getting better," Jackson Kemble said, though his words were immediately followed by a hollow cough.

Tristan seized on this event, handing his best friend a clean cotton square before uncapping a flask. "Travel is not helping. Drink this."

"You want me to die drunk?" Jack retorted, nevertheless taking the flask and sipping from it. He took a few breaths that seemed to come easier. "Well, it may actually help."

"I hope that a good long stay in the country will help more. I've sent word ahead for the staff to have everything ready, and I contacted a doctor in the nearest village."

"Most grateful, your grace."

"Oh, shut up." Even after a year, Tristan was still not used to being addressed as *your grace*. His elevation to duke was damned inconvenient, in fact. Tristan was content with a soldier's life, and wanted nothing to do with whatever it was lords did all day—hunting, he supposed.

Or visiting other lords and ladies, seeing who could bore the other to death first.

Tristan had liked the life of a soldier…until the day Death nearly found him. The enemy launched shell after shell. Most landed far short of the tent where the officers gathered to gauge the battle's progress, but the risk was real. It was afternoon, the sun beating down, when Tristan sensed *something* plunging from the sky. He didn't remember much of what happened. But when he came to, he was virtually deaf in his right ear, his head hurt like hell, and he couldn't feel his right side. He was told he'd saved lives—and more importantly, superior lives, those of officers happy to still be breathing and happier still to tell stories of English bravery to those back home. Tristan was pinned with medals, offered commendations, and toasted at parties. He was a hero.

He hated being a hero. Being a lord, of course, made it even worse. He was expected to be gracious and speak proud words about how British victory was inevitable and the enemy should just admit defeat.

Tristan knew it was all lies. He wasn't a hero. He was lucky. He was lucky that he looked up at just that moment. He was lucky there was a line of sandbags to his right when he hit the ground, turning certain death into mere disfigurement and constant pain. How *lucky*.

"Stop doing that," Jack told him.

"Doing what?"

"Brooding."

"I'm not brooding."

"Yes, you are. And what's more, you're brooding so loudly that it's distracting me from any thinking I might do on my own."

"All right, no more brooding. I shall think on…" Tris stopped, because he couldn't think of anything happy or pleasant.

"Try thinking of women," Jack advised. "I find that helps."

"Women won't look at me."

"Ha." Jack wheezed out the laugh. "You're an idiot. Women love a tortured hero. They'll be flinging themselves at your feet."

"God, I hope not. And anyway, I'm sure that any flinging will be solely the result of wanting to land a duke. I swear, Jack, I should have changed my name in the field hospital and let Tristan Brooks be dead, like all my relatives."

"Brooding again," Jack warned. Then he straightened up in the seat. "I say, I think we may be getting close. Those gateposts have lions on them."

Tris twisted in his seat and caught sight of a large stone lion perched on top of a brick pedestal the size of a horse cart. Iron fencing met it and stretched into the distance. He saw a mirror image out the other window of the carriage.

"We must be here," he said, suddenly nervous. Tristan had heard of Lyondale, the ancestral seat of the Dukes of Lyon, but he had no idea what the estate actually looked like. Pastures and woods and distant hills swept past him, and then he heard Jack sigh in relief.

"That's the house," Jack said, pointing.

The carriage followed the curve of the drive as it passed by a pond, and suddenly Tristan could see his new home.

It was unimaginable. The size of the house was massive, larger than some palaces. Rows upon rows of windows glittered in the sun, and the white stone walls practically glowed.

"Sweet Christ," he muttered.

Jack was impressed. "You may want to think twice about giving this up, Tris. As duke, you could do a lot of good with the influence you'll have."

"What influence? I'm an imposter. I fell into this title by sheer bad luck."

"Luck is what you make it. Practicing law taught me that."

Just then, the carriage came to a halt, pulling up smoothly at the very center of the wide stone steps. An army of servants stood in lines outside, ready for inspection.

Tristan stepped out of the carriage, hiding the arcs of pain through his body after sitting in cramped quarters for so long.

A man stepped up to him and bowed. "Welcome home, your grace. I am Mr. Wynston, majordomo of Lyondale."

Tristan nodded, then looked over the sea of eyes, the many black-and-white-clad servants who were all staring at him without seeming to do so. He was at a loss for what to do next, and briefly considered heading back to the carriage and fleeing to London.

A woman stepped forward. By her outfit and her manner, she was no servant. Her hair was bound up simply and her features were pleasant, though her whole attitude was faded, as if she'd been left in a closet and long forgotten. She curtseyed to Tristan. "Your grace, I am Miss Wallis. We corresponded these past months, and I have worked to ensure that everything you need is ready for your arrival."

"Miss Wallis," he said politely. She was related to him in some distant, tangled fashion. All he knew for certain was that she'd been living at Lyondale at the behest of the old duke. "How good to meet you at last."

"You and your guest must be quite fatigued, your grace," the majordomo said smoothly. "Allow me to show you to your rooms. A tour of the house can wait until you are fed and rested."

Tristan nodded. "The first order of business must be to get Mr. Kemble to his bed. Don't fight me on this, Jack," he warned in a lower voice. "You look like you've got one foot already in."

Jack nodded in silent agreement, which was the most alarming thing he could have done.

Everything moved quickly from there. Tristan was swept along on a tide of servitude. Footmen carried bags, maids hurried ahead to open windows and doors. Jack was suddenly supported on both sides by two hulking footmen, helping him to walk.

As they all advanced into the house, the majordomo kept up a running commentary, explaining where such and such room was, and how so-and-so in the portrait was the second duke, and when this and that piece of furniture was brought back from a Roman ruin.

Tris didn't register a word of it. He cared only that his friend could be made comfortable as soon as possible.

"I sent word ahead that a doctor— " Tris began to say.

"He's here, your grace," the majordomo assured him. "Dr. Stelton, the best in the county. Edinburgh man." That fact eased Tristan's mind. As he had cause to know from his lengthy recovery, Edinburgh was renowned for its medical schools.

Dr. Stelton was actually in the room where Jack would stay, and he proved to be a large, confident, genial bear of a figure.

"Ah, patient's here at last," he boomed out. "Excellent! Let's get the poor creature to bed so I can take a proper look. With your pardon, your grace, I'll get to work now."

Tristan nodded, pleased that the doctor didn't waste time on small talk.

"See you soon…your grace," Jack said in farewell, as the footmen worked to follow the doctor's orders.

The tour was not over. Tris was taken along yet more corridors to a set of double doors at the end of a hall. Two more footmen rushed ahead to open them. Just how many people did he employ?

Beyond the doors, he saw the ducal suite: a massive chain of rooms, far larger than the entire house that Tristan had lived in during his early life.

He stared at the four-poster bed, each corner pillar looking as sturdy as an oak tree. Quite probably six people could sleep comfortably in it. Tristan had no plans to test that theory, though.

"What the hell am I supposed to do with all this space?" he muttered.

"Did you say something, sir?" one of the footmen asked, leaning in. It would never do to ignore a duke.

Tristan thought fast, saying, "I said I want to speak to the doctor when he's done. Show me to a more suitable room where I can wait. I don't like to be in a bedchamber during the day." He'd lain in a bed for almost a year—he was sick of it.

Again through the halls. Again down the wide marble steps of the main staircase, into a blessedly normal-sized place filled with shelves and books.

"This room was used most by the late duchess, sir," the footman explained. "The small study, we call it. I'll inform the doctor of your location."

Tristan paced in the library, waiting for the doctor to finish his examination.

At long last, Stelton entered. "Sorry to keep you waiting, your grace. Your friend is sleeping now, thanks to a bit of laudanum. The travel was difficult for him."

"It's not consumption, is it?" Tris asked abruptly.

"No, no fear of that. No sign of blood in the lungs, which would be the death knell. His illness is serious, but not fatal. However, he'll need to take things very carefully if he hopes to recover. No strenuous activity, no distressing conversations, nothing to worry him at all."

"How long will he need to rest like this?"

"Weeks," Stelton said bluntly. "Could be months. The slightest strain could set him back, so see that he's coddled like a baby."

"He'll hate that," Tristan muttered.

"Better a warm blanket than a cold grave. I'll stop by daily to check up on him." Stelton added, "And you, sir? How do you fare?" He gestured to Tristan's scarred face.

"Well enough," Tris said. "After all, I was wounded nearly two years ago."

"But you still feel the pains," Stelton guessed. "Nasty business, this modern warfare. I've seen men come back —" He stopped, his expression haunted. He shook himself and said, in an overly hearty tone, "Anyway, let me know if you require anything for yourself. I'll be back tomorrow."

Then he left and once again, Tristan was alone, with little to do but brood.

A familiar feeling of being suffocated crept up again. He had to get out of doors. After going to his bedchamber once more, startling the maids who were unpacking, he changed his outfit and said to the nearest footman in his line of sight, "Show me to the stables."

"This way, sir!" The young man, still a boy, really, led Tristan through the byzantine hallways and finally outside. Tristan could smell the stables now, the comforting aroma of hay and horse and manure. That smell never changed, whether it was the army or a duke's estate.

"My horse, Stormer, is here, yes?"

"Arrived last week, your grace. He'll be wanting to gallop through new fields, I'll warrant. Good to have the stable filling up again. The old duke hadn't rode for years."

The stableboy dashed away to saddle Stormer and lead him out, which he did with obvious reverence. Quite possibly Stormer was the finest and most expensive creature the boy had ever seen.

"I'll return by dark," Tristan said, mounting up.

Tristan wore his usual riding gear, which was more suited to a hostler than a duke. For him, riding wasn't a social activity. It was solitary meditation. He didn't care how he looked.

He was glad to be riding out on his own. While recovering from his wounds, Tristan had discovered that riding was one of the few activities that didn't cause him pain, so he rode as often as he could. Stormer was the one indulgence Tristan granted himself upon receiving his inheritance. He loved horses, but the idea of owning one as fine as Stormer was an impossibility for most of his life.

And he had to admit, the estate of Lyondale was perfect for riding. Almost reason enough to keep the title...

As Tristan rode over the estate, he was doubly glad he wasn't in company, because the state of the place was beginning to make him angry. Farmhouses looked in need of repair, and many fields were untended. Tristan wasn't a farmer, but he knew there was no chance that all these fields could be lying fallow intentionally. What could be hindering the tenants from tilling them?

When he happened to see a few men working, he rode over and introduced himself. It took a while for him, as

Lord Lyon, to get a real answer out of the nervous farm-ers, but at last a picture emerged. The rents were high enough so only land absolutely certain to yield enough crops was tilled. Farmers were afraid to risk buying more seed than they might be able to harvest, and they lacked more modern techniques to speed up work, though at least these men were keenly interested in acquiring good equipment.

Leaving the farmed land, Tris rode miles farther on, crossing through meadows and forests. He was impressed by the natural beauty of this part of the country, where'd he never been before. Then, in a thick stand of old oak trees, he stopped short, pulling Stormer up as he caught sight of an unknown house tucked in the middle of the woods.

"This wasn't on the map," he muttered.

The place was strange. It looked much like the old Tudor-style manors, but shrunk down to almost nothing. He'd be surprised if the cottage could accommodate more than three people. The walls had once been plastered white, but now were cracked and sagging.

But why was it here at all, so far from any other estate or village? As Tristan rode closer, he was puzzled to see that the house was also surrounded by a lush and obvious-ly well-cared for garden that seemed at odds with the de-teriorating structure. Someone had to be tending it. Gar-dens simply didn't last without constant attention—weeds and wild animals soon took over. So what was this place, and who could possibly live there?

"Good day, young man," a voice called.

Tristan startled, causing Stormer to shift a few steps, neighing in concern.

An old woman emerged from the woods, bearing a brace of rabbits. For someone who'd obviously been poaching, she looked quite calm about it. But then, the old lady probably didn't know who Tristan was.

"Good day," he returned. "I didn't expect a house here."

"Been here longer than you've been on this earth, my boy," the woman replied with a chuckle. "Come down and have a drink."

Tristan dismounted before he thought twice. Stepping though the verdant garden, he was assailed by a wave of green scent. Flowers and herbs he couldn't name surrounded him, intoxicating in their aggressive beauty.

In the stories, witches live in the woods, Tristan thought.

"Hang those up on the branch," the old woman instructed him, handing him the brace of rabbits. "I'll cook them tonight. Stew for a week!" She sounded delighted.

She disappeared into the darkness of the cottage, leaving Tristan in the garden. He noticed a log placed on end, and sat on it. His right leg was tingling, so he stretched it out carefully, kneading his calf.

The woman emerged again, bearing a tin tankard. She handed it to him, saying, "Drink up, for who knows when you can drink ale again?"

It was remarkably close to what the soldiers used to say to each other, and Tristan took a long pull of the ale, which was cool and hoppy and faintly fizzy.

"Thank you," he said, wiping his mouth. "But you must have to haul this a long way. I can't drink all your ale."

"Bless you, I brew it myself. No distance at all."

"You live out here all alone?"

"Oh, I've plenty of company when I wish it," she said with a wink. "Folk do happen by."

"Do you fear that thieves or ruffians might harass

you?" Tristan thought it very odd for an old woman to live in such a solitary way.

"They'd never find this place," she said. "Only such folk I want to see me can see me."

That answer made no sense, but Tristan didn't argue. He took another sip of ale. It was excellent.

She gazed to the west, where the trees had been lit up like stained glass. "Ah, look at the slant of the sun. Time for you to be moving on. Don't want to be late."

"Late for what?"

She ignored his inquiry. "When you ride out, young man, you'll follow the track until you encounter a stream running west. There's a tree that divides the flow into two. You must take the left turning. Understand?"

"Certainly. But where does the right turn lead?"

She brushed his question away impatiently. "That is for another day. Go left! And don't dawdle!"

"Yes, ma'am." He was amused by the old woman, and didn't want to spoil the encounter by mentioning his title, which would no doubt make her curtsey and apologize for being so familiar.

Tristan mounted Stormer once more. The horse stepped merrily, evidently rejuvenated after the meal of green grass in the clearing. Tris was feeling surprisingly refreshed himself. Maybe he could persuade the old woman to brew ale for Lyondale.

But not today! She had practically pushed him out of the yard, telling him once again to mind the sun. *It's nowhere near dark*, he wanted to protest. Instead he bid her goodbye and rode on. After a while, he saw the fork she was so obsessed with.

"Turn left," he muttered, seeing the huge tree that split the water into two separate, tumbling brooks.

He glanced down the righthand path, feeling a bit contrary. Who was that old woman to tell him where to ride?

But then he heard something, and paused. Singing? The sound was faint and far away, but something about it was enchanting. And it came from the direction of the left-hand path.

So that is where he rode.

Chapter 2

❀ ✿❁✿ ❀

AT ABOUT THE SAME TIME that Tristan and Jack were pulling up to the steps of Lyondale, another scene was unfolding not far away.

Rutherford Grange had been the home of the barons of Rutherford for centuries, so entwined with the family that locals often skipped the full name of the place and referred to it simply as "the Grange." The land behind the great house was forested, and the green trees were just beginning to blush with color as the summer closed and autumn entered. Beyond the trees, a range of hills rose, bare stone peeking out in patches. Birds sang in the high branches and a soft breeze rustled the dry leaves and grasses. It was as fine a day as anyone could ask for.

Daisy Merriot didn't get to see any of this glory, for she was working in the kitchens alongside the house's servants.

Daisy plunged her hands into a washtub of scalding water and scrubbed the next dish vigorously. Soap bubbles flew out, but she paid no mind. This task needed to be finished quickly, or the servants would fall behind schedule, and that made the lady of house quite cross. No one wanted this, least of all Daisy, who faced her wrath more often than anyone else.

"Here, Elaine," she said, pulling the clean dish out of the water and handing it to the other servant to dry. "We're almost done."

"We're never done," Elaine grumbled, taking the dish.

"Well, then be happy it's so, for we have stable work to keep us occupied," Daisy said, trying to look on the bright side.

"It's not right, my lady," Elaine insisted, slamming the dry plate down a little too hard. "You ought to be up in the great hall, instead of that...*woman*."

Daisy sighed, for this was an old, old conversation among the servants of Rutherford Grange. "You mean to say *Lady Rutherford*."

"Aye, *Lady Rutherford* up there, while you toil as a scullion in your own home."

It was true that, at the age of twenty, Daisy never expected for her life to look this way. But then, she never expected her father to remarry when Daisy was twelve, or for him to die so soon after, or the news that the last will and testament of the Baron Rutherford turned out to be quite different than expected. Rather than Daisy inheriting the title and estate, it seemed that the baron's surviving spouse would receive them instead, as well as the guardianship of Daisy until her twenty-first year.

A few days after her father's funeral, Daisy learned that she was not to be addressed as the Honorable Margaret Merriot anymore, but rather as plain Miss Margaret, or (by more and more folks) simply as Daisy. And she would not return to school at Wildwood, but would instead remain at Rutherford Grange to help the family through this difficult time. Somehow, that meant Daisy taking on the management of the house and the lands, while performing ever more daily tasks that kept her among the servants and the tenants instead of with her stepmother and stepsister, Lady Rutherford's own daughter, the Honorable Bella Merriot by courtesy. How quickly things changed.

The young, grieving Daisy was bewildered and confused by all the sudden upheavals following her father's death. Those first few weeks were a blur of despair, and the next few months not much better. Her great love for the estate of Rutherford Grange was all that kept her going—she knew this land better than anyone else, and she knew how to manage the house and the grounds to keep the income relatively steady, and to keep the tenants working and fed.

All that was six years ago, and it now seemed like another person's life. Daisy once dreamed of marrying and having a family and growing old at Rutherford Grange. Now, only one of those things would likely happen, and not in the manner she first imagined.

Still, she thought, *it's home. And it's better to be here than in some strange and cold building far away, where no one knows me and no one cares about me.*

"Miss Daisy," a man said. "Her ladyship wants to speak with you."

"Thank you, Jacob." She smiled at him. Jacob was married to Elaine, and they'd been at Rutherford Grange since Daisy was born. She couldn't imagine doing all this work without them to help her. Yes, there were other servants in such a great house, but not as many as there used to be, and none so dear to her heart.

As Daisy climbed the servants' stairs from the kitchen to the first floor, and then moved to the grand staircase that led to the parlor, she passed several portraits of her family. At the top of the stairs, she paused in front of the large oil painting of her father.

"Good day, Papa," she said quietly. She always greeted him when she passed by, fancying that he still watched over her.

Her schoolfriend Poppy had expressed (in very colorful terms no young lady should know) that the late baron must have been mad when he placed Daisy under the care of her stepmother.

Daisy had dutifully replied, "I am certain Papa thought he was acting in my best interests. After all, I have a home and I am fed and clothed."

"You would have had those things as Lady Margaret," Poppy had said. "Now you have a pallet by the embers."

"That's an exaggeration—I have a bedroom, just as before. And as a young baroness with no guardian, I should have been a target for fortune hunters," Daisy pointed out.

"That sounds much more fun,'" Poppy had noted with a sly smile.

Now, as Daisy gazed upon the portrait of her father, she wished she could speak with him just once more, even for an hour. She had so many questions, and no way to find answers. The image looked out at her, almost as real as the man himself. The baron was not a tall man, nor could he have been termed a Corinthian in any way. But he possessed an amiable smile and kind eyes, and the painter had captured these qualities in oil. In the painting, he sat in a dark leather chair, wearing a black jacket over a snowy-white shirt. His cravat had been tied simply, as he'd done in life. Her father had not been a fussy man, nor overly concerned with details. Perhaps that was to Daisy's detriment.

She continued on to the parlor. The main part of the house was of course much grander than the kitchens and servants' quarters. The floors were marbled and the walls

hung with expensive silk. However, the last several years
had been difficult, and Daisy noticed some troubling signs
of neglect. The corners should be dusted more often, the
runners taken out and cleaned. She saw wax splotches on
the floor beneath a candle sconce and sighed. If only Lady
Rutherford would agree to hire a few more housemaids!
The Grange deserved to look its best. But Lady Rutherford said that it was quite impossible, explaining, "The
late baron, bless his sweet heart, did not invest as well as
he ought. We must make do, and hope that Bella makes a
splendid match."

Bella Merriot was the product of Lady Rutherford's
first marriage (she'd been Bella Dunley until her mother
married the baron, taking his family name instead). Based
upon her beauty alone, it seemed likely that she could
marry a prince. Next to her, Daisy felt like a little field-
mouse, dull and dingy and utterly invisible.

Now, upon reaching the parlor door, Daisy paused,
hearing her stepmother talking.

"—his arrival is nothing less than a sign, Bella. Long-
delayed but inevitable, and we must seize the opportunity
at hand. During the London Season, all is chaos and com-
petition, with gossips everywhere to thwart your efforts.
Here in the country, you will command every room. Who
is more beautiful than you, sweeting? And you must
school yourself to never reveal what you may think of his
own appearance."

"Yes, Mama," a softer voice answered.

Daisy knocked on the door, idly wondering who they
were discussing. Lady Rutherford always seemed to know
who among the local gentry was coming or going.

"Enter!" Lady Rutherford called in her resonant alto
voice, before dropping back to the conversational tone she
was using before. "Remember, darling, this is what you

want."

Lady Rutherford sniffed when Daisy came in and approached where she was sitting, as though she smelled something unpleasant. "Oh, there you are, Daisy. I asked for you some time ago." The implication that Daisy had somehow failed her lingered in the air.

"I came as soon as I heard. What do you require, my lady?" Daisy asked politely.

"Tomorrow, Bella and I will go into Lyonton, for she is in need of some essentials and we must not delay in ordering them. I trust the carriage will be ready at nine."

"Yes, my lady." Daisy knew that a wheel needed to be replaced, but Jacob could do that early, if Daisy took over the feeding of the animals and fetching water.

"Just eggs and toast for our breakfasts tomorrow," Lady Rutherford went on. "Bella is so delicate, you know, and she must not eat too much before a ride. Isn't that right, darling?"

"Yes, Mama." The agreement came from the young lady sitting in a chair near the window. She was embroidering while the light was strong. Bella Merriot looked like a porcelain doll, with perfect blonde ringlets and wide sea-green eyes that at least one suitor had declared to be "the perfect calm turquoise of the Mediterranean," though he himself had never been there.

Perfect and *calm* described Bella very well. She was the model of a young lady of the aristocracy: beautiful, accomplished, well-mannered, and well-spoken. Daisy had never once heard Bella express an opinion of her own.

Lady Rutherford went on, "The vicar is joining us for supper tonight, and he does so like mushrooms. See to it that they are in at least three of the dishes."

Alarmed, Daisy said, "Oh, no! We haven't got any in

the kitchen. I could go get some in the village if you would give me next week's marketing money early…"

"Daisy!" Lady Rutherford said, in a shocked tone. "This is why we must all be grateful that you do not have charge of the finances here at the Grange. *Buying* mushrooms when they can be had for free in our very own woods? Nonsense. You must go and harvest them. You always seem to know where they are growing among the dirt."

"Yes, my lady." The added task would mean not doing something else today. Could she put off the mending? Or the repairs to the chicken coop?

"What would we do without you, Daisy?" Lady Rutherford said then, smiling in satisfaction. "To think you wanted to run back to that school. This house would not be the same if she were not here, would it, Bella darling?"

"Indeed not, Mama," Bella agreed, snipping a thread with a pair of delicate brass scissors.

"That will be all, Daisy," Lady Rutherford said, dismissing her from the parlor and her mind. Daisy dipped into a little curtsey and left.

"Mr. Hornthwaite here for dinner again!" Elaine cried out when Daisy returned to the kitchens and gave her the news. "That man can eat enough for ten, and you'd think he doesn't have a perfectly good cook of his own at the vicarage. Why that woman enjoys his presence is beyond me."

"I am going to the woods to find some mushrooms," Daisy said. "With luck I'll be back in time, but I think the closest patches are bare. I may have to walk quite a ways."

Daisy put on her old straw topper to cover her hair, and grabbed the wide basket she liked to use for gathering mushrooms. Perhaps if she was fortunate, she'd find some late berries as well. Anything that could stretch the larder would be welcome.

At this time of year, the most likely place for mushrooms was along a stream in the woods that more or less defined the border of Rutherford Grange and the even grander estate of Lyondale, the seat of the Dukes of Lyon. However grand it might be though, the place usually had an air of desertion. As far as Daisy knew, no one had lived in the great house for years. The last duke chose to spend most of his time in London or abroad, until he died a year ago. Daisy assumed the new duke had the same preferences, for she'd never even heard that he came to view his holdings here.

Abandoning propriety, Daisy picked up the hem of her skirt several inches and ambled along the narrow track leading to the stream. As a child, she spent many hours there in the summer, watching fish and gathering flowers to weave into delicate crowns. The sun kissed the tops of the distant western hills, and the air was cool. She sang as she walked. Daisy's voice filtered through the trees, but nothing answered her besides the birds. She was totally alone.

That thought brought her sadness as well as relief.

Though she appreciated these few brief moments to herself, when no one could ask her to perform yet another task or tell her one more piece of bad news, she was lately conscious of a loneliness that had never bothered her before.

Now twenty, Daisy was long past the age most daughters of the gentry would have had their debut and entered the marriage mart. She often dreamed of what that path would have been like. The beautiful gowns, the parties, the young men seeking her attention, perhaps a forbidden kiss in a moonlit garden, and perhaps a little more than that...

But what was the use of dreaming now? Daisy had none of the assets so essential for a good marriage among the gentry. She had no title, no dowry, no expectations. True, her lineage was impeccable. Her father had been a baron and her mother's family traced its origins to the Norman Conquest. But who married for a bloodline when it didn't come with an estate to match?

Her stepsister, Bella, fielded so many suitors during her first two Seasons that she often forgot their names. Daisy (who never officially had a coming-out) had no suitors at all. The servants and tenants and villagers near Rutherford Grange considered Daisy to be some strange creature—not one of them, but also not one of the society they all served.

She recalled a recent letter from her old schoolmistress, Mrs. Bloomfield. Among the news from Wildwood Hall, the lady had also extended an offer. If Daisy wanted a change, she could teach at Wildwood. *Your French is excellent and you have always had a quick mind for figures and calculations,* she'd noted. Daisy understood that Mrs. Bloomfield was also offering her escape, for there were almost no options for a woman in Daisy's position.

Teaching at Mrs. Bloomfield's school held a certain appeal. Daisy had always been happy there as a student, and she might have a chance to meet a man of the emerging middle class who would appreciate Daisy's accomplishments and not be so concerned about her lack of dowry.

"Lack of mushrooms is all that I should worry about today," she reminded herself out loud. And dreams of a different future were just dreams. Daisy belonged at

Rutherford Grange, and nothing would change that. Ever.

She sang for a little while, a cheerful, lilting tune to restore her spirits. Then she continued to hum as she zigzagged through the patch of woodland, arrowing in on likely places for mushrooms. She took a few here, a few there, careful to always leave a little so that they'd continue to produce. She sang as she went, switching between French and English as the tunes came to her.

Daisy climbed into a little hollow to gather a few more mushrooms, and she was still in it when she heard hoofbeats from beyond. She thought little of it as she emerged. People were always coming and going, and locals knew the best shortcuts through the trees to shave a little time off their errands.

The hoofbeats slowed.

"Excuse me, are you lost?"

Daisy turned around at the question, and then she *was* lost, because she saw who asked it.

Before her, mounted on a gorgeous black stallion, was possibly the most intriguing man she'd ever seen. He sat easily in the saddle, looking as if he was born to do so. Daisy noticed that while his hair was rich brown, his eyes were a startlingly pale blue, like that of someone who stared out at too many horizons.

He wore a loose white shirt of fine linen. Perhaps due to the heat of the afternoon, or the exertion of his ride, his shirt gaped open at the neck, revealing an expanse of chest. Daisy had never seen that much male skin before in her life, and rather than modestly avert her eyes, she instead stared like a dolt.

Finally, she dragged her gaze lower, only to realize that the man's riding pants were fitted to a degree that seemed unattainable for a mere mortal tailor to accomplish, and that the man's thighs, though covered, were still far too interesting for an unmarried woman to view safely. His riding boots thus became a focal point of last resort, reassuringly workaday and spattered with mud.

Daisy glanced down at her plain wool gown, which was muddy at the hem, and blushed. Her jacket had been reasonably fashionable three years ago, but was no longer. And her hat was nothing more than a straw topper with only a ribbon to secure it. Hardly an outfit to make an impression on a man.

"Didn't mean to startle you," he said, bringing his horse up a little closer. "But I noticed that you're out alone, and you're zigzagging as if you're not sure of your direction."

"I'm going to where the mushrooms are," she explained, holding out the basket.

He leapt down from the horse, taking the leads loosely in one hand. He was at home with the horse, so he must be a groom on one of the nearby estates. He asked, "Was it you singing before?"

"Did I bother you?"

"Not at all. I was just surprised at how...populated these woods are. First the old lady at the cottage, and now you..."

"You met Tabitha! How lucky. Her house is certainly off the track. I can't tell you how many people around here can't seem to find it, even when they have perfect directions. Anyone delivering to her usually just brings it out to Rutherford Grange instead. Rutherford Grange is easy to find."

Just then, the horse stepped forward and stuck its muzzle into the basket.

"Don't you dare!" Daisy cried, pulling the basket away. "I spent a long time picking those. They're not for you, handsome as you are." She lifted one hand to stroke the horse's powerful, glossy neck.

"His name is Stormer," the groom said. "Would you like to give him a treat?"

"May I?" she asked, even as she accepted the carrot the groom produced from the leather satchel. She held a hand to the horse's muzzle and fed him the piece of carrot. The horse ate it happily, and she fancied she could see appreciation in the deep brown eye regarding her.

"Such a magnificent creature," she breathed.

"One worthy of a duke, so I am told."

"Oh, it's the duke's horse," Daisy said, enlightened. "You're so lucky to be able to exercise him!" Now the man's mix of garb and his casual, confident manner made more sense. If he was in charge of the stables, and had access to the finest animals, it accounted for why he was so comfortable in the saddle.

The man was giving her an odd look, but then he smiled. "Yes, I *am* lucky, Miss…"

"Forgive me. I suppose there's no one to introduce you to me!" Daisy laughed, thinking of the formal education that instructed how a lady must never meet a man without the buffer of a formal introduction, preferably given by a dragon of a grande dame who approved the potential acquaintance. "Mrs. Bloomfield would say that in the light of unexpected circumstances, I must make do. I am Miss Daisy Merriot."

"Tristan Brooks, at your service." He offered a little bow from the waist, and a smile that might have been sarcastic. It was hard to tell. The right side of his face was marked by a scar that pulled at his mouth. Nevertheless, his lips seemed designed for smiling, being full and mobile and expressive. She wondered if she could make him laugh, and then she realized that she was staring at him quite shamelessly. Again.

Then he asked, "Who is Mrs. Bloomfield?"

"The headmistress of the school I attended when I was young," she explained, glad of the distraction. It was rare for her to be so flummoxed by a man. Then again, it was rare for her to be near a man...

By habit, she started walking toward Rutherford Grange, and the man kept pace with her, holding the horse's lead in one hand.

"To be honest," he said, "I'm not sure exactly where we are—"

"Oh, we're at the border between Rutherford Grange and Lyon—" Just then, Daisy stepped into a grass-covered hole, and she stumbled. Before she could fall, the man moved and took her by the arm, pulling her to his side to steady her.

"Careful," he murmured.

She was too aware of his closeness to reply. Something hot shot through her—a feeling of aliveness that she'd never felt before. His gaze locked with hers, and Daisy leaned nearer, entranced by his crooked, now faintly sad smile.

Then he said, "I am sorry to tell you that your mushrooms are escaping."

She blinked in utter confusion. "What?"

"Your harvest." He gestured to the ground.

Daisy looked down to find that she'd been so distracted that she'd managed to tilt the basket and spill half her collection out on the ground. He released her, and she crouched immediately to gather them up.

"Oh, no. Stupid goose," she muttered to herself, echoing her stepmother's common complaint.

He knelt down to help her, grabbing several that had rolled toward Stormer.

"The mushrooms are for dinner," Daisy said, brushing

the stray hair out of her face as she stood again. Leaning into him like that! What was she thinking? She'd been about to make a fool of herself.

"You must know the area well, to find these whenever you want."

"Well, I've lived here nearly all my life! I could tell you about everything growing at the Grange...except that wouldn't be very interesting to hear about." She felt flushed and flustered.

"Why should it not be interesting? I find that most topics are more fascinating when they are explained by someone who truly cares about the subject."

"Oh, that's so true," Daisy agreed, having experienced the same thing herself. "But it's getting later and I really must get back home, or it will be too late to make use of the mushrooms."

"How far is home?"

"Less than two miles. I should hurry."

"Then you must accept a ride. Stormer would barely notice your weight."

"Oh, I couldn't. He's the duke's horse."

The man laughed softly. "The duke would insist. I know his mind. Come. I'll help you up."

In a blur, Daisy found herself astride the great black horse. The man offered the refilled basket to her, and then swung himself up.

Even with the weight of them both, the horse pranced as if he were totally unburdened. Daisy adjusted to seeing the world from this slightly higher vantage point. It had been quite a long time since she'd been riding. And she'd *never* ridden with a man seated so close that she could feel his heartbeat.

Then his arm slipped around her waist, and Daisy gasped.

"Just to hold you steady, miss. I certainly don't want you to fall. Again."

There was amusement in his tone, but it was warm and gentle. His breath tickled her ear. She inhaled the smells of hay and horse and leather, and couldn't decide if this situation was merely improper or completely scandalous. Riding pressed against a total stranger...gallant as he might be.

Daisy couldn't have told anyone what she saw on that journey, because her whole mind was consumed with what she was feeling. First the pleasure of being astride such a fine animal, and the relief of not walking. But more than that was the sensation of having this man so very close to her, his legs grazing her hips, his chest so near her back, and his arms encircling her as he loosely held the reins.

Stormer barely needed reins, for he proceeded down the road at a steady but sedate pace. Clearly, Brooks was in no hurry himself.

"You lived in London?" she asked, questing for a safe topic.

"And abroad," he noted. "The war."

That must have been when he got hurt, she supposed, and thus discharged.

"Are you happy to be back home?" she asked.

"If this is home. Didn't think I'd like it here," he said at last, his tone musing. "But the outlook is improving."

The last line was unmistakably flirtatious, and Daisy replied, with uncharacteristic punch, "Don't expect that every ride will include a local resident."

He laughed, the sound rumbling in his chest. "I hope not. Now that I've got you, I don't need any others to distract me."

Daisy turned her head, surprised at the words. "Got

me?"

His gaze met hers. "Just for two miles. I'm not going to kidnap you."

"Good, for you'd get no ransom."

The corner of his mouth quirked. "You have a quick tongue."

As his gaze dropped to her lips, Daisy was conscious of a desire to dart her *quick tongue* along her lips, moistening them in anticipation of a kiss.

He lowered his head a fraction, and her breath caught. *He could kiss me*, she realized with equal parts delight and panic.

Just then, Stormer whinnied and sidestepped. Brooks twitched the reins and focused on the road ahead. The moment was broken. And of course, he'd not been about to kiss her. How absurd, to think it.

Daisy allowed Mr. Brooks to take her all the way home. She told herself that it was the polite thing to do— and deeper down, she knew that she was delighting in Mr. Brooks's nearness, in the novelty of having a man pay attention to her, plain old Daisy, even for a short while.

Brooks asked questions about the countryside and village and the people living hereabouts. Daisy told him as much as she could fit in during the journey.

"You're a treasure trove, Miss Merriot. You said you lived here your whole life?"

"Other than the years I went to school, yes. This little corner of the world is my home, though. I could never leave it. I think you'll come to appreciate it, Mr. Brooks, though it is vastly different than London."

Outside the gates of Rutherford Grange, she half turned and said, "I think, sir, that it would be best if I returned on my own two feet. To avoid…any misunderstandings."

"Very wise." He dismounted and helped her down, both hands lingering at her waist.

Daisy felt her cheeks burning. "Thank you."

"Don't forget your mushrooms."

She had in fact completely forgotten the mushrooms, but managed to rescue the basket before Stormer could raid it.

Mr. Brooks walked with her down the drive, saying that he could not escort her halfway. "That's nearly the same as not doing it at all. I'll let you go when the house is in view."

Just then, they came into view of Rutherford Grange itself. Daisy glanced at the main house, conscious of how dismal it looked, how much it needed repair and attention. She was normally able to ignore the flaws, her view colored by love and nostalgia.

But in the late afternoon sun, the peeling plaster, sagging roof, and dank, overgrown patches in the yard were difficult to ignore.

Mr. Brooks brought Stormer up short and gazed at the scene. "So this is Rutherford Grange. It looks like it's been here since the Normans. That central tower where the main door is could be an old keep. Remarkable."

"You're right!" she said, surprised. "Most people never see that…too much has been added on over the centuries. And it doesn't look as it should. There's not enough money to keep it up."

"Is that your concern? My offer is still open. Say the word and I'll kidnap you."

She shook her head at his teasing. "Never, sir. Rutherford Grange is my home. If I am not here to care for it, who will?"

"A lot of house to care for," he mused, looking at the building again. "I've been learning more about big old houses than I ever expected," he said, "and I hope—"

"Daisy!" a voice interrupted, and her stepmother appeared through the main doors in question. She was resplendent in a burgundy-colored silk gown, but her expression was stormy as she approached. "Where have you been, girl? The vicar will be here in less than an hour, and Elaine cannot conjure dinner out of thin— *Your grace!*"

Suddenly, Lady Rutherford dropped into a curtsey in front of Mr. Brooks, leaving Daisy to stare at her open-mouthed.

"M-my lady," she stammered at last, "there's a mistake. This is Mr. Brooks…"

"No, she's right," he said, his voice low.

Daisy spun to look at him, feeling her world turn upside down. "What?"

"I'm the duke," he admitted. His expression was strange, almost regretful.

"It is his grace, Tristan Brooks, Duke of Lyon!" Lady Rutherford declared, her expression now suitably awed and delighted. "What an unexpected honor, your grace, for you to come to Rutherford Grange. So thoughtful for you to call upon neighbors so soon after your arrival here in the county. If I had but known, I would have made arrangements suitable for a gentleman of your stature. But won't you come inside and take some refreshment, your grace? The Honorable Bella Merriot, my daughter, would be most happy to make your acquaintance. Daisy will mind the horse…"

She waved impatiently at Daisy to do just that, but Mr. Brooks—no, *the duke*—stopped her.

"Very kind of you, my lady, but I am merely passing by. Having met Miss Merriot by chance on the road, I thought she should not have to return home unescorted."

Lady Rutherford blinked in apparent confusion. "Darling Daisy, unescorted? Oh my." As if she herself had not sent Daisy alone on the errand to fetch mushrooms.

"No harm done," the duke said easily.

"And I have the mushrooms," Daisy added. "I shall just take them to the kitchen, shall I?" She wanted more than anything to disappear and never be looked at again. Mr. Brooks was the *Duke of Lyon*? And to think she'd mistaken him for a groom! And she rode in his arms, and chatted and flirted with him…oh, Daisy wanted to *die* of embarrassment.

"Mushrooms!" Lady Rutherford said, startled back onto her original concern. "The vicar! Supper!" She looked torn about all her potential options. "Your grace, permit me to extend an invitation for dinner this evening…"

"Alas, I must return home," he said, firmly closing the door on her importuning, with a directness Daisy admired. "But I would be honored if you and Miss Merriot would come to Lyondale soon."

"Indeed, your grace," Lady Rutherford breathed.

"And Miss Daisy as well, of course," he added.

"Oh! Yes, of course," the baroness said, flustered into accepting the addendum.

"I shall have a formal invitation sent over. Good evening, ladies." He mounted up on Stormer and prepared to escape. He looked directly at Daisy when he said, with a tiny smile, "By the way, no ransom would have been asked."

And then he rode out, leaving Daisy standing there with a basket of mushrooms, a furious stepmother, and the knowledge that she'd unknowingly fallen into the embrace of a duke.

Chapter 3

✥ ❧ ✥

IT WAS FORTUNATE THAT STORMER was an intelligent horse who after only a week knew the way back to the stables at Lyondale, because Tristan was so distracted that he scarcely knew where he was. His mind was completely consumed with Daisy Merriot.

How could a brief encounter cause such a reaction? True, it had been a long time since he'd even spent time with any women, never mind being *alone* with a woman.

In fact, he was lucky that he'd managed to conceal the most obvious physical reaction while she was pressed against him, her soft curves fitting all too well in the space between his thighs. Riding with her had been an exquisite torture, as he tried to converse in a coherent manner, all while inhaling the scent of her and keeping his hand from straying all over her. He was painfully alert, hoping for the slightest signal that she would have welcomed more attention. Alas, the young lady was clearly a real lady, in the sense that she was not the type to enjoy an al fresco tumble with a stranger.

Well, not a stranger anymore. Tristan had avoided revealing his title when they met, relishing the interaction with another person who didn't know what he was. It had been so good to *not* be a duke for a few minutes. And surely the fact that Daisy had mistaken him for a hostler was the only reason she'd been so open and friendly. He'd seen the difference in people when they knew his title— they bowed and scraped and wouldn't look him in the eyes.

And indeed, when that woman at Rutherford Grange had suddenly revealed who he was, Tristan saw the shock and horror in Daisy's expression. Never again would he get to have a conversation with her as one human to another. No. Now it was duke and lowly servant.

"God damn my ancestors," he swore aloud, not for the first time.

If only he weren't Duke of Lyon. Why shouldn't he get to converse with someone like Daisy just because he wanted to? He liked everything about her, from her admittedly pretty face to the way she staunchly defended her countryside from any insult. Clearly, she loved her home.

If only he loved his own home, he thought when he saw the lights of the great house over the rise. Sighing, he rode toward his destiny.

That evening, as soon as Tristan heard that Jack was awake again, he went to his friend's room.

Jack looked much better than he had earlier in the day. He was sitting up in bed, the remains of a modest supper on a tray beside him. He actually had color in his face, not the deathly pallor that so alarmed Tris before.

"Glad you're back in the land of the living," Tristan told him cheerfully, as he flung himself into a chair placed near the bed.

"So am I," Jack replied. Then he looked at Tristan, his eyes narrowing. "Hold a moment. What happened to you?"

Tris leaned forward in his chair, trying not to smile as

he said, "I met someone while riding."

"A woman," Jack said. "My lord, I take an afternoon nap and you're already out meeting the beauties of the shire. I assume she's a beauty?"

Tris nodded, and very briefly explained where he'd encountered Daisy in the woods. "She is a neighbor, though her position in the household seems a bit odd. She was very ladylike, and she mentioned going to some boarding school...but she's also foraging for dinner?"

"Perhaps she's a natural child," Jack guessed. It was common enough for some aristocratic families to harbor a few by-blows of the master, depending on the circumstances. Sometimes, the bastards were raised in exactly the same manner as the legitimate children. In other cases, they might be little more than servants. "I'm sure Miss Wallis can tell you more. She's lived here for years."

Tristan had almost forgotten the lady, that slender shadow who greeted them so warily when they arrived. "Yes, I'll do that. Local knowledge is always best."

"She's worried you'll send her packing," Jack said bluntly. "She came by about an hour ago to see how I was doing. We chatted."

"And she told you that?" Tristan asked.

"Don't be daft. A lady like her would never breathe a word against the new master of the house. It's everything she *didn't* say. She's terrified that the new duke will decide that she's an unnecessary drain upon the resources, vast though they must be. The problem with being a useful woman is that it's always someone else who determines when the usefulness ends."

Tristan knew what Jack meant. Though he'd never personally had to deal with excess female relatives until now, he understood that society had very few places for women who were not daughters, wives, or mothers. A small number managed to find positions as "useful women" who minded children who were not theirs, or served as companions to family members more wealthy than they. Miss Wallis had done the latter for the old duke, but Tristan was unlikely to need the same services.

Jack's words also made Tris think of another problem. "Miss Wallis may be right to worry on one point. From what little I managed to learn so far, my resources are not nearly as vast as everyone seems to think."

"But the dukedom…"

"…is in difficulty," Tris said bluntly. "Quite how much difficulty I don't know yet. The solicitor had in-complete information, and the estate manager has been elusive. In fact," Tristan added hesitantly, "when you're better, I was hoping that we could go over the books. You know that when it comes to numbers, I'm at sixes and sevens." Since Kemble studied the law, specifically in chancery, he was much more familiar with the mundane aspects of money management.

Jack smiled. "Of course I'll help. I must earn my keep."

"You're a guest, you idiot. But if you're not feeling well enough…"

"Nonsense. Where are the books and ledgers? Let me at them! And we'll run this estate manager to earth like hounds chase a fox."

"Ha. If the doctor could see you now! All it takes to get you on the mend is paperwork."

Tristan arranged to have all the materials brought to Jack's room. Footmen were kept busy trotting to and fro from various offices to seize more items and papers to examine. Tristan also learned that while the housekeeper kept a massive ring of keys, he had his own ring, nearly as heavy, for all the locked drawers and cases that the duke alone could access.

The men spent quite a while examining the books available. Tristan was out of his depth, though he knew he'd catch on soon enough. What was clear was that Lyondale was not nearly as well-run as it could be. The estate manager's intermittent reports were not particularly informative either.

"Have I made a mistake in coming here?" Tristan asked.

Jack looked up from the ledger book, his expression alert but his flesh looking a bit sallow. "No, of course not. The good news is that you do have money. The bad news is that your predecessor had been tapping into the principal of all the investments. If you don't change the way the estate collects revenue, you'll be out of funds in a decade or so. And that's if you spend wisely."

"So I need to make the place pay for itself," said Tristan.

"Yes. It's not impossible. There's very good land here. It's just been poorly managed since your predecessor's health declined several years ago. This estate manager, Mr. Reed, sounds like he's incompetent." Jack held up one of the sloppily written reports.

"*And* I refused to come here immediately after the old duke's death, exacerbating the problem," Tristan added, feeling the guilt wash up.

Jack shook his head. "No need to cast blame. Be grateful that you have a chance to correct course before it's too late. First thing, I'd suggest letting Reed go."

Tristan nodded, having already come to that conclusion. "I need a new estate manager, then. A good man who understands these things. I know just enough to be dangerous."

"Yes," said Kemble. "You should advertise for one. If

you're lucky, you should be able to interview men and get the right one out here before spring planting. The sooner, the better. And it wouldn't hurt to let everyone know that there will be changes. People get used to the way things are, even if things aren't going well."

Tristan mused, "I need a way to get everyone in one place. I'm not going to repeat my intentions to a few dozen local worthies. I'll say it once and be done with it."

"Throw a party. You can announce things then."

"Ugh."

"And you can invite your Miss Daisy. Get those locals gossiping."

"Oh, no," Tris groaned, remembering the end of his conversation with Lady Rutherford.

"What's wrong?"

"There's another daughter too. I managed to avoid meeting her, but I did promise an invitation to all of them for some sort of dinner." He frowned. "Which means I've got to plan some sort of dinner now. Hell."

"It was inevitable, your grace. Better to dive in now than fear it forever. Miss Wallis can be hostess," he added. At Tristan's blank look, Jack said, "You do remember that it's proper for a lady to preside."

Tristan brightened. "You mean that if I set Miss Wallis up in some other home, I wouldn't have to host a single thing?"

Kemble rolled his eyes. "Let's table that discussion. You made a promise to the ladies of Rutherford Grange, so you'll have to honor it. Start with a dinner, and work up to a full-fledged ball later."

Tristan hated social events. *Hated* them.

When he'd first got back to England, there was a round of foolery in London. He had to attend several functions and greet higher-ups and tell exaggerated versions of the truth and endure the adoration of idiots who had no idea what a war entailed. He had to act pleased that fate tossed him at the top of the heap of aristocracy for no apparent reason.

He could see the doubt and distaste in the eyes of those he met, the people who knew he didn't belong. Tristan didn't go the right schools. He didn't hold the right commission. He didn't have the right jokes, or the right manners.

So finally he told them to leave him alone.

That was the one benefit to being a lord. When he told people to do something, they did. He still had enough money, apparently, to do that. He shouldn't spend a farthing until he improved the situation at the estate.

At least Lyondale was out of the way, tucked in a quiet corner of Gloucestershire. Tristan needed quiet, because one other result of his so-called heroism was that he couldn't hear loud noises without cringing in fear. Things as simple as drums could incite a panic, as he discovered during an unfortunate evening at the Kew Gardens in London.

Yes, it was good that he came here, and brought Jackson Kemble with him. Lyondale was just what he needed. He feared it would be dull, but now that he'd met Daisy…

"She's not a bit dull," he said, abstractedly.

"Who?" Jack asked, confused.

"Miss Daisy Merriot. I was just thinking that I'd like to see her again."

"Tris, you'd better not be suggesting what I think you are," Jack told him. "Finding pleasure where it's offered is one thing. There are plenty of women happy to be a mistress, or just take the money for a night. But to ruin a young lady…"

"Oh, for God's sake, Jack! What do you take me for?

I'm not contemplating setting her up in some love nest."

"Then what? If she's a young lady of good reputation, your options are limited."

"I'm aware of that," Tristan muttered. "I just meant...I liked her. It was one of the first normal conversations I've had with a person since I got hurt."

"If you want to see her, the honorable thing to do would be to court her. But I suppose you've got to think of the title now. A duke must marry a lady prepared to be a duchess."

"Trust me, potential candidates have been flung in my path since the moment I learned I was to receive the honor. Even in London, within a week of learning of my inheritance. God damn it, there were four men ahead of me, Jack! *Four!* Do you realize how much bad luck it took to land me here? I should have stayed on the Peninsula. Perhaps I would have been hit by another cannonball, then some other poor sod would have to deal with this mess."

"Don't say that," his friend warned. "You not only survived something that by all rights should have killed you instantly, you now have a chance to begin life again as one of the most powerful men in the country."

Tristan sighed, shoving the paperwork away, as if that action could also push away the financial problems the papers detailed. "The title may impress people, but there's not much beyond that. If I don't marry an heiress, the next duke will have nothing at all."

Chapter 4

❧ ❧

DEAR HEATHER,

I have put off writing to you only because I feared I had nothing new to say. But now I can fill pages, for I have met a gentleman who I never would have dreamed I might say one word to...and yet I can report to you (please burn this letter as a favor to yours truly) that not only have I spoken with him, I have ridden with him, walked with him, and (please, please burn this) even flirted with him.

Here is the worst of it: he is the new Duke of Lyon! I didn't know, and he did not enlighten me. Until my stepmother saw him and recognized who he was! (You would understand if you saw him, for he was dressed no better than I.)

Heather, you have always been the fearless one among us and so it is you I must ask. What should I do concerning this acquaintance, which is both dizzying and terrifying to contemplate? I am all too well aware of my social position, my lack of wealth, to even attract a gentleman, let alone one so exalted as a duke. And yet, I dare to hope that he has looked on me with a certain regard that is unfeigned. And he does not seem at all what I would have *expected a duke to be. But perhaps I am letting my heart run away with my head. When he sees Bella, he'll no doubt forget me. Advise me to forget him, dear friend, and I will heed your wisdom. Or I will try! But I must hear the thoughts of another whom I trust, for my own thoughts are a maelstrom....*

Daisy put down the pen, wearied by recounting even the bare facts of her encounter with the duke. If she told her friend Heather all the truth—that the man had (maybe, perhaps) nearly kissed her while they were riding—well, even Heather might faint.

All in all, it had been a most disturbing day. Immediately after the duke had left, Lady Rutherford insisted on hearing all the details of Daisy's encounter, mostly to divine any clues that would help her own daughter's pursuit of him. Hence there were dozens of questions about whether he mentioned other ladies in the county, or if he expressed a preference for a certain color, or if he had hobbies.

"Well, he was riding when he came upon me. And the horse is worth a fortune on its own," Daisy said, hoping the scrap of information would placate her stepmother. (It was difficult enough to relate a safer, more boring version of the meeting—one that did not include her memory of riding with her body pressed to his.)

"Excellent," Lady Rutherford had purred. "Bella rides well, and she can use the good horse for any excursion with the duke. I must ensure she has a new riding habit made. Go finish dinner, dear Daisy. The vicar will be here at any moment."

Daisy did not eat with the family most evenings, and certainly never when the vicar, Mr. Hornthwaite, came. She avoided him as much as possible. For a man of God, he was astonishingly petty and venal. Yet Lady Rutherford counted him a great friend, and often had him to Rutherford Grange. Daisy wondered if the vicar's favor was why people in the village were always so polite to Lady Rutherford and her daughter, even the tradesmen who were constantly owed money.

As usual, Daisy ate with Elaine and Jacob and the other servants, then sat by the fire mending clothes while Elaine cleaned up the kitchen, singing Welsh folk songs. Elaine sang as naturally as other people breathed, and her choice of tune signaled her mood. Welsh songs invariably meant she was feeling out of sorts and ready to do battle. Jacob raised one eyebrow at Daisy and whispered, "The vicar's presence always brings out her Welsh side. Don't worry, lamb, she'll be sunny again tomorrow."

After the vicar left and the house was quieting, Daisy went upstairs with an armful of mended clothing. She deposited one gown on Lady Rutherford's bed. A housemaid who was tidying up nodded in thanks. "Oh, you mended that! Thank goodness, Miss Daisy. You've got a finer hand than I do, and those ruffles haunt me. Her ladyship's always treading on them and she refuses to have it taken up."

Daisy knew why it was so. Lady Rutherford wished most passionately that she were two inches taller, and she believed a longer gown would convey the impression that she herself was taller. In fact, the only result was that Daisy mended hems regularly.

She continued to Bella's room with the bulk of the clothing. Daisy put the gowns into the clothespress herself, which was where Bella found her when she walked in.

"Is it true that you mistook a duke for a stableboy?" Bella asked, her voice quiet but incredulous. "Mama told me just before the meal."

"He was exercising a horse when I encountered him," Daisy said defensively. "And he did not once mention his title until your mother saw him and shouted it from the rooftops."

"Oh, Daisy, how could you not put two and two together? His name…"

"How was I supposed to know? He introduced himself as Mr. Brooks, not His Grace, Duke of Lyon!"

"But it's all anyone's been talking about for weeks. The new duke is a war hero, scarred in battle. He's young. And he's finally come to Lyondale, a year after gaining the title. Honestly."

"Perhaps that's the talk over tea, but I'm not taking tea with you and your mother and those who come calling." No, Daisy was usually overseeing the making and serving of the tea. How could she hear any gossip among the society ladies?

Bella was regarding her with narrowed eyes. "How long did you speak with him?"

"Not long," Daisy hedged, sticking to the story she'd offered Lady Rutherford. "He simply happened to be passing me along the track. And he slowed down and walked with me to Rutherford Grange. Out of a sense of chivalry, I suspect. He offered to carry the mushrooms," she added suddenly, remembering her amusement at the gallantry.

"Well, it sounds as if he's got some manners, even if his background is…odd."

"Odd?"

"Daisy, do you listen to anything? That man ought never to become a duke. There were four—five? No, four —men ahead of him, with titles already and breeding besides. He's a third cousin or some such. *Barely* gentry. He's never spent time among society and he's half-savage from serving in the army. But fate plucked him from the heap and placed him at the top of the ten thousand. Like putting a crown on a puppy dog."

"Do you think the new duke needs to be housebroken?" Daisy asked innocently. "Shall we send some old newspaper over?"

"Daisy!" Bella covered her mouth to stifle a laugh. "That is a most improper subject to jest about."

"I shan't repeat it."

"What does he look like?" Bella asked. "The rumor is that he's crippled and twisted up and acts like a brute."

"Nonsense," Daisy declared. "Yes, he's got a scar on his face. But he's tall and rides well and is very hand—" She broke off, scared that she might reveal too much of her raw impressions of the man. "He was quite civilized," she said. "A brute would not have escorted me home."

"That's true," Bella mused. "All the same, I'm afraid of him."

Daisy hadn't felt scared in the duke's presence. And yet she could guess that he would be very intimidating if he chose. A soldier by trade, and now one of the most powerful men in the land…perhaps Bella was right to be nervous.

But Bella would still obey her mother and try to win a proposal from him. *What a strange world*, Daisy thought as she headed to her own bedroom.

She had a chamber in the old Norman part of the house, a square block that towered over the newer structure. Daisy liked it, because it was out of the way and offered a fine view of the forest to the east, which made for a pleasant way to get up in the mornings. It was furnished oddly. The bedframe was a massive thing in dark stained oak, carved all over with little flowers. The bed must have been three hundred years old, and was now horribly out of fashion. The rest of the furniture—a table and chair, the washstand, a small cabinet for clothing— were all similarly mismatched, drawn from other places in Rutherford Grange. Daisy didn't mind at all. Everything in this room belonged to her family, and thus it was part of her.

Daisy had strange, broken dreams in which the new Duke of Lyon appeared quite frequently. In her dreams, she had no trouble responding to his comments with the sort of wit she never mastered in waking life. Unfortunately, all the witticisms evaporated with the dream, and she remembered nothing of what she might have said.

"Not that it matters," she told herself. Lyondale was only a mile or two away, but it might as well be on the top of a glass mountain for all that she was likely to see the inside of it.

Daisy wished she could lie in bed and relive her brief time with the duke, who had been so human and kind when they spoke. But she had to get up. There were many tasks to be done around the house, and several fell to Daisy, who had been taking on more and more as the years passed.

That morning, she harvested vegetables from the garden and picked apples in the orchard. She gathered eggs from the henhouse, and noted the presence of fox pawprints around the outside, though all the birds were accounted for.

"That fox is back," she told Elaine when she returned to the kitchen. "I don't know what we'll do if the hens stop laying again." Meat was expensive and reserved for the baroness and her daughter, so a steady supply of eggs was important.

At the news, Elaine clucked like a hen herself. "We need a dog to scare away those creatures."

"We can't afford a dog," Daisy said sadly. She loved animals. But funds were simply too tight, and a well-trained dog would be difficult to find at a good price.

"Oh, by the way. A cart drove by while you were working outside, and brought a package that had been delivered to you in the village."

Daisy found the large package in the front room and opened it, revealing a bolt of fine cotton cloth. "Oh, dear," she murmured. An envelope fell out, and she recognized the handwriting of her friend Poppy St. George.

"Well?" Elaine poked her head around the corner. "What is it?"

Daisy read aloud:

Dear Daisy,

I hope this message finds you well. As you might remember, I have stepped in to help two days a week here at my stepfather's shop, following my older sister's marriage. It is quite a change from just living at the house with Rose, but I bring her samples of the fabric to touch when I come back, and we make a game of it. In any case, the business is much involved in cotton imports. I have included some samples of a new product, a cotton produced only in one province of India. It would be most appreciated if you could evaluate the cloth and offer us your sincere opinion on its quality. I remember well that you are an excellent seamstress.

Do put the fabric through its paces (please do not tell anyone how I am mangling my metaphors) and write to me when you have time to consider its worth. If you find it acceptable, I will advocate for importing it in greater quantities. I hope the value of the cloth will compensate you suitably for the time you spend evaluating it. Take care, my dearest Daisy. I hope to visit you someday, along with Rose, who says she'd love to spend time in the country. Perhaps our families can arrange for us to come out next spring. Or you can come to London and stay as long as you like. Sometimes I wish we were all still at Wildwood, snug and happy with Mrs. Bloomfield to guard us against the world! But alas, we all must grow up. Do write and tell me your news!

I remain your affectionate friend,

Poppy StG.

Daisy put the letter down and felt the quality of the cotton again. It was a lovely pattern, varied rosettes and faint stripes, all in yellows ranging from pale sunshine to mellow gold.

"A sample, is it?" Elaine said. "That does look like fine fabric, miss."

"Indeed." Daisy read between the lines perfectly well. Though couched as a matter of business, the gift was just that—a gift. She did not like charity, but neither could she deny that she needed the fabric. "I can sew a new dress from this, and there will be enough left over to line the hood of your cloak."

"That would be a relief once winter sets in," Elaine said, pleased at the notion. "Such a bright color will be warming all on its own."

However, winter was still a ways off. The afternoon proved warm, and Daisy spent the time weeding the vegetable garden to allow the best growing for the remaining crops. In a month or so, the mornings would be rimed with frost, but early fall still felt like summer, and she relished the golden days.

When she returned to the house, the mood was strangely ecstatic. "Daisy, come here at once!" Lady Rutherford called. (If another, lower-born woman had done this, it would be considered a shout. But Lady Rutherford *never* shouted.)

Daisy hurried into the parlor where both Lady Rutherford and Bella stood, their faces glowing. Lady Rutherford gestured impatiently. "Come here and read this."

"An invitation came," Bella said, forestalling any mystery.

Daisy took the invitation, feeling the weight of the heavy, expensive paper. She read the line her stepmother indicated with one long bony finger.

The Duke of Lyon requests the presence of Lady Rutherford, the Honorable Miss Bella Merriot, and Miss Margaret Merriot at dinner on Thursday the 20th.

"I'm invited too," she said, not believing it until she read her own name on the paper. How had he known her full name? Oh, doubtless Miss Wallis told him. Daisy often saw the woman at church.

"Yes." Lady Rutherford wrinkled her nose. "The duke is exceedingly generous. Well, you may come. Bella may need assistance with her ensemble. You have that green gown still, don't you, Daisy? That should serve."

It would barely serve. Daisy thought of the dark green dress with a slight shudder. The gown looked acceptable from a distance, but anyone sitting near her at dinner would see how many times it had been patched and mended and let out and remade. The gown had once belonged to Lady Rutherford, but it was now Daisy's, since the baroness declared it was far more frugal to reuse things than "waste" money on new clothing.

"Bella, that new cream silk gown will look stunning at a dinner," Lady Rutherford went on. "The candlelight will cast such a perfect glow on your skin. You'll wear my pearls for the evening."

"Oh, Mama, may I?" Bella asked, her eyes widening.

"Certainly, darling. This will be a very important night. The night the duke first sees his future bride!"

Surely he'd be so dazzled by Bella's beauty that Daisy would fade to nothing in her secondhand gown. But then she remembered the bolt of yellow cloth. The twentieth was soon, but the new style of dresses made for quick work. The bodice was simple and the skirt loose and flowing. Daisy even had some jewelry that had been given to her upon her mother's death. The collection lay in a locked box that Daisy hid at the bottom of her basket of mending. She rarely had a chance to wear any of it, but there were fine pieces she could use for a dinner party. Not the beautiful ruby necklace, which was too fancy, but there was a lovely pearl pendant...or the silver locket with her mother's hair curled inside. Yes, that would work very well. Daisy could also make an impression that night!

"I'll go see that Bella's gown is aired properly," Daisy said quietly. "And I have some sewing to do as well."

The others weren't even listening, chattering about the potential guest list and who might wear what on the twentieth. Daisy slipped away, quiet as a mouse.

A mouse with a plan.

Chapter 5

❦ ⁂ ❦

YOUR GRACE—

Deuced odd to have to call you that in a letter, but pleased as punch too. My friends ought to mount in the world. But duke! You've been keeping secrets from your friends! And you're not the only one with a secret. I've got one too. But I have to share it with a few trustworthy men. Will you believe it? I have stumbled upon a diamond mine in the region of Golconda, which is not where my mother lives. It's all mountains and rocks and damned snakes. I haven't had to deal with one yet, but the locals kept yelling "Pamu!" at us. I finally learned it was "snake" in Telugu, which I don't speak, as Mama taught me Hindi growing up. Dangers aside, there are reasons worth going. Diamonds are one such reason. I've partnered with another man, Joseph Rait, who I don't know well, but he's smart as a whip and has the eye for an opportunity. We have a line on a new source of diamonds and Rait bought the land quick as a wink, after I secured half of the amount. We appraised the few rocks found on the surface, and the jeweler said he hadn't seen one so pretty in decades.

We're already starting work but it will take some capi-

tal to really get the mine going, especially since I intend to do it right and pay a proper wage to everyone down to the boys feeding the donkeys that haul out the rock. You'd be shocked by how little most of these owners get away with paying their workers. And they're not careful enough with safety either. I aim to show everyone it can be done another way. Of course, that means more investment up front, but I'm confident we'll be repaid. Yes, we! I thought of you straight off. You saved my life in Spain, and don't think I'll forget it. I suppose that as a peer of the realm now, you won't care to grub in the dirt (or finance the grubbing in the dirt, for it's all these local lads who do the real digging). But I wanted to make you the offer first out of the great debt I owe you, ~~Tris~~ your grace. As a partner, you'd have a full third interest in the mine. You, me, and Rait, and all the diamonds we could dream of. Just think of it! I'm so excited I can scarcely hold a pen. It's been two days since the jeweler appraised and I'm still as giddy as a schoolboy.

Yours truly,

John Cater

John Cater! It had been a few years since he'd heard from his old childhood friend. Cater's mother was Indian, so after his army service and the death of his father, he took her back to her family. But Tris and John had grown up in the same street in London, playing together whenever they could escape their chores.

Even now, he could summon up John's image: a slight but sinewy figure, always in motion or about to leap into motion. He had a narrow face and smooth, deep brown skin like his mother, and a ready smile. Anyone who looked at John Cater could see the spirit burning inside. As a boy he was always looking for adventure, and that same impulse for excitement was part of why Tristan once had to save his life in Spain.

Tristan reread the letter once more, still dazzled by that one word: *diamonds*. It was so very different from the dull round of life in the English countryside.

That said, Tristan was slowly adjusting to life at Lyondale. Tucking the letter back into his jacket pocket, Tristan turned his mind to more immediate matters. As he'd mentioned to Jack, one unavoidable part of being Duke of Lyon was that he had to socialize with the local gentry. He'd paid no house calls so far—a duke did not have to stoop to visiting others. But guests seemed to call upon him with depressing regularity. He was actually relieved when Jack suggested that he hold a larger dinner for all the local worthies; it seemed to be the easiest way to be attentive to several people at once.

With the assistance of Miss Wallis, who chose the guest list to reflect the people in the area Tristan ought to know, invitations were sent. Almost within hours, replies were tendered, and Tristan tried to prepare himself to be congenial. At Jack's recommendation, Daisy Merriot was specially invited. This met with Miss Wallis's cheerful approval.

"She is a very sweet young lady. Miss Bella Merriot is the beauty, of course, but Daisy has lived at Rutherford Grange her whole life. She's part of things here."

"Miss Bella is not?" Jack asked curiously.

"Oh, Miss Bella is quite popular. She's very charming, you'll see. But the baroness is keen for her to marry high, and it's inevitable that she'll be gone soon, off to some great lord's home as his lady wife."

"Does the baroness have plans for Miss Daisy to marry as well?"

Miss Wallis shrugged. "I don't think she'd object if

Daisy accepted a proposal. But I can't think what gentleman would offer for her, since she spends all her time running the estate. I believe it would fall to pieces without her."

Clearly, Miss Wallis knew all the details of local life, so Tristan probed a bit further. He asked, "Can you tell me about exactly how the title fell to the current baroness? I'm surprised it didn't go to the nearest male relative, no matter how far from the tree…as in my case."

"Oh, the title for the barony of Rutherford is entirely different. From the very first, it has gone to heirs general, not just male heirs. According to legend, the barony actually began with a woman—a very strong-willed one, rumored to have defended the original castle against a siege with only half a dozen retainers. She insisted that a daughter was just as worthy as a son."

"Strange though, that the late baron changed the will to not go to his daughter."

"He was besotted by his second wife," Miss Wallis said shortly. "I expect that had something to do with it. And of course, he could do as he wished."

"He could have split the property."

"As a matter of fact, he couldn't. That's the one thing no Lord or Lady Rutherford could have done over the centuries. The land can never be parceled out or sold off in pieces. It's all or nothing. It has a certain logic—the land was fought for and defended with blood and sweat. To divide it is to weaken the family."

Tristan nodded, though he wasn't sure he agreed. According to such logic, it seemed as if someone was destined to lose.

On the day of the event, he almost called it off, annoyed by some little thing in the morning. "No one wants to come here for a meal, Jack," he said to Mr. Kemble.

"It's all just theater. A table full of people I don't know and will likely despise."

"But Miss Merriot will be here too," Jack pointed out. "Miss Daisy, I mean. It's very confusing, you know. Miss Daisy is the elder, but it is Miss Bella who will be next in line, so she is to be called Miss Merriot…how does anyone know *what* to address them as?"

"The locals seem to muddle through," Tristan noted. "Of the irregularities in that succession, I imagine who gets called Miss Merriot is not very important."

"Clearly, you've not spent enough times around ladies," Jack said with a snort. "The pecking order is *everything*."

The addition of Daisy to the guest list was all that kept him from canceling the event. Tristan wasn't sure if he was excited or scared to see her again.

"I made a fool of myself in front of her the last time I saw her. It was stupid to not tell her who I was."

Jack shook his head. "Under the circumstances, it was natural to avoid the awkwardness of insisting on being addressed as a duke. She'll forgive the lapse. You didn't look a fool."

"When a lady is more in command of herself than I could be, what else could I look like?"

"Like a lord, which is what you are, like it or not," Jack said. "But that's for another time. First, you must survive this dinner."

And the fateful evening duly arrived. Tristan was dressed in an appropriately lordly manner. His new clothes still mostly felt stiff and uncomfortable to him, despite the fine fabrics they were cut from. That evening he wore a jacket in a deep tan broadcloth, which complemented both the white linen shirt beneath, and the lighter-colored, close-fitting pants. It was well-tailored, because all his clothing was well-tailored now, but he felt as if he were about to be strangled at any moment.

"Stop twitching, Tris," Jack told him in the corridor before they walked down to the ground floor.

"I can't help it. I'm not used to this formality of dress."

"It's no more formal than the military, and you never complained then."

"One doesn't complain in the army."

"So you make up for lost time now!" Jack laughed. "Don't worry. And don't lose your temper."

"It's easy for you to talk about formality. You're not going to face the gauntlet." Unlike Tris, Jack wasn't dressed for dinner, and in fact it was something of a triumph that he got dressed at all.

Jack had had a bad morning, coughing constantly until he was too weak to even stand. Tristan had decided that Jack was not to be allowed among the guests. He needed rest, not the stress of chatting with strangers. It was too bad—Tristan had been relying on his friend to deflect some of the worst questions that would inevitably be asked.

Instead, he ensured that Jack would be installed comfortably in the garden, on a chaise with a number of blankets to keep warm after the sun set. Tristan was taking the advice of Dr. Stelton, who recommended that Jack get as much fresh air as possible. A maid servant named Alice was under strict instructions to check on Mr. Kemble every half hour. Tris walked Jack down to the gardens and saw that he was settled.

Tris felt the crinkle of the letter in his pocket. He pulled it out. "Did you hear that Cater went out to India?"

"John Cater? Haven't heard from him in an age."

Tristan opened the letter. "He took his mother back to

India so she could be near her family again. I don't think she ever loved England, and as a widow, she had little reason to stay. But listen, Cater found a diamond mine. Or a place to dig a mine. He wants me to be a partner."

Jack sighed. "A hundred to one it's nothing at all. Even if there are diamonds, it takes a long time to develop such things."

"He's got a local partner, a man who knows the area. And Cater never let someone go hungry. He's going to pay the workers well, so we can sleep at night, knowing that we're not relying upon virtual slaves."

"It sounds nice, but don't get pulled into this, Tris," Jack warned. "There are better ways to waste money."

"I don't have a lot of money to waste," he said quietly. "If an investment like this did pay off, the returns could be astronomical."

"*If. Could.*" Jack looked skeptical. "Those are not re-assuring words. Let it go, Tris. If you must, give Cater a couple hundred as a gift to get things started, out of friendship. I'd say he deserves that, for he was always the sort who'd jump to help someone in a rough spot. But stay well away from any madcap scheme where you can't even verify the facts."

"You're right, of course," Tristan said, folding the letter back up. "I suppose it's just the image, like a scene from the *Arabian Nights*…caves filled with jewels, just waiting to be picked up."

"Fairy tales!" Jack said from his comfortable chaise. "Cater's a good man, but good men do not always make good businessmen. Now put this nonsense behind you. Go and greet your guests."

Tristan returned to the house. The first guests arrived moments later. The village vicar, Mr. Hornthwaite, a man of around forty or forty-five, looked distinguished but austere in his mostly black clothing. Then another local worthy, Lady Weatherby and her eldest daughter, Lady Caroline, arrived. Lady Weatherby was short and plump and never closed her mouth. Lady Caroline was short and plump and never opened her mouth. Indeed, after she got one good look at Lord Lyon upon being introduced, she barely raised her eyes again. His scars ached suddenly, but Tristan smiled inwardly. That might put a crimp in Lady Weatherby's obvious plans to make her daughter the next chatelaine of Lyondale.

There were a few other local gentlemen and a wife or two. Lord Dallmire, the young Lord Fothergill...all people he needed to know in order to function well in this corner of the world. He would either impress them or intimidate them, and he didn't much care which it was.

Luckily, Miss Wallis helped to oil the wheels of social nicety. She chatted amiably with the Weatherbys about the approaching holiday season, and if the village ball at Christmas could hope to outdo the last one. Tristan listened with half an ear.

The vicar kept sidling up, clearly hoping to ingratiate himself with the new duke.

"So you are the duke's cousin?" the vicar was saying to Miss Wallis, having settled for a discussion with her until he could scale that final rung to a chat with the duke himself.

"Second cousin, once removed," Miss Wallis replied primly. She added nothing else, and Tristan got the distinct impression that she did not like Hornthwaite. Interesting. The vicar seemed personable enough, and he supposed the man could be called handsome (in an ecclesiastical sort of way). And yet, he didn't like the vicar either...or else why did he avoid him so? Tristan put that thought away for later. Perhaps Miss Wallis would tell him more after the guests left.

And then, finally, Miss Daisy Merriot entered.

She wore a plain, almost shabby cloak, while the two ladies with her nearly glowed in the brighter colors they each wore.

The other young lady was fragile and beautiful. She allowed a footman to take her cloak, revealing a gown that looked like something a fairy princess would wear. Meanwhile, Lady Rutherford was regal, gowned in a rich purple frock and a headdress that featured three peacock feathers.

But he only noticed them because they were with Daisy.

"Hurry up with your cloak," Lady Rutherford was saying to Daisy in an annoyed tone. "Bella must meet the duke as soon as possible."

As Tristan approached the trio, Daisy removed the cloak…and revealed that she was just as alluring as the first time he saw her.

"Where did you get that gown?" Lady Rutherford hissed, clearly shocked at Daisy's appearance.

"I made it from the fabric bolt my friend Poppy sent," she explained in a soft voice.

"You should have told me—why, your grace!" Lady Rutherford said, affecting a sweeter tone. "Good evening. We were just saying how wonderful it is to have Lyondale open again."

An obvious lie, but Tristan had no option to pursue it, since he was immediately introduced to Bella Merriot, who was all but offered to him on a platter.

To be fair, she was a very pretty young lady. If Tristan ordered an artist to paint an ideal woman, the result would probably look like the Honorable Bella Merriot.

Daisy Merriot was dressed more simply than her stepsister, but everything about her said gentry: her manner, her voice, her looks. Her blonde hair was bound up properly, but it would spill everywhere if that one ribbon were to be undone—an image he found he quite liked. She had a heart-shaped face and lovely, big dark eyes, and an intriguing bow of a mouth.

"Thank you for coming." He looked at her and smiled. "A question, if you'll indulge my curiosity. Did I hear your stepmother call you Daisy the other day?"

"My given name is Margaret, as you must know, for it was on the invitation," she said shyly. "Daisy is just a pet name."

"It suits you very well," he said.

Daisy's eyes widened. She was shy, and obviously nervous, which Tristan found charming, if only because it gave him a bit of confidence. He wasn't a great talker himself, but she was nearly tongue-tied. He wondered if a kiss would untie her tongue or silence her completely, and then decided either outcome would be interesting.

Before she could respond to his comment, the bell rang for dinner.

Chapter 6

❀❧❀

DAISY FOUND HERSELF BEING ESCORTED into dinner by the duke himself, and she was so stunned by this event that she couldn't talk. She felt Lady Rutherford's gaze boring into her back. It wasn't her fault that the duke happened to be speaking to her just as the dinner gong sounded! It was polite to offer to escort the nearest lady, regardless of who she might be.

She wore her new gown for the occasion, the one she sewed from the gifted fabric. Lady Rutherford glared at her when Daisy removed the cloak, but Daisy had no idea why she really cared. Bella's gown was far more impressive. In fact, everyone's outfits were more expensive and showy than Daisy's. She was a moth among butterflies.

Soon, the guests were seated in a large, windowed room with a long dining table. Tristan led Daisy to her seat, which was of course *not* next to the end, where he would be sitting. In a duke's home, seating arrangements were all made in advance, accounting for the rank and influence of every guest.

Through the glass windows, one could see the pond below the house, and the fields beyond it, all now turning golden and russet in the fading sunlight. Daisy wished she could be out there, rather than in the dining room among strangers. With the exception of Lyon himself, she felt no one wanted her there. Indeed, she still wasn't sure *why* she was there.

The meal was not a happy one, though the guests certainly never allowed it to become a silent one. Bella commented only rarely, perhaps thinking her pink-and-white English rose looks—all fair skin and blonde hair and limpid blue-green eyes—conveyed all she needed to. Daisy was acutely conscious of the other girl's impeccable gown and jewelry that murmured rather than shouted of wealth. Lady Rutherford was equally well-draped. It all left Daisy feeling out of place and vulnerable.

The conversation ranged wide and often included topics Daisy knew nothing about—nor did she wish to.

"Governess, my foot!" Lady Weatherby said at one point, speaking of a local resident. "That woman is Mr. Billing's natural daughter and the job a merest fiction."

Miss Wallis choked on her tea.

"I beg you pardon, ma'am," Lady Rutherford said in agreement, "but it is the truth. At least he's providing for her, that all I can say."

Miss Wallis still looked appalled at the coarseness of the discussion, and the duke must have realized a change in subject was called for.

"I noticed that a number of fields at Lyondale lie fallow. Is that common in this area of the country?" He looked at Lady Rutherford and asked politely, "How are such matters handled at Rutherford Grange?"

Lady Rutherford looked blank, then turned to Daisy and repeated, "How *are* such matters handled at Rutherford Grange?"

Daisy put down her cup before saying, "The management of the land is of course considered from several factors, and what is done at Rutherford Grange may not suit Lyondale. Both the tenant farmers and the estate's own fields are scheduled years ahead, with some going fallow to restore the land between plantings. I believe ten percent are fallow at any particular time."

She had begun speaking directly to her stepmother, but then turned to Tristan, who'd asked the original question.

"It sounds as if considerable planning is required," Tristan said. "I wonder if I might arrange for my estate manager to speak to yours."

Daisy had no answer, for the fact was that Rutherford Grange had no such manager. The last man had been let go a few years back, and Daisy handled everything now. But it would be embarrassing to admit that in such company. Both Lady Rutherford and Bella were staring at her in alarm.

At last, she squeaked out, "I am certain that everyone at Rutherford Grange would be most pleased to answer whatever questions come up."

"Indeed," Lady Rutherford jumped in. "We will do anything in our power. His grace has but to ask. Isn't that right, Bella darling?"

"Of course, Mama," Bella said, peeping at Tristan beneath lowered eyelashes.

"Miss Bella," the vicar said then, with an unctuous smile. "May I say that you look particularly charming tonight. Is that the much-vaunted gown your mother was telling me about?"

"It is, sir," Bella said, her eyes modestly downcast. "Mama indulges me."

"You are my only daughter, darling," Lady Rutherford replied, ignoring Daisy completely.

Lyon cleared his throat, but Lady Weatherby managed

to ask Lord Dallmire something and diverted the conversation before Lyon could step into a very awkward subject. Thus saved from being the center of conversation, Daisy did her best to chat with her neighbors, and managed to not embarrass herself, though she knew she was no salon wit.

Thankfully, attention never returned to her. Hornthwaite asked Lord Lyon if he had plans to attend services in the village. "The late duke did, you know. Until his illness prevented."

"I shall add that pilgrimage to my responsibilities," Lyon said.

"It would be advantageous, your grace."

"For whom?" Lyon asked.

Hornthwaite looked flustered, but then said, "Is it not always beneficial to attend church?"

"Not if a man needs to catch up on his sleep after a night of cards," Lyon replied.

Daisy saw the set of his jaw, and wondered if Hornthwaite would have the sense to stop questioning the duke about his habits. Thankfully, the topic changed soon after.

The meal progressed to the dessert without mishap, though Daisy for one was ready to flee from the tension in the room. All the personalities vying for control, all the people asking favors from others and trying to find favor with Lord Lyon…she had no part in it, and felt like a deer among wolves.

After the meal, the ladies went through to the drawing room, while the men remained for the customary smoke and drink.

A maid handed out tea or sherry to the women. Everyone chatted while Lady Rutherford stared daggers at Lady Weatherby, and Bella and Caroline exchanged pleasantries as if their mothers were not about to go to war.

Daisy accepted a tiny glass of Madeira wine, unsure if she even really liked Madeira.

"Perhaps a little music?" Miss Wallis asked hopefully. She looked to Daisy, who unfortunately did not count pianoforte among her accomplishments.

Daisy, still holding her glass, gestured toward Bella, about to explain that her stepsister was the one gifted in music. Just then, Lady Weatherby sneezed, knocking Daisy's elbow. The glass of Madeira went flying…directly toward Bella.

The red wine exploded all over the pale gown.

"Oh, no," Daisy whispered.

"Oh, *no*!" Bella wailed at the same moment.

"You clumsy little girl!" Lady Rutherford cried in dismay. "You've ruined your sister's new gown!"

"I didn't mean to!"

"Of all the things to do, Daisy. You ought to be ashamed of yourself. Poor Bella deserves better."

"It was an accident, Mama," Bella said, grabbing at a serviette Lady Caroline thrust at her. She dabbed frantically. "Oh, the stain is spreading…!"

Indeed the deep red of the Madeira was rapidly expanding on the thin, highly porous silk, causing Bella to look as if she wandered through an abattoir. Tears glistened in her Aegean-blue eyes. "Mama, I look *hideous*."

"This is your doing, Daisy," Lady Rutherford hissed. "Get out of my sight."

Daisy was only too eager to obey. Turning, she fled down the hallway not knowing or caring where she ended up, only that it would be far, far away from her stepmother.

Daisy instinctively sought out the darkest, most solitary location she could find at Lyondale, which was the garden. Though near the great house, it was blessedly deserted, since all the guests were currently inside, probably making jokes at Daisy's expense.

"I never should have come here," she said out loud.

"What's so bad about Lyondale?" a male voice asked from the darkness.

Daisy gasped, whirling around to discover who or what was speaking.

"Over here," the voice continued. "By the roses."

She could smell the roses, and a moment later, she could see them too, for there was a dim light from a lantern placed on a low wall nearby. Next to the lantern, a figure lay on a chaise.

"Hello?" Daisy asked, approaching it.

"Good evening," the figure replied. "I didn't mean to frighten you, but in my defense, I didn't want to eavesdrop on your conversation with the plants. I'm Jackson Kemble, at your service."

This little speech was delivered from a prone position, as the speaker was clearly not well enough to get up. Daisy now saw that he was covered in a wool blanket and that he was uncommonly pale. This must be the convalescing friend Tristan had mentioned at one point during dinner.

"How do you do, Mr. Kemble?" she said, remembering her manners. "I'm Miss Daisy Merriot. Shall I leave you in peace?"

"Were you hoping to escape into the darkness?" he asked. "I wouldn't recommend it. Some of the plants in these gardens are carnivorous."

"They are not," Daisy objected, but with a laugh, for it was absurd to think about.

Mr. Kemble laughed too, a thin sound compared to the size of man he was. "Very well. But it could be true somewhere." He held up a book. "I've been reading about some discoveries of amazing plants in the tropics. Alas, reading about them is about as close as I'll get for a long time. Travel does not agree with me lately."

Daisy stepped closer. "His grace spoke of a friend who was quite ill, and therefore could not join the dinner party. Was that you?"

"Indeed. I've known Tris—excuse me, the duke, since we were schoolmates. He was kind enough to haul me along when he decided to see Lyondale at last. The doctors say the air in the country is better than that of London."

"I've only been to London a few times," Daisy said, "but I must agree with the doctors. Do you feel any improvement?"

"I'm coughing less," he admitted. "And I can sometimes sit up in a chair for an hour or two, which is more encouraging than it may sound. However, it will be a long time before I can return to Chancery."

"You're a solicitor?"

"Was. Now I'm an invalid." He smiled. "But that is dull talk. Tell me why you told the plants you shouldn't have come here. For myself, I'm quite happy you have."

She sat down on a wrought iron chair a few feet away from Mr. Kemble. Though he was a virtual stranger, Daisy felt instantly comfortable with him. And while she ought not be alone with a man, one could hardly object to her sitting with an invalid who couldn't do any harm.

"The matter is a trivial one," she explained. "I made an embarrassing scene. Only I was harmed and the harm shall not last long. I am not important enough for anyone to care if I humiliate myself. Well, it is likely that my sister's gown was ruined, but she has plenty in reserve."

He chuckled. "That sounds like comedy, not tragedy. But if she is your sister, won't she forgive you?"

"In fact, Bella Merriot is my sister by marriage only," Daisy said, to clarify the matter. She added, "We do not have much in common."

"Ah, the Merriots of Rutherford Grange," he said. "I've heard mention of them. I'm a bit confused, though," he went on. "Because if those Merriots are here by marriage, how are you connected to the late baron?"

"I'm his daughter from his first marriage."

He frowned. "And yet you are not the baroness now?"

"It's all a bit tangled," Daisy said, "and I'm afraid that I am not very good at explaining the details of all the legal aspects, especially to a lawyer."

"Try me," he said kindly.

So Daisy related the basic facts as she knew them. As she spoke, she was reminded of those first few months of numbness and pain after losing her father. She'd disregarded so many things then, and it was all still a haze.

"You never read the will yourself?" Kemble asked at one point. His tone was mild, but Daisy could tell that he was incredulous.

"Well, I may have, and I simply don't recall. I was only fourteen. Much of the language of the documents was quite beyond me." She tried to think of another subject, one that was less mournful. So she asked, "How did you meet the duke?"

"We were at school together, and remained friends after he went off to the Continent to join the fighting, and I stayed here in England to study the law," Kemble said. "As it happened, Tr—that is, his grace returned on a medical discharge. I had space, so I insisted that he come live with me while he recuperated. Unfortunately, I seem to have got rather run down, and I took very ill just as he was recovering." He looked frustrated. "At least he's back on his feet. I feel like I may never be."

"Was it very bad?" Daisy asked hesitantly. "The duke's injuries, I mean. He looks strong now, but I gather that he might have…died?" She didn't even want to imagine the possibility.

Kemble nodded. "It was as dire as one can get without meeting one's Maker. Did you hear how it happened?"

"Only some garbled rumors."

"Well, I'll tell you, both to set the story straight and because he never will. He's too modest."

Kemble paused, recalling the details, and then began to relate what had happened.

"Tristan Brooks—as he was called then—was part of a company defending a mountain pass that the French were keen to take. Our boys had the high ground, which helped. But the enemy had brought along some nasty machinery, setting up barrages of cannon fire to make life difficult for the defenders. Tristan happened to be walking with a few of the most senior officers one day as they surveyed the camp and were trying to make plans for new defenses. How Tristan knew something was coming— even he can't explain that. But he shouted and hurled himself at the major general, who was in the direct line of fire. Knocked him and a couple others to the ground just before the shell struck. Tristan saved the lives of more than one man that day…but he was closest to the shell, which exploded on impact and hurled out scraps of burning metal. Many of them hit Tristan."

"It must have been so painful for him," Daisy whispered, imagining the horrific scene.

"More than he's ever admitted out loud," Kemble agreed. "He was taken to the field hospital first, where they said he wouldn't last until nightfall. But he did! And a few days later they sent him to recover farther away from the front, still thinking he'd succumb to the wounds, or fever, as so many soldiers do. But he survived that too. And then the word came down on high, and Tristan was promoted to lieutenant and offered an honorable discharge on account of his wounds being so severe that he could never return to the army. He resigned his commission and went to his home in London to recuperate. And that's where the solicitors of the Lyondale estate found him… and told him he was the next in line for the dukedom."

"What an astonishing turn of events. I'm so happy for him," Daisy said, meaning it. "It's evidence of Providence, that he is now duke. He'll be able to do so much good with that influence, and an understanding of life's difficulties that few other men in his position have. Perhaps you could tell him that for me."

"You can tell him yourself, if you like." Mr. Kemble gestured to something behind Daisy, and she turned to discover the duke standing there, his presence making her shy all over again. Had he been listening? She couldn't imagine speaking so boldly to the duke himself, telling him how he ought to live his life!

But if he overheard, he didn't show it. He said, "I came out to see if you were still here, Jack. It's dark now, and too cold for your health."

"Mother hen," Mr. Kemble muttered, but with a resigned expression. "I should have gone in earlier, but I was quite distracted by this young lady's company."

At that moment, two footmen and a housemaid arrived, obviously there to help Mr. Kemble inside and to gather all the accoutrements he'd been using. Mr. Kemble stood with the assistance of the footmen. Still, he managed a polite little bow in Daisy's direction.

"Pleasure to make your acquaintance, miss. I do hope to see you again."

"I should like that very much," she replied warmly.

She glanced at Tristan, realizing that any such visit would entail her being invited to Lyondale again. "That is, if his grace would permit it."

"Anything for a friend," he replied, with a cryptic smile.

"Watch over Miss Merriot, will you?" Mr. Kemble told Tristan.

"Certainly," the duke replied. "Perhaps she'll allow me to take her for a turn around the garden path."

Daisy felt a little thrill. Of *course* she'd want to spend more time with him! But, she thought out loud, "Won't your other guests miss you?"

"What other guests?" he replied, making butterflies suddenly take flight through her stomach. *That* was a flirtation, she realized. Whatever had happened between them on the afternoon they met was not merely in Daisy's imagination. He felt something too.

The housemaid bustled about, gathering the blanket and lantern as she hurried after the others. As she began to walk along the path away from the house, Daisy noticed that the book Kemble had been reading was left behind, and she stooped to pick it up.

"She missed this, and books ought not be left outside," Daisy said. She looked at the cover and smiled, telling Tristan, "He said that the book details some very dangerous things! I wonder if it's even safe for me to hold it," she joked.

Tristan took the little book from her, saying, "There are other books I could think of, far more dangerous to a young lady's innocence than this one."

"A book can't be so corrupting."

The corner of Tristan's lips quirked. "Oh, some can. Not that you can know what I'm talking about," he added hastily.

Daisy was a little indignant. "I know exactly what you mean!"

"Oh?" His eyebrow arched, and she blushed in embarrassment. "Just how might a proper young lady like you know what I mean?"

They'd just reached a turn along the path, and they were now concealed from the house by several tall yew trees, providing a green wall of privacy that made Daisy aware of just how alone they were.

And Tristan had stopped to look at her, awaiting her answer.

"Well, in fact," Daisy said haltingly, "Mrs. Bloomfield had a particular bookcase...which was locked...but I found the key one day..."

"...and you found an interesting collection of bedtime stories, is that it?"

"I don't think this is a topic of conversation that we should pursue." How mortifying, to wander into such a topic.

"On the contrary, I'm fascinated," he said, not allowing an easy escape. "What exactly did you learn from these books?"

"Nothing!" she said, far too quickly to be believable.

"How many did you read?"

"Um...all of them." Some had been illustrated, and Daisy had been both shocked and utterly amazed at what they depicted.

"And you learned nothing? I'm not sure I believe you."

"Please...I can't talk about this sort of thing with you."

"Then we won't talk."

He brushed his lips against the back of her hand, very lightly. Daisy's eyes slid closed as she savored the feeling of the kiss, so unlike anything the forbidden books had mentioned. The glide of his lower lip along her knuckles made Daisy faint with desire.

"Did you read about that?" he asked softly, pulling away.

"I read about kissing," she answered, dazed. "But none of the books said a kiss on the hand felt so... special."

"A major oversight." Once again, he treated her to that half kiss, that teasing sensation. Daisy was suddenly aware of a desire to touch him, to run her fingers along his skin and see if she could evoke the same sort of reaction. How did men feel when touched like that? Was it the feeling of growing warm and slightly dizzy, of wanting more of the same until some unknown threshold was reached?

"Speaking of special," he murmured, his lips sliding to her wrist, and then the inner part of her forearm. Daisy inhaled, her nerves singing.

It was an experience entirely different than any she'd had before. Alone with a man in the darkness of the gardens, with the vast presence of the great house behind them. Daisy's heart was beating rapidly, her breathing uneven in the wake of Tristan's attention. She never wanted it to stop.

But he's the duke.

The reality of the situation felt like cold rain on her consciousness. In her haste, Daisy almost shoved him away.

"I am so sorry," she said in a rush. "I should not be alone with you! It's most inappropriate, and what you must think of me..."

Tristan stepped back, his manner shifting from passionate to aloof in the space of a breath. "Then let's get you back to your family." He offered his arm, the gesture cold and proper.

Daisy slipped her own hand around it, feeling her cheeks hot with shame and embarrassment. She'd done something very wrong, and she was sure that she'd somehow hurt or disappointed Tristan.

Before their mutual absence could be remarked upon, the duke escorted Daisy back to the drawing room, where the guests had gathered. However, neither of the Merriot ladies were present.

"They left, your grace," a footman informed them when the duke inquired.

"Left? Without one of her daughters?" he asked, puzzled.

"It was my fault," Daisy interjected. "Earlier, I spilled wine on Bella's gown. It was an accident, but I'm afraid I quite ruined her evening."

The footman nodded in confirmation. "The baroness called for their carriage immediately. The lady said her daughter couldn't be seen in company after the… incident."

From the footman's tone, it seemed he was glad they were gone. So was Daisy, except for the fact that they'd taken the carriage, leaving her stranded. She gazed at Tristan's hand, since he was still arm in arm with her, though the pretense for any kind of formal "escort" had evaporated the moment they'd stepped into the house.

He noticed her gaze and put his hand down, out of her sight.

She looked at his face again, and was caught by his eyes, which were shadowed in the poor light of the foyer, but still watching her with an indecipherable expression. Daisy had never been good at conversation, and definitely not with a duke, or any man who insisted on looking at

her so *steadily*. "I should go. It's a long walk back, and—
"

Tristan was incredulous. "You'd walk three miles in the dark wearing evening slippers, Miss Merriot? Not likely."

Before Daisy could object, the duke ordered for his own carriage to be brought up to the front of the house.

"Certainly, your grace," a footman said. "It will take a quarter hour—we'd not been anticipating needing any carriages until tomorrow."

"Fine, that shall give me time to bid good-night to the other guests."

This task was performed with startling efficiency. The guests had obviously been expecting to stay much longer —an evening in the drawing room with some music or entertainment, and no doubt more of the duke's excellent food and drink. But instead, they found themselves hustled out to the foyer, and draped with their cloaks and outerwear while nearly stepping over themselves to thank the duke for his hospitality.

The duke kept Daisy near him as he bid the other guests goodbye. When he spoke to Lady Weatherby and her daughter, he thanked Lady Caroline for her scintillating conversation, sarcasm that neither woman appeared to notice.

Hornthwaite left after reminding Lyon once again that it would be well for the lord to appear in the village church sooner rather than later. Tristan gave a noncommittal answer. The last of the guests besides Daisy left, and Tristan sighed with relief.

"*That's* done," he said. He turned to the majordomo. "From now on, only people I actually enjoy being around are allowed on the property. Have the footmen shoot anyone else."

"Yes, your grace," the majordomo replied.

"I believe he's joking," Daisy added hastily.

"Yes, miss. I'll supply the footmen with blanks to maintain the effect."

Tristan laughed. "That will do," he said. He seemed entirely recovered from any annoyance by Daisy's behavior in the garden or the hassle of unwanted dinner guests. "Is my carriage ready now?"

"Yes, your grace."

"Excellent. I shall take Miss Merriot home."

"Yourself!" Daisy said in surprise. "But I can't bother you further, your grace."

"No bother at all. I would not have it said that I would allow a young lady to be sent off alone into the night." With a nod of his head, Lyon indicated his wishes, and the staff all leapt to accommodate him.

Well, Daisy thought. He may not have been Duke of Lyon very long, but there was no question that he was the lord now. He walked with Daisy to the coach and helped her in himself, leaving a slightly startled footman in his wake.

In the carriage, he sat opposite her as the driver urged the horses on. "Once again, I must thank you for coming tonight," he said in a low voice.

"I have a question about that, your grace. Why was *I* invited?"

"Jack—Mr. Kemble, that is—thought you'd be a good addition to the party."

"Ah," she said. So Tristan had nothing to do with it. "I am sorry to have disappointed him."

"Disappointed? What makes you say that?"

"My conversation is thoroughly provincial. I talked about crop rotation."

"Your conversation wasn't why we included you. Miss

Merriot, your *presence* was key. On three separate occasions, I nearly yelled at the whole party to get out."

"Why didn't you?"

"Because you were there." He looked a bit sheepish. "I thought I should prove that I can endure a whole conversation without losing my temper or fleeing the scene."

"Oh." Daisy wasn't sure what to say to that. "You might have started with a less challenging group, then."

His face broke out into a smile, and he laughed, which made her laugh too. She shook her head. "Now I'm being rude."

"No, just accurate." After a moment, Tristan said, "I can see why Jack took such a liking to you. You must come back to chat with him. I'm terrible company most of the time. But you…any man would rise from the grave if you were expected to drop by. How about Thursday afternoon?"

"I should like to, your grace. But I do not have much time to myself. The running of Rutherford Grange keeps me busy."

"Are you politely putting me off?"

"No! It's just that the marketing must be done Thursday."

Tristan said, "You will come to Lyondale for that afternoon. No excuses—Elaine and Jacob can do the marketing." Somehow she wasn't surprised he knew the names of her servants. Tristan Brooks seemed dedicated to making up for the time lost before he moved to Lyondale.

"In that case, I will be here at the appointed hour. I know better than to argue with a lord." All at once, she giggled, thinking of the Duke of Lyon posting footmen as guards to keep the guests away.

"What's so amusing?" he asked.

"You are. You can't post guards to keep society out."

He leaned forward, looking more serious. "Then what should I do?"

"Why ask me?"

"Because this is the world you're from. You understand them. Whereas I grew up among commoners, and then lived among soldiers."

She sighed. "It's been some time since I've been part of that world. I'm neither fish nor fowl now. I have the name but not the wealth to be accepted among society. I don't fit in among the village, because they're afraid to insult me by treating me as if I'm not gentry. So you see, I'm not the one to seek advice from."

He reached out impulsively, and took her hand. "Is that how it seems to you? You fit in perfectly back at Lyondale, during supper, as if you did that every week."

Daisy swallowed nervously. Tristan was looking at her intensely, and it was hard to think when all she could notice was his eyes, the blue color all dark in the dim light of the carriage. "I would soon be unmasked if I had to do that every week, if only because I've just this gown for the occasion."

He looked her over approvingly. "It suits you."

"I hope so. I made it," she added shyly.

"You look lovely." He hadn't let go of her hand, and she just noticed that he'd threaded her fingers with his. Definitely *not* approved etiquette, but she didn't want him to stop. In the darkness of the carriage, it was a very intimate and interesting sensation.

"I have to ask for your forgiveness," he said then. "What happened in the garden was very much my fault."

"I cannot forgive you, because I enjoyed it," Daisy whispered. "I'd be lying if I said otherwise."

He looked surprised. "I thought I offended you."

"I thought I offended *you*," she admitted.

Suddenly, they both laughed. Tristan said, "Ever since...I got hurt, I assumed no woman would tolerate my interest."

"A woman so shallow does not deserve your interest," Daisy retorted.

Tristan looked quite surprised, then cautiously pleased. He seemed about to say something, then he simply raised her hand to his lips again. "May I?" he asked, his eyes locked on hers.

"Please," Daisy whispered.

Tristan peeled the glove off before kissing her fingertips. It was even more sensual than before, and when he actually took one fingertip into his mouth and sucked, Daisy felt a reaction in her very core.

She let out a little gasp.

Tristan kept teasing her, but moved from where he was sitting opposite, to kneel in front of her. Daisy took a ragged breath as he finally let her finger go, his mouth curving into a sensual smile, made crooked by the scar on his cheek that pulled one corner down. But Daisy was already learning to read his particular expressions, and this one was pure pleasure.

On his knees, Tristan still commanded her attention. He trailed his fingers along her jaw. "That's a thank-you for possibly the nicest thing I've heard in a year and half."

"It was just truth," she whispered.

"Well, I liked it." His gaze dropped to her mouth. He said, "Do you know how tempting your lips are?"

She shook her head, feeling far out of her depth. "How...how tempting is that, your grace?"

He lowered his mouth to her own, and suddenly Daisy got a taste of what temptation meant. All her clandestine reading did not measure up to the intense swirl of feeling from Tristan's kiss. His lips on her hand earlier was enticing, but this was astonishing.

She needed more, so she raised her head and pressed her mouth to his, demanding greater contact. She parted her lips and felt a jolt through her whole body when his tongue grazed hers.

"Christ, yes," he moaned, the blasphemy sounding sweet in her ears. She put her hands on his upper arms, feeling the muscles ripple beneath her touch.

Then she felt him press against her, his hands running along her thighs. She realized that she'd parted her legs to allow him closer, and their entwined position was now far more scandalous than anything they'd done before. If anyone saw them now, Daisy would be ruined.

Would it really be so bad to be ruined? Daisy thought. She was unmarriageable as it was. She was poor and no man wanted to take on a dowry-less woman. Why not enjoy one night of pure abandon? It was all she'd ever get.

Daisy kissed him back hungrily, her brain swirling with conflicting arguments. Why argue when she could simply enjoy the moment?

Unfortunately, the carriage came to a halt then. Daisy gave a startled little moan of protest, and glanced outside to see the familiar sight of Rutherford Grange. She was home.

"I wish you lived farther away," he murmured, then released her. "Or much closer. You're a little distracting."

"I don't mean to be." She quickly set her gown to rights and pulled her glove back on— why did the removal of one glove somehow feel as naughty as removing everything?

"That's part of your appeal." He smiled as he moved to help her out of the carriage. As she stepped out, he said,

"Good night, Miss Merriot."

"Your grace...if you like, you could call me Daisy."

He smiled slowly. "I would like that very much. But I will only do so if you call me Tristan."

"Oh, your grace, that would be far too forward..."

"After what we just shared?" He smiled lazily. "Besides, I want to hear you say my name."

"Tristan," she whispered, trying it out.

"There. Was that so difficult? Don't forget our next meeting...Daisy."

Daisy would certainly not forget that. As she drifted asleep later that night, she imagined that she could still feel Tristan's lips on her own.

Chapter 7

❧❀❧

Dear Daisy,

I was recently looking through my trunk of old school things, and I pulled out nothing less than the Crown! Can you believe it? I forgot that I had it, but I must have been the last Fairy Tale Queen before we all left Wildwood Hall. I remember when you first made the Crown out of the old pasteboard hatbox and the glass beads. How carefully you sewed them in, and I teased you the whole time, thinking that the thread would rip through that pasteboard in a fortnight. Well, the joke is on me, for all these years later, the Crown's "jewels" are holding fast. I put it on my head and looked in the mirror, and how I laughed at my silly image. And then I wanted to cry, because you didn't get enough chances to wear it yourself, leaving school so soon. I still say it was cruel of your stepmother to keep you there. You missed too many turns as Fairy Tale Queen, being able to tell us others to pick up your plates and to fetch you more tea. I may send you the crown in the post, so you can wear it. Or perhaps I'll send it to Poppy first, for sprucing up. She's got the millinery connection now, and though the beads are still on, the silk is looking a bit worn! I suspect Poppy would have a scrap or two to spare.

Write to me soon and tell me all the excitement in Gloucestershire, for I assure you there's none here, hence my pawing through the old trunk....

Much love,

Heather

Daisy chuckled as she read the rest of the letter, remembering the funny old "crown" she'd created for make believe. The girls had dreamed up a whole kingdom to go with it, and they took turns playing Queen, rotating every Saturday. Whoever had the crown could order the others about, directing them to perform small tasks and silly tricks. But one had to be very careful and not abuse the power, for another head would wear the Crown soon enough!

It had been so long since those days. Daisy sighed, thinking of how happy she'd been at Wildwood Hall, and how much she missed her dear friends. It was good to be reminded...especially now.

A few days had passed since the dinner at the duke's home. Daisy had been distracted for most of her waking hours, and by night her dreams had got quite out of hand. In them she walked at Tristan's side while he presided over Lyondale during the days, and at night...well, Daisy awoke feeling hot and flustered, aware of new desires that she'd never been bothered by previously in her quiet life.

Yet no matter how she felt, work remained to be done.

One afternoon, Daisy had just walked into the parlor with a tray holding tea things and put it on the low table between Bella and the baroness, when a housemaid entered behind her, bearing another little tray. She carried this directly to Lady Rutherford.

"Just arrived, my lady," the maid announced in a

breathless tone. "It bears the duke's seal!"

Hence the excitement, Daisy thought. Even the household servants were interested in the activities of this new duke. To be fair, this corner of England was not generally overwhelmed with news.

The maid stepped back, but hovered, clearly hoping to glean information about the contents of this letter. So did Daisy, for that matter.

Lady Rutherford broke the seal and read the paper. An expression of real joy spread across her face. "An invitation from the duke to join a riding party! How wonderful."

"I don't always like riding when the weather turns," Bella said, with considerably less joy. "The ground gets so muddy."

"Nonsense, dear. With your new riding outfit, you will look ravishing next to the duke."

"He's invited me particularly?" Bella asked, her eyebrows arching.

"No, the invitation is addressed to all the ladies of the house." The baroness looked chagrined as she realized that included Daisy. Clearly, she'd not meant to reveal that in Daisy's presence.

But Daisy had no intention of joining the party. She knew that she did not truly belong. "That was most polite of the duke to include me, but I could not join anyway. I've no outfit that would suit the occasion." Daisy in fact hadn't owned a riding habit since her school days, and she'd look like a ragamuffin in her country clothes, a laughingstock next to the aristocratic guests in their finery.

"Oh, you may borrow my spare habit," Bella said, the offer surprising both Daisy and Lady Rutherford.

"Bella!" her mother chided.

"No, I couldn't. Anyway, I've much to do here at the Grange that day," Daisy added quickly, not wanting to incur the wrath of her stepmother by inserting herself into the event.

Bella ignored Daisy's objection. "Mama, it would not do to appear that *any* of us are ungrateful for the invitation. Who refuses a duke? And Daisy will fit into my old brown habit. It was too loose on me."

"The brown habit," her mother mused, growing calm again. "Yes, that would be fine, I suppose." She smiled, probably thinking of just how awkward and out of place Daisy would be at the event, even in better clothes. Daisy barely rode anymore. "I shall accept the invitation on behalf of us all."

Daisy wasn't sure why Bella offered the use of her old outfit, and she suspected it was out of pity. But as her stepsister noted, it was not the thing to refuse a duke. It looked like Daisy was going riding after all.

On the day of the ride, the trio of women arrived at Lyondale at the appointed hour. A small crowd of others had gathered—the duke's riding party was evidently rather grand. Miss Wallis, looking very modish in a pale blue riding habit, greeted the guests with her usual grace.

Several grooms were present to lead the guests and point out obstacles, and to serve the inevitable requests that the guests would make. In addition to the grooms, there was a phalanx of younger boys, who were in charge of holding the guests' horses and tending to their needs. Nearer the house, maids stood ready with various accoutrements—fresh water, cloths to wash off dirt, even sewing needles in case one of the female guests required assistance with her appearance.

So many people just to allow a few riders to enjoy the day, Daisy thought. Rutherford Grange was a great house too, but the difference between what went on there and what was needed for a duke's lifestyle was remarkable. Tristan truly lived on another level, one far above Daisy's.

The now-mounted group milled about in the meadow, waiting for the sign to begin riding. Daisy felt particularly mousy in her borrowed riding habit. How was it possible that Bella even had a riding habit of drab brown when she favored lighter, bolder colors? True, the habit was a rich velvet, delightfully warm on such a raw day. But Daisy glanced at Bella's new habit in a cardinal red wool, which brought out the pink in her cheeks and made her skin glow, and knew that everyone would look at Bella today, not Daisy at all.

When two figures emerged from the stable area, Daisy straightened up in her saddle. Tristan looked as if he'd been born to ride. He wore a riding outfit crisp with newness—this was probably the first time it had been worn. Daisy remembered the more casual clothes he'd been wearing when he rode up to her in the woods that day. He looked so different now, so aloof and aristocratic. Her heart shrank a little even as she admired his magnificent appearance. As if Daisy needed a reminder that Tristan was far above her…

Next to Tristan, she was surprised to see Jackson Kemble. He appeared to be much healthier and stronger than the last time she'd spoken with him. But horseback riding? In the cold? She frowned, watching the two men converse.

"What are you pouting about, Daisy?" her stepmother asked, noticing her expression.

"I'm worried that Mr. Kemble is being too optimistic in attempting to join the group today. His health seemed so fragile."

The baroness looked over at the approaching pair, a

calculating gleam in her eyes. She said softly, "That is a very wise observation, Daisy."

Daisy was surprised at this praise, but even more surprised when Lady Rutherford turned to her daughter and said, "Bella, you should stay close to Mr. Kemble today."

Bella blinked in confusion. "You wish me to ride with Mr. Kemble? Not the duke?"

"Use your head, Bella," Lady Rutherford said. "This Mr. Kemble is the duke's closest friend. If you earn his good opinion, it will no doubt further your appeal in the duke's eyes. And you will appear to be most concerned for his health, which will reflect favorably on you as well. For a successful marriage, all advantages must be considered. Now, he's about to look over. When he does, smile and nod. Just a little."

"Yes, Mama." Bella cast her gaze under her lashes to watch the approach of the men without seeming too bold. Then, just as Jackson Kemble lifted his hand to the brim of his hat, Bella gave him a sweet smile.

"Good morning, Lady Rutherford, Miss Bella. And Miss Daisy." He still looked very pale in Daisy's estimation. "It should be excellent weather for a ride."

"Indeed, Mr. Kemble," Bella responded. "Do you ride often?"

"Not so much lately," he admitted with a laugh. "Perhaps I ought to have a minder."

"I should be glad to take on the task, Mr. Kemble," Bella said demurely.

He looked nonplussed for a moment, but then said, "That would be very kind of you, my lady."

Behind Lady Rutherford's austere expression, Daisy could recognize a certain giddiness. She was relentlessly executing her plan to make Bella a duchess within a year.

And all Daisy could do was watch.

Tristan said, "The grooms have laid out a path for us. I'm still not familiar enough with the estate to pick out my own route."

"Ah, then I shall ride beside you," Lady Rutherford said, pouncing on this opportunity. "For I am well acquainted with the whole area. It would be my pleasure to point out the other houses and estates you'll want to know."

Tristan nodded in agreement, his eyes flickering only briefly to Daisy. She'd never felt more invisible.

The signal came to begin the ride, and the whole party started off, stretching naturally into a longer train as various riders found the pace that suited them. At the head of the group, of course, the duke himself rode, joined by the baroness.

Daisy, no longer a very confident rider considering it had been years since she'd ridden for pleasure, allowed her own mount to choose its speed, which was slower than most of the others. *Just as well*, Daisy thought. *This is where I am supposed to be.* Trailing along behind, only able to watch while others do what they wish.

* * * *

About a half hour into the ride, Tristan was so tired of Lady Rutherford's chatter. The woman passed judgment on literally every topic that came up, and Tristan wondered how anyone could even have that many opinions on such trivial matters. When pointing out the distant sight of the home owned by Lady Weatherby (who rode somewhere behind them), Lady Rutherford added that the place was cramped and depressingly dark inside. When gesturing to Lord Dallmire in the course of another conversation, Lady Rutherford noted that he looked very fat.

Tristan wondered what the lady said about his own appearance when he was not present—surely his scarred face was a matter of disappointment to her.

He tried to steer the conversation to a safer place, reminding the baroness that he'd still very like to arrange a meeting with the estate manager of the Grange. The baroness looked almost offended or alarmed, and then hastily promised to sort it out soon. "After all, no one wants to think about such mundane things if they don't have to. Certainly, I don't worry about it. Oh, look at that ramshackle building over there. It ought to be burned down."

Seemingly, nothing and no one could please her…other than her daughter, Bella. Lady Rutherford praised her to the skies, telling Tristan that she was a perfect angel, schooled in every little thing a lady would need to know to run a great house, even one so grand as Lyondale.

It was all very obvious, and Tristan resisted the urge to roll his eyes. In fact, Lady Rutherford's behavior actively repelled him. Bella might be the most beautiful woman in England for all he knew. But she'd be a lot more beautiful without a mother like Lady Rutherford hovering nearby.

At last, he couldn't take it anymore. He suddenly wedged one heel into the flank of his horse, causing a startled whinny.

"Oh, no," Tristan said. "He might have injured a hoof." Immediately, Tristan dismounted and pulled the horse to the side of the path. "You go on, my lady," he ordered firmly. "I'll catch up as soon as I can. I mustn't deny you the pleasure of the ride."

Without a clear reason to stay, Lady Rutherford was forced to continue on with the group. Tristan knelt by Stormer's front leg, picking up the hoof and examining it closely. The horse was perfectly fine, and clearly confused by Tristan's behavior.

"Sorry, boy," he whispered. "It's a necessary deception." A chunk of apple went a long way to mending Stormer's mood, and the horse crunched on it happily while Tristan pretended to be worried about his leg.

Just then a young groom rode up, concern on his face. "Your grace! Is the horse lame?"

Tristan motioned him over. He was one of the brighter boys who worked in the stables, and Tristan decided he could be trusted with a small covert operation.

"Listen here, Timothy. It is Timothy, yes? Good. I want you to ride back and fetch a farrier's rasp. Bring it back here."

"Sir? Will that help?"

"No, but it won't hurt. And it will give me some breathing room. Now go, not too fast... and not a word to anyone."

"Yes, sir!" The boy wheeled about, his horse trotting back toward the house at a pace that looked more frantic than it was.

Tristan waved other riders by, telling them that a groom was already handling the issue. He actually enjoyed the moment of quiet in the woods.

Then Daisy rode up. "I do hope Stormer isn't hurt!" she said, looking over the horse for damage.

"He's fine. I simply needed an excuse to not ride at the head of the group."

Daisy understood his unspoken point instantly, and covered her mouth to hide a smile. She looked behind her, but there was no one. "I will wait with you, if you don't mind. I was last in the group, and alone anyway."

"That's a shame," he said, helping her dismount. The pleasure of holding her waist as he lowered her to the ground made his hands linger there, feeling the soft velvet of her jacket. "You're denying others your company."

"They do not care for my company," she retorted. "They all wish to be near you. Or plot and plan ways to make you notice them."

"Your stepmother certainly prevented all others from an opportunity," he said, again relieved that he'd evaded her.

"But I seem to have stumbled into one," Daisy said with an impish smile.

"I'm glad." He reached out and pulled her closer, using the bulk of the horses to hide them from prying eyes. "It's near impossible to get a chance to see you without a dozen others lurking around."

Daisy looked shy as she said, "I've spent more time alone with you than I have with any other man."

"Good. I'd hate to have to hunt someone down."

"Tristan!" she objected, alarmed.

"What? I'm jealous of the very idea."

"There's absolutely no reason to be. No one is courting me."

"What is wrong with the men in this county?" Tristan muttered. It had been days since he'd escorted her home in the carriage, and learned exactly how good it felt to kiss her, and how much he wanted to be with her for a much longer time.

Now, he took the opportunity to lean down for a kiss, hoping to rekindle the feelings he remembered so well from the carriage ride.

Daisy's lips were just as soft as before, and after a little sound of surprise, she opened her mouth and let him deepen the kiss.

Oh, this was not going to be enough. Tristan drew out the kiss as long as he could, feeling very annoyed that breathing was so essential to life. He pulled back to get his breath.

Her eyes opened, and she regarded him in a dazed, delighted way. "Why did you do that?" she asked, blinking slowly, as if coming out of a dream.

Because you're irresistible, he wanted to say. But the words stuck in his throat, because he heard something else...distant hoofbeats.

"Damn it," he swore under his breath. He stepped back and looked Daisy over. She was wearing velvet, and the imprints of his hands were all over the fabric. Like evidence of a crime.

He ran his hands over her, smoothing away the marks into long streaks.

Daisy looked down and gasped, realizing the problem. She pushed his hands away and completed the job herself, quickly erasing all his touches. Then she smoothed her hair and straightened her jacket, obviously worried. "Do I look all right?" she whispered.

"Beautiful," he replied instantly.

"I mean..."

"No one would guess," he corrected, then looked to where the sound of hooves was coming from. He breathed a sigh of relief when he saw that it was only Jack.

But no, it was not *only* Jack. Bella Merriot rode beside him. If she suspected that Tristan was just ravishing her stepsister, it was likely that the news would make it to the baroness in less than an hour. And Tristan did not want that.

Putting on his blandest expression, he hailed Jack.

His friend came to a halt nearby, clever eyes taking in the scene and silently questioning Tristan about his intentions. But Tristan gave nothing away and seized on a more obvious question.

"How is the ride for you?" he asked. "I see you're not

exactly pressing your mount."

"I'm well," Jack said, though Tris could see a pallor in his skin that hadn't been there this morning. "Miss Bella has been most tolerant of my slowness."

"Nonsense. I don't like to race anyway," Bella said. She was the picture of feminine propriety, maintaining a small distance from Jack's horse, but still obviously paying close attention to him. "It has been a very pleasant outing, but perhaps it would be best for us to return to the house."

Bella gave Tristan a look, and made a tiny nod toward Jack. So she was worried about him too. Tris decided this was a perfect opportunity to get out of the mess he'd put himself in with Daisy, nearly allowing them to be discovered in a compromising position. Idiot.

Tris helped Daisy onto her own horse (keeping his hands very firmly where they should be and not allowing his touch to linger this time). Then he remounted Stormer.

Jack said, gesturing to the horse, "I thought…"

"He's perfectly fine," Tris said quickly, loud enough for all of them to hear. "I had first thought he'd hurt his front hoof, or got a stone under the shoe. But he's fine. Let's all ride together back to the house. Mr. Kemble has certainly exceeded the doctor's orders for fresh air today."

Jack's eyes narrowed, but he said nothing. The four of them rode slowly back toward the great house, the conversation innocuous. After Bella made a chance remark about Daisy doing so well at managing the harvest this year, Tristan suddenly realized something he should have picked up on before.

"*You* manage the estate," he said. "During the first part of the ride, I asked the baroness to set up a meeting with the Grange's man, and she nearly cantered off to avoid the topic. That's because the manager is you."

"Don't tell anyone, please," Daisy pleaded. "Lady Rutherford would be mortified. The fact is that the last one left a few years ago and she's never replaced him. I know what to do anyway, so it seemed unnecessary."

"Unnecessary? Daisy, it shouldn't be *your* job to sort through ledgers of crops and livestock. You're a lady."

Daisy gave a little, sad smile. "Am I?"

"To me, yes." Tristan grinned, his mood brightening. "Oh, this is actually perfect. I've got so many questions, for it turns out Lyondale's manager was completely incompetent. I sacked him."

"Personally? What an honor for him."

Tristan laughed at the unexpected remark, but then proceeded to ask a half dozen questions about Daisy's methods and her plans for Rutherford, and how he could do the same for Lyondale. Before he realized it, they were practically to the stables. He hadn't even noticed the slow passage back, because Daisy had somehow made winter wheat an intriguing topic.

"Are you two chattering about farming?" Bella asked then, with a musical laugh.

Tristan noticed how Bella looked between him and Daisy, probably considering her suspicions about a man and woman found alone in the woods. She rode closer to Daisy and reached out, smoothing the arm of Daisy's jacket.

"That's the problem with velvet," he overheard her say to Daisy. "It does show every little mark."

Bella's tone was mild, but Tris saw the alarm in Daisy's eyes.

Luckily, just at that moment, the young stableboy Tris had sent on the errand earlier came riding up, distracting Bella.

"Sir!" he called out. "You're riding Stormer?"

"A false alarm," Tristan announced. "I feared he had injured himself, but he soon recovered."

By the time the quartet reached the house, an array of servants stood prepared to retrieve the horses (Stormer was fussed over, which pleased Tristan). Footmen were ready to help Jack walk back inside. He protested all the while that he was perfectly fine, despite labored breathing.

Daisy and Bella both looked after him worriedly. Daisy said, "Riding is too vigorous an activity for someone in his state of health."

"I agree," Bella said. "A walk around the pond would be much better for him."

"Excellent idea, my lady," Tristan said, walking up to them. "Perhaps you would both join us on an afternoon soon to do just that. When Mr. Kemble is feeling up for it, that is."

He was thinking that such an occasion would be another opportunity to see Daisy, but it was Bella who replied in a pleased tone, "We would be delighted, your grace."

"I'll arrange it," he promised, casting a look at Daisy —who looked less delighted than her stepsister. Tristan wondered why, but then decided that she was still concerned that Bella might have realized what Tris and Daisy had been doing during their brief time alone.

No matter. It was a kiss, nothing more. Daisy would not suffer for it. He hoped.

Chapter 8

❀ ༺༻ ❀

REMEMBERING WHAT TRISTAN HAD TOLD her about Jack Kemble's illness, Daisy slipped out of the house very early the next morning to go visit Tabitha in her cottage. The old woman couldn't have known she was coming, yet she was there in the doorway, smiling at Daisy when she walked up.

"Hurry on in, girl. Got the kettle on and some lovely mint tea in the pot for you."

Daisy entered the dark cottage, not questioning Tabitha's foreknowledge, only grateful for the warm beverage offered to her on such a frosty morning. She blew over the surface of the tea, saying, "Winter's on its way."

"Aye, cold dark times coming," Tabitha agreed, scowling. "Going to be rough for many."

"Are you worried about the weather?" Daisy asked. "You can always move to the Grange for the season, you know."

"The weather? Bah! That's no concern." Tabitha bustled around the cottage kitchen, putting various dishes in their place. "Now tell me what's on your mind, Daisy girl."

"Well, if you remember that February a few years ago,

when I came down with that terrible cough? You had some medicines that helped quite a lot."

"*Medicine* is too fancy for what I make," Tabitha objected. "But I do remember the simples I brewed for you and the others that winter. Why? Someone got that sickness so early in the autumn?"

"Not exactly. The duke's friend had been suffering from an illness for a few months, and he's got a cough that seems similar. Those drops and the syrup you made would help him."

"Surely the duke has a high and mighty doctor at his call."

"That he does. It's Dr. Stelton from the village, who is very good. But every time I hear Mr. Kemble coughing, it sounds as if he's dying!" Daisy hoped that was not the case, since Mr. Kemble was such a nice man.

"I happen to have a bottle of syrup and a batch of the drops on hand," Tabitha announced, a bit smugly.

Daisy had little doubt of it, for Tabitha always planned ahead, and she'd be ready for the very first of the seasonal maladies that plagued the locals in the colder months. "Wonderful! May I take some today? Tell me what you'd like in return and I'll see that it's sent over from the Grange."

"Well, a bottle of wine would be a treat, for that's a thing I can't make on my own. But as for payment, Miss Daisy, what I want from you is your word."

"My word?" she echoed, puzzled by the cryptic request.

"Yes," the old woman replied, pulling a small dark green bottle out of a cupboard. "I'll give you the simples to take to this friend of the duke. But in return, you must promise me that when you flee from the Grange, you'll come here first."

"Flee the Grange?" Daisy asked, incredulous at the very idea. "Tabitha, what are you talking about? The Grange is my home! I'll never leave it."

Tabitha held the bottle close to her chest. "Promise me."

"Very well, I promise," Daisy said, mostly to appease the older woman. Perhaps it wasn't so good for her to be living all alone in the woods. She was growing eccentric. Well, *more* eccentric.

"Promise made is a payment paid!" Tabitha said. She held out the bottle and a small paper sack that contained the sweet throat drops that tasted of mint and honey. "See to it that the poor man gets these. By my word, he'll feel better within hours."

"I certainly hope so." Daisy tucked the medicines away in her bag. She finished her tea, telling Tabitha of the ordinary goings-on of the village and the Grange, scrupulously avoiding mention of the duke, since the very thought of him made her heart flutter. Riding with him had been a pleasure, and with Bella and Mr. Kemble close by, it was entirely proper and even felt...familial, which was a novelty for Daisy.

Then she hurried back to the Grange, knowing that she was late for the morning's chores. But when she returned, the baroness was already awake, looking alert as a hawk in a very fashionable midnight-blue dressing gown.

"Where have you been, Daisy?" Lady Rutherford asked, as she entered the front foyer of the house.

"Just visiting Tabitha," Daisy explained, putting her bag on the table as she took off her bonnet. "I wanted to get some syrup for Mr. Kemble to help with his cough."

Lady Rutherford picked up the green bottle, curious. "Is that what this stuff is?"

"Yes, and the paper sack holds candied drops to soothe

the throat."

"Hmmm." The baroness put the bottle back. "Interest-ing. But don't you have some tasks to attend to, Daisy?"

"Yes, ma'am." Daisy hurried to the kitchen, thinking of the breakfast to prepare.

Later, when she remembered the medicine, she couldn't seem to find it, and she nearly tore the house apart in her search. How very vexing, to lose something you intended to give to another person!

"It'll turn up at some point," she told herself. "Proba-bly someone just misplaced them."

The next day, Bella and Daisy were invited for a pic-nic at Lyondale. The duke sent one of his own carriages to pick them up at Rutherford Grange. Daisy was harried, for once again she'd been looking all over the house for the medicines she got from Tabitha, intending to offer them to Kemble on arrival.

"I am so chicken-brained lately," she huffed out, look-ing into a kitchen cabinet for the third time. "I swore I put them near the door so as not to forget them, and now I've forgot where I put them!"

"Daisy, hurry!" Bella urged, looking nervously at the carriage. "It would be very rude to keep the gentlemen waiting."

Daisy resolved to do a more thorough search later, and until she found the items, she wouldn't mention anything to Kemble, so he didn't get his hopes up.

Traveling toward Lyondale, Daisy and Bella sat on the forward-facing seat, each looking surreptitiously around the opulent compartment. Bella hadn't seen it before at all. Daisy had, since the duke had taken her home that night after dinner…but that had been in the dark, and also with the distraction of Tristan kissing her so sensuously that Daisy had nearly melted, and therefore she'd been quite unable to appreciate the conveyance itself.

The closed coach featured paneling between the sparkling glass of the windows. The seats were padded in heavy brocade, and the whole coach rode smoothly, despite the pitted road. Daisy tried to guess at the cost of the vehicle, and gave up—the amount was probably the equivalent of several tenant families' annual incomes.

Bella looked over the coach's interior with curiosity in her eyes. "After this, our own carriage will seem even shabbier." It was a mere statement of fact, and Daisy had to agree.

"Well, it's only needed to go to town and for church on Sundays," she said. "Surely if your mother wanted a new one, she'd purchase it."

"I've asked," Bella said. "I never quite understood why Mama spends so much on some things, but not enough on others. She says that my wardrobe is the most important thing…until I'm married. But I think that she ought to put more thought into the appearance of Rutherford Grange. My suitors do call on me there, after all. A house is like a wardrobe," she concluded. "Where a lady lives matters just as much as how she looks."

Daisy felt the words with a sting. She had slept in the alcove of the kitchen last night since she'd dozed off while mending clothes, and woken up feeling sore and cramped, not to mention covered in the soot of the fireplace. Where a lady lived did matter…and Daisy was one step away from living in the stables.

But Bella wouldn't have known that, and her words were probably not intended to censure Daisy. So she tried to ignore her hurt and asked, "Have you told your mother that? She does so very much want you to marry well."

"That's true, but she seems to think that I will soon have a proposal in hand."

Bella didn't add the rest of the statement, because it was obvious. The expected proposal was going to come from the duke, who, after all, just invited Bella to a picnic with Daisy in tow to chaperone her.

"Have you…have you cause to believe a proposal is imminent?" Daisy nearly squeaked out.

"I should not presume to know any gentleman's intentions," Bella said primly. "Though the duke certainly has been attentive since he came to the area."

Daisy bit her lip, remembering that Tristan had been very attentive to her indeed. But only when the two found themselves alone.

Then Bella said, looking out the window, "You know, Mr. Kemble has never once told me that I am pretty."

Daisy raised an eyebrow, though Bella wouldn't see it. Was the girl so vain that she cataloged each time a man complimented her?

When the women arrived at the steps of Lyondale, both Lord Lyon and Mr. Kemble were ready to greet them at the front of the great house.

"We're ready," said Kemble. He stood next to what looked like a very large hamper of food.

"Are you expecting many other guests?" Daisy asked on seeing it.

Mr. Kemble smiled back. "No, just you two. But the kitchen staff seems to think we're planning to picnic in Wales. We have *several* meals' worth."

Two footmen did the work of carrying the hamper down to the location by the pond, which had been chosen for its view across the water and to the fields beyond. Trees grew at the far end of the pond, their leaves shining gold as they drifted away in the breeze.

When they sat, Bella's gown pooled around her like a perfect white cloud. Daisy felt as if she was getting tangled in her dark green wool. Still, the mood was cheerful and quite casual compared to the previous dinner party. The absence of Lady Rutherford no doubt helped this effect.

To Daisy's surprise, the picnic was actually a very pleasant affair. Bella was skilled at guiding a conversation, hitting all the social niceties while steering away from difficult topics. It also helped that Tristan and Jack were good friends, and had many stories to tell. Bella seemed fascinated by Tristan's younger life. In particular, she listened raptly to stories of the rougher years of his childhood, before his destiny as a duke was revealed.

Daisy liked hearing his stories too, though she could sense the elisions in his tale that Bella clearly missed, the way he didn't mention missed meals or the prospect of not knowing if the next quarter's rent could be paid. It was odd how her and Tristan's lives had flipped. Daisy grew up in comfort and luxury, expecting to become a baroness in her own right. And now she lived a life closer to a servant than an heiress. Tristan's life was just the opposite, growing up in modest surroundings, unaware of his bloodline until the truth was given to him so abruptly. And now he lived like a prince. She hoped he was happy with the change. Sometimes she got the impression that he would rather run away from it all.

After the group tested the desserts (eclairs, cream puffs, a lemon cake...the array of choices went on and on), Tristan asked Daisy about how she'd chosen a particular breed of sheep, remembering the last time when she mentioned it in passing.

Jack sighed. "If you two are going to drone on about livestock, please take a walk around the pond while you do."

"I certainly could not contribute on that topic," Bella

said. "It is quite beyond me. But do feel free to stretch your legs. I will see that Mr. Kemble is not abandoned."

So Daisy and Tristan walked at a sedate pace, and since they were in view of their picnic companions or the great house, the stroll was quite safe. They followed a path near the water, and Daisy was pleased to have Tristan to herself. After a few moments of conversation that ranged from sheep to corn laws, she said, "Your grace, I was actually wondering…"

"Yes?"

"Oh, never mind."

"Tell me."

"I don't wish to summon any painful memories," she said.

"Curious about what happened to me? During the war, I mean."

"Oh, no. Mr. Kemble told me what happened."

"He only knows what I told him," Tristan said cryptically.

"What's the truth?" Daisy asked.

He flexed his injured hand subconsciously. "The truth will likely disappoint you."

"Why is that?"

"Because the truth is I don't know what happened." Tristan took a deep breath. "I saw something—a cannonball, a shell, I didn't know—and I just reacted. I shoved down whoever it was standing next to me. And I shouted. Together, it gave enough warning to the others around us to scatter. The shell hit right where we'd been grouped together. But I was knocked unconscious, so I don't know details. When I woke up, my head was ringing so badly, I felt like I'd been packed inside a cathedral bell. But the man I shoved was a general, and he remembered everything, or least he told the story like he did." He sighed. "It wasn't any great act of bravery on my part. Just luck."

Daisy said nothing for a moment. Her mind was on the possibility of Tristan's luck going the other way. The idea of his dying made her shudder.

"Not a pleasant story," he said apologetically, mistaking her reaction.

"I liked the ending," she said. "The part where you lived."

His mouth twitched. "Is that so?"

As they completed their circle of the pond, they made the final turn in the path, and Daisy could again see Mr. Kemble and Bella, sitting on the blanket. She was listening to some story he was telling, and then let out a silvery peal of laughter as she heard the final line.

"Jack is looking so much better," Tristan said then. "I think Miss Bella's presence must have a positive effect."

Daisy glanced at him, catching an odd light in his eyes. A little part of her despaired again. Despite the way he'd kissed her before, despite the connection she felt to him today...all it took was the appearance of the beautiful Bella Merriot to turn his attention away from Daisy. She remembered her stepmother's plan—for Bella to dote on Mr. Kemble as a way to gain the esteem of the duke. It seemed the plan was working perfectly.

Since Tristan was expecting her to comment on Bella's effect, Daisy began to reply, but was stopped short by a loud slamming sound echoing over the water of the pond.

"Oh!" she cried, instinctively putting her hands to her ears.

Alarmed, Daisy turned toward the great house and saw two workers standing by a pile of boards in the lawn, which had fallen from the height of the roof. Thank goodness everyone else was well away from the area.

"What happened?" she called. "Is anyone hurt?"

"No, miss!" one called back. "The rope broke and the boards fell. That's all."

"Please be more careful! That could have hurt someone!" she reprimanded them. She turned back to Tristan, who had gone completely still. He'd shrank from the sound, squeezing his eyes shut. A look of pain crossed his face. He was standing as if frozen in place, and something in his breathing suggested that he was far more affected by the clatter than she had been.

He shook his head as if to clear it. "What happened?" he whispered.

She hated to see him distressed. Hoping to restore his mood, she said, "Don't worry. No one was hurt. The sound was just the boards falling from where your men are repairing that roof."

"That sound..." he said, still looking haunted. "It's too close..."

"Your grace? Sir?" Daisy asked. She paused and tried again. "You hate the noise, don't you? You hate anything loud."

He refused to look at her. "You should go, Daisy. Take your sister and get away from here."

"But you just said that Bella was good for—"

"I said go!" he roared. "Why are you still here? *Get the hell away from me!*"

Chapter 9

❧🙦🙤❧

WHEN THEY RETURNED TO THE house, Tristan insisted that Jack go rest in his room, despite his friend's protests. The ladies had left immediately, of course, and he'd been too rattled to apologize or make amends for anything. Less than an hour later, though, the majordomo interrupted Tristan in his office, while he was puzzling over John Cater's latest missive about the diamond mine venture, which involved a lot of numbers that he could not quite parse.

"Your grace, Miss Bella Merriot has come to call. Are you at home? She said she has something for Mr. Kemble."

"Something for Kemble?" Tris echoed. "Show her in."

The majordomo bowed and left. Shortly after, he reappeared with the doll-like Bella in his wake.

Tristan stood up. "My lady."

"Your grace." Bella dipped into a graceful curtsey. She looked unnervingly perfect, her hair curled into those shiny, stiff ringlets and the lace of her gown starched to withstand a gale. *She must be damnably uncomfortable*, he thought.

It was strange how Bella was considered the far better

catch, when it was Daisy who drew him. Daisy had a spark of life, a curiosity about the world that he loved to see. Whether she was discussing the weather or music or simple village news, she always expressed interest in the tiniest details, and she clearly cared about the outcome of each event. In contrast, Bella seemed like a paper doll.

"I have some local remedies that may benefit Mr. Kemble in his convalescence. I didn't mean to disturb you, but perhaps you could see that they're given to his nurse…"

"I'm sure that he'll derive even more benefit if he has a visit from a friendly face, especially after you had to leave so quickly before." *Now that's talking around the issue*, Tristan berated himself. "Come with me, my lady."

Bella nodded quickly. "Happily, your grace."

Kemble sat up in bed when he saw them enter the room.

"Visitor for you, Jack," Tristan murmured. Louder, he said, "Miss Bella has brought a gift."

"Not a gift, Mr. Kemble," Bella said, blushing prettily. "Just a few medicines that may help relieve some of your symptoms."

"I'll take all the help I can get," Jack replied. "That was a very kind thought, my lady."

Bella paused, then said, "In fact, it was not my thought. Daisy arranged to get them from our local healer. I think she meant to give them to you herself, but she must have been distracted. My mother found them and told me to come posthaste. So you see, I am only the errand girl."

"Then I am grateful to you both."

Bella approached the bed and placed the basket on the extreme edge. "The syrup is to be taken at bedtime, and will ease coughing so you may sleep through the night.

These drops can be used anytime. I remember using them myself last winter, and they are wonderfully soothing for the throat."

"Perhaps we should let the doctor go and bring this healer to Lyondale," Tristan said. "It seems that's exactly what you need."

"This is why it helps to know your neighbors, your grace," Jack replied, with an arched eyebrow.

"I am sorry if I interrupted your reading, Mr. Kemble," Bella said. She seemed to be more human now, and Tristan regretted thinking her a doll earlier. Very probably, she was just being extremely careful to behave herself around a duke. Kemble *was* much more approachable. He always had been.

"Not at all. In fact, I can't read for long. Even the weight of the book is hard to hold up for a while, and my eyes get tired."

"Then you must let me read to you!" Bella exclaimed, then glanced at Tristan. "That is…if your grace does not object?"

"On the contrary." Tristan grabbed one of the chairs by the fireplace and dragged it to the bedside before he remembered that dukes weren't supposed to do those sorts of tasks. "Pop one of those sweets in your mouth, Kemble. My lady, is this light sufficient?"

"Quite, your grace." She allowed Tristan to seat her in the chair.

"I'll have tea sent up shortly."

"Very good, your grace," she said, already opening the book. "The ribbon is marking the page at chapter four, Mr. Kemble. Shall I start there?"

"Please." Jack smiled at her, and Tristan got a jolt when he realized that there was something besides simple pleasure in his friend's expression.

Oh, God, Jack's falling for her.

And why not? Bella Merriot was a beautiful woman. But she was aiming to marry as high as she could, certainly higher than a mere solicitor. Whether she intended to or not, the Hon. Bella Merriot was going to break his friend's heart.

Just as Daisy was going to break his own.

For several days, Tristan nursed his anger at himself for letting Daisy witness his weakness. He stayed exclusively at Lyondale and sought out only Kemble for company. He buried himself in estate business and tried to forget embarrassing himself in front of Daisy. It was difficult, because he thought of one reason after another for why he wanted to see her. Partly, he knew, it was that he just enjoyed being with her. Daisy was such a calming presence, and a delight to talk to—for it turned out that he really did like learning about agricultural practices when it was Daisy doing the lecturing. He had been planning to invite her to a supper soon, hoping it would be a suitable excuse to see her again. But it was all ruined when that *noise* pieced his skull.

After the worst of it, he did write to Daisy, asking to call on her so he could explain. She gave no reply, which made him cross and reclusive. However, he couldn't hide forever. Though Tristan had literally no interest in hearing Hornthwaite's homily that Sunday, he decided that he ought to go to the village church at least once. It seemed to be expected, and he *was* the new Duke of Lyon, after all. He'd put in one appearance, and then he would consider his duty done.

He took Jack with him, because he believed misery loved company.

When the two men arrived outside the church building, however, they both stopped to stare upward in dismay.

Kemble spoke first. "I studied the law, Tris, not Christian doctrine. But I have to tell you that from what I understand of tradition...this church looks broken."

He was absolutely correct. The steeple of the building was completely gone, and ugly wooden boards covered the hole where it had once met the peaked roof. The effect was like a bandage on a wound.

"Let's see how bad the inside is," Tristan said, moving into the flow of parishioners who were all heading toward the doors, dressed in Sunday best.

Inside fared better. They were ushered to the special pew reserved for the duke and his guests. Several congregants greeted him in a respectful manner, but within minutes, the crowd settled. Hornthwaite took his place in the pulpit and the service began.

The vicar was born for the task of speaking ad nauseam to a crowd that could not politely escape. Tristan was soon bored by Hornthwaite's dull talk, which was full of platitudes about Christian charity, but little actual comfort for a soul in torment. Tristan's mind drifted back to his army days. While he'd been laid up in the hospital tent after being injured, the chaplain came to visit him every day. Tristan wasn't a devout man even before having half his body shelled, and he had a lot of questions about a god that would permit such suffering. The chaplain, who was named Langdon, had sat and listened to Tristan's bitter words, his rage, his self-sorrow. He'd prayed for Tris, but he'd also talked with him. And he was open about the gaps in cosmic knowledge. No, humanity did not know why suffering was permitted, why evil existed, why a loving god did not simply create a world without pain and sorrow.

"I believe," said Mr. Langdon, who was a gaunt, greying man even in his early forties, "that the truest expression of God's love for us is that He trusts us to experience pain and suffering and yet to still choose to value that which is good in the world. That he made us strong enough to endure pain and death and still feel love and hope ourselves. I think Jesus himself must have had a few moments of doubt during his supreme suffering. Would this mad attempt for salvation really work? Could a sacrifice by one truly save all? But in his human incarnation, he went ahead with it—he used his own faith to live through death itself. That is the message, Tristan. That suffering is not fated to triumph over us, but that we can triumph over it, simply by *enduring* it."

"You're not lying in a bed with half your face gone," Tristan had growled back.

"No, and I won't pretend to understand what you're going through. But you are alive, and that is a gift. Think on that. I'll be back tomorrow."

In contrast to the army chaplain's words, Hornthwaite's speech was insipid. Tristan couldn't imagine this man visiting the sick and dying. He knew better than to peer around at the congregation, but he wondered if Daisy was in attendance that day. Sadly, he didn't get a glimpse of her. Perhaps she had to stay home.

At the end of the service, Hornthwaite was there at the door, bidding all the parishioners goodbye. When Tris came up to him, the vicar offered a slightly smug smile. "So gratifying to see you today, your grace. I was certain you would show the same respect for the church as your predecessor, despite the concerns of some parishioners." Parishioners he declined to name, Tristan noted.

"I prefer private devotions. Isn't that right, Mr. Kemble?"

"Very private indeed," Jack agreed with a wry smile.

"Is that so?" Hornthwaite said, with a pinched expression.

"You requested that I look at the church building itself," Tris went on. "Am I correct in thinking you hope for some financial assistance from me in order to repair some of it? Does the parish not provide for such needs?"

"The spire was struck by lightning this spring, your grace. Most unexpected. And expensive to replace."

"No doubt."

"And I heard you are making improvements at your own estate. You've shown such zeal in making changes to Lyondale, not at all like the old ways. Rutherford Grange has always maintained tradition in both the house and the fields. And speaking of Rutherford Grange, I heard that you've been seen with Miss Merriot."

"I've been seen with half the shire," Tristan retorted. "But yes, the Misses Merriot both joined us for an afternoon not long ago."

Hornthwaite said, "I trust you found Miss Bella to be as presentable and charming as we all do."

"No one could complain of her," Tristan admitted. "She has been coming to the house to read to Mr. Kemble here, no doubt speeding his convalescence."

"She is the apple of Lady Rutherford's eye," the vicar said, warming to his subject. "The baroness has reared perhaps the most perfect young lady in all of England. She will be a prize on the marriage mart. The smart man would offer for her quickly, or risk losing her."

"And what would she bring to a marriage?" Kemble asked in his mild tone.

Hornthwaite turned to him. "Aside from the expected title and her own personal charm, there is a substantial dowry. I believe it is some thousands."

"And that is from the inheritance from the late baron?

Or does she have previous expectations?" Jack pressed.

"All from the baron," Hornthwaite said. "Her mother is very clever with money. It will all be managed well, right up to the moment of the wedding."

"She will no doubt make some man very happy," Jack replied.

Tristan glanced at his friend, wondering what he was about. On their own, the questions were innocuous enough—every marriageable woman knew her worth down to the penny, for that was one of the most important aspects of a contract. But why did Jackson Kemble care?

"At the moment, I'm not thinking of the social scene, but of the actual scene." Tristan looked up pointedly at the broken spire. "The church does not look its best at the moment. It does not inspire confidence. I'll let you know if I can do anything to improve the situation."

"Why, thank you, your grace!"

"Don't thank me yet."

With that, Tris and Jack returned home.

Jack, lying back in his seat in the carriage with a worrying pallor to his complexion, said, "The vicar seems to think you've got sacks of gold lying about the place."

"I suppose I should be grateful that my financial situation is not obvious to everyone in the county. Speaking of gold, what was all that about Miss Bella's dowry?"

"Ever since Miss Daisy told me of the events surrounding her father's death and the subsequent news of the will, I've been curious," Jack explained.

"Miss Wallis explained it to me as best she could," Tristan said. "The barony of Rutherford was one of the few to specifically descend to the oldest child, whether male or female."

"Yes, that's what she told me too. It's a barony by writ, so that's possible, if not usual. And I asked Miss

Bella what she knew about the changed will, but she has no knowledge of the matter at all. She takes her mother's word for everything, and never questions it, or if she does, it's buried quite deep. But what I find odd is that he turned his back on generations of tradition to gift the title to his *second* wife and her line? It would be one of the most unusual dispositions of title and property that I've ever heard of…and having spent years in Chancery, I've heard of many."

"It's bloody unfair to Daisy," Tristan said. "Especially because she's so devoted to the estate. Whenever I hear her talk about the fields, it's like she's talking about a friend. I think leaving this part of the country would kill her."

"Well, the baroness certainly seems to want to keep her stepdaughter close, if only to handle the day-to-day workings of the place." Jack sneered, disapproving of Lady Rutherford's cost-saving measure of using Daisy as an unpaid estate manager. When Tristan had first told him about it, Jack had said a *very* rude word to describe the woman.

"You must be feeling better, to worry at the minutiae of a country estate. A few weeks ago, I couldn't get you to care about what to eat for dinner." On the other hand, Jack didn't look much better, especially not at the moment.

"The air agrees with me," Jack said, with a slight smile

"Even so, I'm afraid I shouldn't have dragged you along to the church. You're worn out."

"Nonsense."

Tris shook his head at his friend's stubbornness, but then remembered something else. He pulled out a letter from his coat pocket. "Did I tell you that John wrote again? He sent along a whole packet of papers this time,

He must have been waiting at the docks to get the message on a ship to England!"

"That means he needs money," Jack replied, looking interested despite himself. "How much does he want?"

"Only ten thousand."

"Only!"

"It seems reasonable considering the expenses in starting a new mining venture. And the terms are very favorable. Though there are three partners, I'd get forty percent of profits, in light of my initial contribution to the funding."

"For the love of God, Tris. A diamond mine thousands of miles away, on another continent, overseen by people you can't check on, not to mention the corruption that surrounds such ventures with precious stones? It has all the makings of a fiasco. I beg you to put this mad notion aside."

Tristan paused, and his expression must have tipped Jack off to the truth.

"You already did it," he accused Tris. "You invested ten thousand pounds without thinking twice."

"I thought many times," Tris protested. To be honest, he thought about offering Daisy a spectacular necklace or rings to dazzle her. "It's a rare opportunity!"

"It's a scam," Jack said bluntly.

"That's unworthy of you. John would never do such a thing."

"I meant he's the *victim* of a scam."

"It's real," Tris snapped back. He pulled a small object from his pocket. "Look."

Jack took the pebble he was offered, surveying it with raised eyebrows. "A rock I could have picked up outside the church this morning."

"It's a diamond. Cater sent it along with the papers.

It's not impressive now because it has yet to be cut. But it's five carats! Think of how many more diamonds must lie below."

His friend bit his lip, frowning at the stone. "You could send it to London to be appraised, I suppose. But with the money sent already... Tris, I wish you had spoken to me first. I could have looked over the papers at the very least."

"You're not well enough yet for such work," Tris told him. "I didn't want to strain you."

"It's a strain to think that you've thrown away ten thousand on a lark. Wait, do you even have ten thousand available?"

"It's not as if one sends coins in the post! I arranged it all with my bank. They have an office in Calcutta." Tris hesitated. "If I need more money anytime soon, though, I'd have to cede some land to the bank."

Jack paled further, and Tris knew why. Land was power, land was money. For the aristocracy, it was the source of all their income—the crops themselves, the rents, the simple fact of owning real estate. Most people would give up everything else before selling a parcel, which would be lost forever, along with any future income that came from it. Tris was too new to this world to fully appreciate the risk he'd taken, though now he was realizing that he'd been a bit hasty to leap into a proposition from an old friend.

"But it's not worth worrying about now," Tris went on. "If all goes well, I'll be the duke of diamonds, and I'll never have to worry about money again."

The expression of doubt and horror on Jack's face said it all.

"*If* all goes well..." Jack muttered. "Is this part of some plan to court your Miss Daisy?"

"Hardly. She won't even answer the letters I've sent."

"You sent letters?"

"A few. At first I thought she might be too busy and it simply got overlooked, but after the fourth, I fear she's quite done with me. I suppose that's what I get for losing my head and yelling at her just because I heard a loud noise." He shifted in his seat. "I hate it, Jack. It's like the war's still going on in my head."

"I'm sorry," Jack replied. "Perhaps time will make it fade. It really hasn't been that long, you know."

"It feels like forever." And it was worse without Daisy to brighten his days. He didn't fully appreciate how much he enjoyed her company until he suddenly lost it.

Chapter 10

❦ ⚶ ❦

DAISY DIDN'T SEE THE DUKE for several days following the ill-fated picnic, though she thought about him far more often. She wished there was a reason to run into him somehow, and she imagined making some clever remark that would make him laugh, to bring him out the dark mood she last saw him in. Something that would make him notice her, and forget Bella, who had apparently been invited to Lyondale any afternoon she wished to come — an invitation she'd taken advantage of, for a carriage was sent by the duke every day at noon, and Bella got into it wearing a stunning new outfit each time.

If only Daisy could compete with that. If she had the wardrobe of a lady…

"Enough daydreaming," she scolded herself. She tried to distract herself by reading the latest issues of *The English Farmer* and *The Register of Cultivation*, to which she subscribed in order to stay aware of trends in agriculture that she could use at the Grange. But now, all she could do was mark pages that she wanted to show to Tristan.

"Ugh!" Daisy put the journals aside. Why must everything make her think of him?

Fortunately, ordinary tasks still had to be done to keep

the Grange running. So Daisy helped Elaine with the washing. She mended clothes while Elaine worked in the garden (Elaine was an attentive gardener who never let a fruit go overripe or a root unharvested). Then there was the marketing, when Daisy went into the village to buy what they couldn't make at the Grange.

The journey to Lyonton and back normally didn't take very long, but on this day, she found herself hurrying along the path almost an hour later than usual. And because the days were growing shorter, the light was already turning golden—beautiful for the moment, but heralding a swift nightfall.

She wished she had accepted the offer of a ride from one of the nearby farmers. But Daisy had been suffering a bout of pride, and she could just hear her stepmother's disappointed tone: *Oh, Daisy. You're the daughter of a gentleman. You mustn't ride in the back of a hay cart as if you were a ragamuffin.*

The bags were heavy, and Daisy had to stop often to rest. But then she stopped for another reason entirely. The Duke of Lyon stood in front of her, leaning idly against the broad trunk of a tree. He looked perfectly at ease, his body relaxed in the late sun.

"Your grace!" Daisy said in surprise.

"Daisy." Tristan was holding a bunch of wildflowers, which he offered to her. "I've been waiting."

"For how long?" she asked, taking the flowers after she placed her bags on the ground. Tristan immediately picked them up to carry them to a safer place than the road.

"Does it matter? I've come here practically every day, hoping you'll pass by. But you're as elusive as a ghost."

"Lady Rutherford has kept me busy," Daisy said.

"So busy you can't respond to a letter?" he asked,

drawing her farther away from the road, where they could have a more private conversation, and not be overseen by anyone.

"Oh, not that busy! I can still write in the evenings when I have a moment. I don't know what I would do if not for writing to my friends."

"But not me?"

She paused, reconsidering his words. "Wait, did *you* send me a letter?"

"More than one," he said, his brow lifting in surprise. "Are you saying you didn't receive any of them?"

"No." Daisy frowned. "My stepmother must be behind it."

"Does she hate me that much?" Tristan stopped walking, having reached a little clearing where Stormer waited patiently, just as Tristan had waited patiently for Daisy at the roadside.

"She doesn't hate you at all, your grace. She can't wait for the day that Bella will be your duchess."

"Bella?" he echoed, his jaw going slack. "She thinks I fancy Bella?"

"Well, you do send for her to come to Lyondale every day, your grace."

"So she can read out loud to Jack!" Tristan ran his hand through his hair. "Which is exactly what I told you, in the letters you never received…"

Daisy had a sudden, uncomfortable realization. "I hope you didn't write anything in those letters that would be, um, awkward."

"Such as how much I want to see you?" Tristan asked, his gaze turning intense. "Such as how many times I wished I could take back what I did at the pond? Such as how I wish that this…nonsense about titles and income could be burned to the foundation?"

"That would be awkward, yes," Daisy murmured. "A duke ought to hold up traditions."

"Hang traditions."

He moved closer. "Daisy, I know I shouldn't keep you here, but—"

She dropped the flowers to put her arms around him, feeling as bold as she ever had in her life. "You're not keeping me here. I *choose* to stay here."

Without waiting another moment, he kissed her.

"Tristan," she breathed, then pressed her lips against his neck, relishing the slight scrape of stubble against her skin. She inhaled deeply, smelling soap and sweat and the leather of the saddle and the scent of the outdoor air. Daisy reveled in the sensation his lips provoked, and she let her eyes drift closed, hoping to enjoy this moment of delicious freedom to the full.

She opened her mouth, and the move elicited a low sound from him, something both very satisfied and very primal. Tristan held her closer, his mouth exploring places on her body that no one had ever touched before. He pulled aside the edge of her neckline with his teeth, and Daisy gasped both at the rawness of the move, and the fact that it sent heat shooting up and down her limbs.

Then Tristan pulled away, murmuring, "Wait here. Half a minute."

He looked very unhappy to leave her arms, but he did so. He walked over to Stormer in three big strides, and raided the saddlebag for a rolled-up blanket. Returning, he spread it on the ground. Then he shrugged out of his jacket, so that he had only his white shirt, which was voluminous but made of thin cotton. Stepping up to him, Daisy ran her hands over his arms.

"Stay with me a little while," Tristan whispered. "I can't tell you how badly I've wanted to be with you, really with you alone…"

Daisy kissed him, silencing his words. Whatever he was asking, she'd already committed to being here with him as long as she dared.

A breathless moment later, he was laying her down on the blanket, stretching out alongside, pressing himself to her. Daisy loved it, and wiggled closer to him, burying her head into his chest and shoulder. The books she'd read in secret had failed to mention how just being next to a person could inspire rapture.

"I wish we could stay here forever. To not have to go back home, to work and all the judgment…"

"…all the eyes staring at you. I know how it is." Tristan brushed a few strands of hair away from her face, his touch light but electrifying.

"But everyone admires you!" she said. "They envy you."

"They envy the position I hold," he said. "Not me. I could die tomorrow and they'd just summon the next heir."

"Don't say that," Daisy said, putting her hands on his face. She pulled him in for another soft kiss.

The kiss stretched out into many. Daisy sighed with pleasure when Tristan proceeded to kiss his way down her neck and chest. He tugged lightly at the edge of her dress, using his fingers this time. "Can you loosen this somehow?" he asked, the frustration evident.

"There are buttons at the back. I can't reach them."

"Then turn over." It was part order, part plea.

Daisy rolled onto her stomach, and Tristen straddled her, plucking at the buttons one by one. She felt the heat of his thighs though her gown, and got a little faint. Anyone seeing them in this moment would be scandalized. *She* was scandalized, but even more than that, she was entranced, excited to discover what she'd feel next.

Tristan pulled the bodice of the gown a few inches away from her body and then bent down, kissing the newly exposed skin of her back.

Daisy let out a soft moan. Who knew how good that could feel? She shivered with pleasure and the growing sense that she needed even more than this. That there was something entirely new that awaited her if only she allowed Tristan to continue.

This is why they tell us men are dangerous, Daisy mused, lost in the lovely feelings Tristan was summoning in her body, his mouth warm and soft on her skin.

Then he moved so his mouth was at her ear. He said, "You have no idea how much I want to take your gown off, Daisy. See you utterly naked."

"I…I'm not sure that's such a good idea."

Before she could say more, he was turning her over again, so she could look at him directly. "I won't," he said. "I want to, but I'll never do anything you don't want, darling."

"What if I *did* say to take off my clothes?" she asked, with the sort of boldness that only comes from twilight. "Or yours? I've never seen a real man naked before. Those illustrations from the books were not terribly accurate, I suspect."

"You'd be scared if you saw me naked."

His voice was gruff, even angry, and Daisy felt a thrill of something almost like fear—but not quite. "I'd never be scared of you," she whispered. "Even when you yelled at me, it was only because you were in pain."

Tristan looked at her a long moment, wonder in his eyes. "You knew that? That it hurt me to hear that sound?"

"Well, wasn't it obvious? You'd never yell at a person

to be cruel."

"Daisy, I never apologized for yelling."

She giggled. "I'd say you're apologizing now. It's certainly much nicer to be kissing, isn't it?"

"Couldn't have said it better myself." He bent his head to capture her lower lip, sucking it gently, until Daisy was panting with a newly awakened desire.

"Tristan," she said at last. "Tell me what to do. It's one thing to read about it, but quite another to actually be with someone…" *you love*, she almost said. Was that what was happening? Was Daisy falling in love with him? Why else would she want to offer herself to him, not just her body, but her heart too? "I want to please you."

"Oh, God, she's going to destroy me," he groaned to himself. Then he said, in a low tone, "If you want to please me, let me touch you."

"You are touching me," she told him, smiling, for he was practically molded to her, his body pressed to hers.

"This will be different." He reached down and found the bottom of her gown, slipping his hand under the hem, gliding along her leg. He shifted, intending to kneel between her legs. "Spread your knees apart a little. Trust me, sweetheart. I won't hurt you."

Hurt her? Daisy wouldn't describe the dizzying rush of warmth as *hurt*. It was pure, honey-thick sweetness.

Tristan ran his hand up her inner thigh until he brushed against the curls between her legs. "I'm going to touch you here," he said. "Tell me if you like it."

Then his fingers were stroking lightly against her body, that hidden core. And his touch felt divine. Daisy sighed as lovely, shivery sensations began to radiate through her.

"I do like that," she whispered, gazing at him. "Oh, yes. I do."

His jaw worked as he watched her respond to his exploration of her body. Daisy accepted each new touch and stroke with a delighted gasp, until she felt his finger slip all the way into her body, and she cried out in pleasure and astonishment.

"Too much?" he asked, withdrawing his finger.

"No! It's...wonderful. The books suggested it would be."

"I have a lot of questions about this school, if those books were so easy to find." He smiled, and slipped his finger into her body once more.

"Mmm, yes." She closed her eyes, enjoying his touch, learning that there was a sort of rhythm to the feelings in her body, and that her hips wanted to move to meet his hand.

He noticed too, and encouraged her. "Yes, press against me, just like that."

The push and pull of his hand against her and inside her was building to something that Daisy was desperate to understand. Tristan kept telling her that she was perfect and beautiful and to continue letting her body enjoy his touch.

"More, Daisy. Don't hold back."

She pressed harder against his palm each time, her eyes closed as she reacted to the new sensations. She was nearly frantic, and then a beautiful thing happened and she cried out as her whole body briefly felt warm and wonderful. She let out a long breath, and then another. Her cheeks were hot, her chest was hot. She tingled all over.

Tristan was watching her with an expression of pure lust. "You come so beautifully," he said, his voice rough.

His breathing was uneven, and he looked almost feverish.

"Tris, what's wrong?" she asked, returning slowly to reality.

"Nothing. Nothing except that I haven't been with a woman at all since before...and watching you now is killing me." He tried to laugh it off, but his jaw clenched, and she could tell he was hiding something.

"What do you need? Tell me, Tris, please."

"I can't, Daisy."

"You need the same release, don't you? That's what this is all about, isn't it?" Daisy suddenly understood a dozen different little things that she'd been half told, half warned her whole life. This is why men and women came together and married and spent their lives together; it was this chance to feel and give a sort of mutual pleasure that nothing else in the world quite matched.

Tristan looked decidedly less happy than Daisy thought he should. He said, "You deserve more than a... blanket in the woods."

"Let me touch you," she interrupted, thinking that there was far too much chatter and not enough doing. Tristan needed her to act.

Daisy reached for him, and at the falls of his pants, she encountered a heavy, stiff bulge under the fabric. At her mere touch, Tristan groaned with pleasure. He put his hand over hers, directing her in short, breathless tones what to do next.

But then a shout in the distance made Daisy freeze, holding tense and wary as a deer. Had someone seen them together? Would someone storm up, furious at the scene?

Tristan swallowed hard, both of them listening for any other sound to follow.

There was nothing, only some fading hoofbeats farther down the path.

"It's all right," Tristan whispered, his words hot breath

in her ear. "Just folk passing by along the road."

Then, before Daisy could do anything more, he moved away from her, farther into the shadow of the nearest tree. "This was a mistake," he muttered.

Daisy breathed deep, her mind returning to the present moment, which was far less pleasant than the fantasy realm she'd just been lost in. What was she thinking, dallying with Tristan here in the woods? It was madness, and to be caught would be disaster for them both.

Daisy looked anxiously at the deep blue of the evening sky. More time had passed than she'd thought. It would be full night when she returned to the Grange. She stood up, feeling the cold air swirl around her. "It's getting dark. I have to go home."

"I'll take you." He gestured to Stormer, who was oblivious to everything going on.

"No! It would raise questions." Such as where they'd been all alone. "I'll walk. That's what everyone expects." She struggled to pull her gown straight again, realizing the buttons were still undone.

"I'll fix them," Tristan said, now standing beside her. "Turn around."

She turned her back to him, and shivered a little as his fingers made quick work of the buttons, holding her gown tightly in place over the stays once again. How were these the same fingers that just wreaked such havoc in her body?

"There," he said at last. "With your cloak over it, no one will see anything out of place."

Feeling a little lost, she turned to find her abandoned marketing bags.

"You shouldn't be hauling goods like a mule," Tristan said, watching her. "You're no servant girl."

"No, but I'm happy to do what needs to be done for

the Grange. And anyway, you were the one talking about burning all the traditions to the ground."

He smiled, but didn't look very happy. "When will I see you again?"

"I don't know. Please, I really must get back. I'm sorry to leave like this…"

He took her in his arms and kissed her roughly, then pushed her away. "But you're right. This was…not smart. Go. Before I change my mind and keep you here all night."

Daisy felt the sting of his kiss all the way home. She was flushed and excited and nervous, and above all, dizzy with desire for Tristan, who waited for her—her!—to walk by.

The courtyard of the Grange was quiet, even sleepy. Daisy knew that most of the servants would be busy tending to the final tasks of the day, and she hoped that Elaine had managed to get dinner prepared without Daisy's assistance. She'd make it up to Elaine tomorrow.

When Daisy entered the foyer of the house it was dark, as no servant had yet come around to light any lantern. Sighing, she dropped her bags to the floor at last, and reached for a candle on the table, while simultaneously striking a flintstone against the wall.

"You fool."

Daisy stopped short at the words, issuing forth from a dark shape in the middle of the hall, framed by the cold, dark stones and low vaulted ceiling.

Lady Rutherford stepped forward, into the meager pool of light offered by the stubby candle Daisy had just lit.

The chatelaine of Rutherford Grange, the baroness herself, had come down to the lower floors, just to lie in wait for Daisy. Her usual fashionable coolness was even more marked down here in the shadowy, flickering light. Her mouth was drawn into a tight, pinched circle, and her eyes glittered with malice.

"You think I am unaware of what you've done?"

Oh, Lord, how could she know of Daisy's secret, unplanned tryst? Aloud, Daisy stuttered, "My...my lady?"

"You are skulking about, insinuating yourself among your betters." She flung a packet of paper on the floor. Daisy caught only a glimpse of Tristan's handwriting, the strokes of black ink marked in great, impatient slashes— the writing of a man who was used to sending missives from a battlefield.

"His grace's letters," Daisy said faintly. "You did intercept them."

"They came to me because at least some of the servants here have a modicum of sense, and knew that a duke had no business corresponding with a"—she checked herself—"a young woman with whom he has no cause for...*special* relations."

"Did you read them?"

Lady Rutherford nodded, saying, "Thank the Lord that they are little more than invitations to write back. But even so, they are inappropriate." The baroness knelt and scooped the letters up before Daisy could do anything. She then held one above the candle flame. It caught fire, illuminating the small foyer with a sudden, painful light.

"You are attempting to undermine your sister's prospects," the older woman said. "How can you hate Bella so much that you'd destroy her best chance for a marriage?"

"I don't hate Bella!"

"Then why are you constantly hovering near his grace? The Duke of Lyon may find you diverting, but his destiny and yours are utterly separate. Forcing your attentions upon him makes you look foolish at best, and may even tarnish his own reputation. Do you want Bella to marry a man to whom *rumors* have attached themselves?"

"Bella is not engaged," Daisy protested.

"Not yet," Lady Rutherford admitted. "But the day will come very soon. And until the words are spoken and she is contracted to the duke, I will ensure that you are out of the way."

"Out of the way?" The phrase was ominous.

"To begin, you are confined to Rutherford Grange. No accepting invitations to Lyondale, or anywhere else without my express permission. No dallying in the woods. No jaunts to the village to do the marketing, or to visit mysterious old crones."

"But—"

"Don't you dare speak back to me!" Lady Rutherford glared at her, but then her expression softened. "I'm doing you a favor, Daisy. You may have your head turned by this man. But trust me, men think only of themselves. If by some chance he were to encounter you alone, away from the protection of society, he'd seek only one thing, and if he were to get it, you would be ruined and cast aside."

A hidden tremor shook Daisy's body. It was as if her stepmother had been watching…

"Men are the same everywhere," Lady Rutherford added with a little sneer. "They speak sweetly until they get what they're after, and then they're off on the next hunt, without a thought for the broken hearts and shattered reputations they leave behind."

Daisy stood speechless, unable to even formulate a thought amid the horror her stepmother painted for her. Tristan had been waiting for her in an out-of-the-way place, and he had begun a seduction that she responded to all too eagerly. Only the sudden shock of hearing others nearby had ended the tryst. But if Daisy hadn't left, would Tristan really have continued the seduction? He certainly spoke of how much he wanted to.

The older woman seemed to come out a reverie, and then said, "Stay here at the Grange, Daisy. That is an order. If you disobey, you will regret it until the end of your days."

Chapter 11

❀ ✿ ❀

TRISTAN ARRIVED BACK AT LYONDALE well after dark had fallen. No one asked where he'd been, no one questioned his decisions. That was his life now, so different from living the life of a soldier, where every aspect of the day was tightly regulated and there was always a superior officer ready to jump on your neck for a minor infraction.

Perhaps there were a few benefits to being a duke, he thought, recalling his encounter with Daisy. He'd never meant for it to go so far, but one thing had led to another, and Daisy's innocent enthusiasm and her utterly bewitching lack of prudery led Tris much further than he'd intended. Before he could think twice, he was so deep into lust that he was absolutely ready to take her virginity, right there in the woods.

That's what this is all about, isn't it? she'd asked, not accusingly, but certainly with a clear-eyed realization that Tristan was taking advantage of her. It didn't much matter that she wanted him to—if he'd listened to her and made love to her then, he'd still be a heel. Tristan could name a dozen soldiers in his regiment alone who had left young women ruined or pregnant, not through malice but sheer stupidity. Men did not exactly think straight when alone with a woman. This simple fact was undoubtably why the daughters of the gentry were kept under lock and key until they were engaged. If Daisy hadn't lost her inheritance, Tristan wouldn't have been allowed within a hundred feet of her without a chaperone.

He'd have to guard himself closer in the future, at least until he could figure out how to formally propose to Daisy without the whole shire going up in flames. Because Tristan was certain of one thing: if he wasn't going to have Daisy, he wasn't going to have any woman.

Tristan entered the parlor, drawn to the sound of music. Inside, candles glittered in crystal sconces while Miss Wallis played the pianoforte with admirable skill. Jack was there as well, sitting in a velvet upholstered chair, listening attentively, though a book lay facedown on his lap.

Tristan waited until the song ended before stepping through the doorway. "Good evening," he said. "You play wonderfully, Miss Wallis."

"Thank you," she replied with a nod. "His grace bought this piano for me." She stood up, tidying the loose sheets of music on the top of the pianoforte. "If you'll excuse me, I do think it's time to retire. Good night."

Jack stood up as Miss Wallis left the room, and Tristan was glad his friend was feeling well enough to be able to observe the little niceties of etiquette again. Tris knew it killed Jack to be thought impolite, even though it was quite clear that his illness was the cause.

As Tris walked to the side table to pour himself a brandy, Jack sank back down to the chair. "You missed supper," he noted. "I think Miss Wallis was worried that you'd fallen off your horse and snapped your neck somewhere. She was only playing so long to keep me company, and to keep her own mind occupied."

"I was perfectly fine," Tristan said with a laugh. "Just

a long ride, that's all." But the words made him realize once again that his actions did matter to other people, even the simple action of staying alive affected the whole household and estate. He added, contritely, "I suppose I should make an effort to return before dark." And after all, soon he wouldn't need to haunt the woods, waiting to run into Daisy because his letters all somehow went astray. Soon, it would all be solved!

Jack gestured to the desk. "By the way, your correspondence is there, just in case you don't want to wait till morning. Including a package from London, I note."

He eagerly moved to the desk, putting down the glass of brandy and picking up the slightly bulky package from London. Yes, there was the name of the appraiser he sent the diamond to. Tristan felt a thrill of excitement. This note would contain the confirmation he needed to live life his way. He could take care of the declining estate. He could set Miss Wallis up with an annual income so she never need fear being made homeless. He could get Jack back on his feet and ready to open his own law office, if he liked. He could ask Daisy to be his wife, with no concern about her lack of dowry or the cries of the local worthies that he picked an unsuitable girl. Daisy—Miss Margaret Merriot—was eminently suitable, and everyone would know it when they saw her dressed as a duchess, dripping with diamonds from the duke's very own mine.

"Well?" Jack's voice interrupted his reverie. "Are you going to open it?"

"Yes, yes." Tristan shook himself. "I was just…thinking of all this means."

He could see that Jack was as impatient as himself, so he cut the string and opened the package. The diamond half rolled out of the paper it had been wrapped in, and Tristan picked it up and cradled it as he took the letter in his other hand. He skimmed the first paragraph, then…

…I wish to assure you, your grace, that I took all possible care in examining this stone, to be sure that a mistake was not made. The most detailed tests were conducted. I regret to report that although it superficially resembles a diamond in the rough, and to most eyes would be assumed to be a diamond, this stone is not of the same mineral composition as a true diamond, even a low-quality one with multiple imperfections. It is a variety of quartz, which has no value on the market for precious minerals.

Unfortunately, it is all too easy to mistake this type of stone for diamond. The fault is certainly not your own, and I am glad that I could correct any misapprehension at an early stage. A full report of the examination is enclosed. If your grace has any further questions, my firm stands ready to answer them at your convenience, and of course we are most happy to conduct business on your behalf if you are interested in purchasing or selling real diamonds. It is an honor to serve your grace in this matter….

Tristan read the words over and over, trying to fit them into his universe, and failing.

"What's it say?" Jack asked anxiously. "What is the conclusion? Is it not a good diamond?"

"It's not a diamond at all." Tristan swallowed, his throat painfully tight. "It's just a stone. A rock. A piece of trash. Cater now has ten thousand pounds of my money to dig up some useless rock."

"Give me the letter."

Tristan handed the Jack the letter and the folded report. He could barely think. How was this possible? John Cater wouldn't lie, not a good friend like him, but the partner, this man who Cater met… He could be a swindler ready to steal from all of them.

And like a fool, Tristan walked right into the trap.

Paper crinkled while Jack read over the report, his legal mind no doubt taking in every word.

"I'm so sorry, Tris," he said at last, a soft and un-lawyerly phrase that made Tristan understand that things were dire indeed.

"There's no way to get the loan recalled, is there?" Tristan asked.

"No. By definition, any such investment is a gamble, and—"

"And I lost. God, what am I going to do now?"

"I don't know, Tris. It was a nice thought, having a source of income that would free you from the usual expectations of your position, and the financial issues you're facing. But I warned you…"

"You did," Tristan said, gripping the stone in his fist. That damned stone. He'd dreamed of having it cut into a fabulous shape, put in a necklace, and offering it to Daisy on the day he married her.

But the stone was nothing. In a sudden fit of rage, he hurled it into the fireplace. It bounced against the fireback and dropped into the flames. He hoped it melted and disappeared forever.

"I'm never going to get the money back," he muttered. The bank could come down on him at any moment, demanding repayment or taking the very land from under him. Land he now realized meant something to him after all, land that kept people working and fed. And he was so stupid that he risked it all on a whim. "What am I going to do?"

"Hold a ball."

"What?"

"Listen to me, Tris. You tried one way, and it didn't work. Now it's back to the old reliable. *You have to marry well.* Find some eligible lady who's got the income you need, and you'll give her the title she needs. This is how things work."

"I hate how things work."

"You don't have to love it, but you do have to do it. People are depending on you."

Tristan knew Jack was right. He knew it all too well.

* * * *

Daisy heard snatches of rumors through the network of servants in the region, since servants made for the very best gossips. Every time something was delivered to the Grange, people talked. Every time Elaine went to the village, people talked. Apparently the duke was planning something, something big enough to get the whole county murmuring. In the kitchen of the Grange, Daisy kept to her work and was merely glad that none of the gossip was about the duke meeting a certain young lady in the woods one afternoon.

The stolen hour she'd shared with Tristan seemed more and more like a dream with every passing day. Was it possible that they'd really lain that close together and touched each other the way they did? Was it possible that Daisy exposed her body and heart in such a shameless way? Was it possible that she was hopelessly in love?

The last question was what occupied her day in and day out. Daisy worried very much that she'd let her heart run away, all the way to a duke. And considering her situation, there was no hope of winning him. He would court some daughter of the gentry in a calm and proper manner. He'd marry her and bring her to Lyondale, where she'd be the new duchess, all while Daisy watched from the servants' quarters of Rutherford Grange, her heart broken and battered.

How could she have let this happen? The first meeting was pure chance, but after that...she'd allowed herself to believe in impossibilities. And Tristan took her interest as any man would, and enjoyed the clandestine moments without promising anything. And honestly, what could he promise? Was it Tristan's dream to marry the impoverished daughter of a dead neighbor, who now had no title and no legacy to speak of? No. He liked Daisy, and she was clear-eyed enough to know that he had taken risks to spend time with her, risks he should have avoided.

But the end of their story was inevitable. Daisy might wish otherwise, but what good could a wish do against the full force of society and tradition?

Then one morning a footman from Lyondale arrived at the Grange with a letter for Lady Rutherford. Daisy happened to be in the parlor when the baroness received it, and thus was present for the woman's cry of delight as she read the news out loud.

"Ah, at last! The Duke of Lyon is holding a ball. A masquerade ball, at Lyondale!"

"When, Mama?" Bella asked.

"In ten days. My goodness, that's not much time. We shall have to ensure that you look absolutely perfect, darling. This is a very important event, I don't have to tell you. When the duke sees you arrive, he must be dazzled."

"If it's a masquerade," Daisy asked, "how would he know who has arrived?"

"Silly Daisy," the baroness said indulgently. "You've never been to such an event. Yes, the guests are masked. But everyone is announced the same as ever. The costumes are merely for fun."

"What do you want your costume to be, Daisy?" Bella asked. "I've got no notion what I should go as."

"Daisy is not attending." The baroness's words were soft, but attracted the attention of both girls.

"Am I not invited?" Daisy asked, feeling her heart contract. Would Tristan do that, perhaps to send her a message that their brief dalliance was over?

"Technically, you are. The Merriot Family, it says, and you are a Merriot."

I'm more of a Merriot than you, Daisy thought, rebellion, so long held in check, now rising in her all at once. *I was born a Merriot.*

"But my dear, what would you wear? You have nothing and ten days is not enough time. The inclusion of you in the invitation is simply the result of how it is worded. A politeness, nothing more."

The matter-of-factness in her stepmother's tone made Daisy want to cry. Was that it? She was nothing, just an appendage who had been inconveniently named Merriot, so that her stepmother couldn't simply toss her out with the rest of the rubbish.

Bella was silent, staring at them both with wide blue eyes. What thought lay beyond them—if any—Daisy couldn't tell.

Then the baroness folded the invitation back up and smiled. "Well, we've a lot to do, haven't we? Bella, we must go to your room and see what gown will be best adapted for a costume. There is just no time for one from whole cloth. That sky-blue one with the pearls is your finest. Perhaps we will make you into a snow princess? With a silver and pearl tiara and a long fur-trimmed cape. Wouldn't that be pretty?"

"Yes, Mama," Bella murmured, and her mother swept her along to the upper floor, leaving Daisy alone in the room.

The silence surrounded her, a vast, empty feeling that left Daisy cold. Her eyes pricked, and she was suddenly having difficulty breathing. So this was what it was like to be forgotten.

Just then, Elaine popped her head into the parlor. "There you are, Miss Daisy! Jacob's been asking for you, he needs help with…what's wrong?"

She hurried to Daisy, who was barely holding in her sobs. Daisy started to explain, discovered that tears were running down her face, and she could barely speak.

Without waiting a moment, Elaine hustled Daisy down to the kitchen, which was warm and filled with the yeasty odor of baking bread. As Daisy calmed down enough to relate what happened, especially hearing Lady Rutherford's pronouncement that she would not be allowed to attend the ball, Elaine tutted sympathetically. She gave her hug after hug, telling her that the Grange couldn't do without her and that fancy lady upstairs didn't appreciate Daisy as she ought to.

"If I was given an invitation, you'd bet I'd go!" the older lady declared, heedless of the flour decorating her cheeks.

Daisy smiled sadly. "Well, the baroness is right about one thing. I don't have an appropriate gown."

"What about that lovely yellow one you just made?"

"That's not a ball gown," Daisy said. "I'd need something much different, not to mention that it's a masquerade, and I certainly don't have something that would suit as a costume. I'm afraid my attending really is out of the question, no matter how much I may want to go."

Elaine sighed, shaking her head at the unfairness of it all. Then she said, "Now I hate to make you work, my dear, but the fact is that Jacob had to fix the fence for the

chickens—again!—and he's had no time to dig in the garden. And I'll do that, but that means I can't go to the village to do that marketing. I know her ladyship wants you
to stay on the estate, but it's not as if we've got extra
hands sitting idle!"

No, Daisy thought to herself, *there were fewer workers
every year, as the baroness let some go to save the cost of
paying them.* "You're right. As long as no one sees me go
or come back, I should be fine. It shouldn't take long to
harvest some mushrooms or nuts."

"Oh, thank you, miss. That's all I really need for
tonight—the rest of the marketing can wait till
tomorrow."

In fact, Daisy was glad of the task. It would give her
something to do, instead of wringing her heart dry by the
kitchen table.

Daisy took a basket and plunged into the woods. For
once, she hoped that she would not meet Tristan. She
didn't think she could stand to see him, knowing that it
might be for the last time.

The pickings in the woods were growing slim, as the
autumn advanced and all the creatures of the forest hunted
for their own sustenance. Daisy got some late nuts and a
few mushrooms, but this would likely be her last foray
before winter set in. Then she realized she was approaching Tabitha's cottage, and she hurried her pace, hoping to
see the woman while she had the chance.

"Tabitha!" she called out when the cottage came into
view. She spied the woman tending a leaf fire in her front
garden.

"Why, hello, child!" Tabitha's face crinkled up with
pleasure. "What a nice surprise. Come in and sit awhile, if
you can spare the time. I just made some raspberry tea."

"That sounds lovely." Daisy kissed the old crone on

the cheek and then set her basket down by the door.

"Out picking nuts?" Tabitha asked. "I got a good crop of chestnuts, too many for my taste. You'll take some back home when you go."

At the word *home*, Daisy felt the despair rise up again. The Grange felt less like home with each passing hour. "Oh, Tabitha, I've had the worst day."

"Did you now? Tell me."

So once more Daisy poured out her sorrows, adding a hint of what she'd concealed from everyone else so far—namely, that her heart twisted every time she thought of Tristan. His wry comments, his discomfort with his title but his determination to do his best anyway. How he kissed her so sweetly. And how she knew it was an impossible dream, but she dreamed it anyway.

"Love is a tricky thing," Tabitha said seriously. "It twists and turns, and it can hurt you before it heals you. But I know that in the end, you'll be happy."

Daisy sighed, picturing what Tabitha must mean: someday Daisy would meet a good, solid man who would overlook her material lacks and make a little life somewhere. Perhaps she would be happy…as soon as she put aside her dream of a life with a duke.

"I just wish I could just go to the ball!" Daisy said. "I know it's a silly wish, but I've never been to one, and I'll never get the chance again. Oh, I'm miserable and I hate it!"

"There, there, my dear. Not every day is full of sunshine, as you know. But not all days are grey, either. You'll feel better soon, and you'll see your path."

Daisy gulped down the raspberry tea, and tried to smile. "I know. I'm just…wallowing."

Tabitha laughed. "Everyone needs a good wallow now and then. Like a pig wallows in mud. It's messy, but it feels good to them."

"I'm glad you're willing to listen. I hate to bother you with my troubles."

"Nonsense. Other people's troubles are no trouble for me. Now you hurry home with these chestnuts. And remember that old Tabitha is always here, should you need me."

Daisy kissed her goodbye and walked off, feeling a bit more like her old, calm self. Tabitha was right, and she was fussing over things she couldn't change. It would be better to take things day by day, working to make the Grange the best home it could be. After all, her father's people had been barons and baronesses of Rutherford Grange for centuries. She had a duty to uphold that tradition, even if the title was no longer going to her.

She decided to walk back along the road, having a full basket now. A short while later, the rumble of a carriage behind her made her step to the side to let it pass. She was surprised, however, to see the phaeton stop.

"Mr. Kemble?" she asked, seeing him lean over to greet her. "Good evening!"

"To you as well, Miss Merriot." He smiled. "This is my new compromise with my doctor. I get to be outside, but with no exertion to speak of."

"That sounds most sensible," she said, pleased to see how healthy he looked.

"May I offer you a ride to the gates of the Grange?" he asked politely. The driver of the phaeton had already leaned over to open the door, so Daisy climbed in, not wanting to be rude.

"Thank you," she said. "I was just gathering some nuts for our dinner." She gestured to the basket.

"Sounds very industrious. Perhaps one day I'll be able to do as much." He looked rather hopeful about it, and

Daisy thought that a good sign.

He asked if the ladies of the Grange had received their invitation to the ball.

Daisy nodded, but added that she herself would not be attending.

Mr. Kemble frowned. "Whyever not? Please come. There will be fireworks. Have you ever seen fireworks?"

"No. I've read about them." Daisy paused. "Forgive me, but wouldn't his grace hate fireworks? They're so close to the explosions during the war." Having heard the story of his experience, and seeing how he'd reacted to the noise while they were by the pond, Daisy doubted if Tristan wanted to hear anything loud or violent.

"It's true," Kemble confirmed. "But I had the idea that if he should see and hear such sounds in a place where he's having a good time, it will help to recalibrate his mind. Of course, that presupposes this party is a place where he'll have a good time." He looked at her. "If you'll be there, the duke's chances of enjoying the evening will improve considerably."

"But you see, I can't, as I have nothing suitable to wear for such an occasion."

"Oh, I hadn't thought of that," Kemble said, looking upset. "We just assumed...since the baroness..."

"Bella will be there," she assured him. "Along with Lady Rutherford."

"Yes, but I know that Tris..." He trailed off, looking preoccupied. "There must be something..."

The carriage came to halt. "Rutherford Grange, miss," the driver said, leaning down once more to open the door for Daisy.

She alighted and then accepted the basket Mr. Kemble handed over to her. "Thank you for the ride, and you mustn't be concerned that I can't come to the ball. It's a very kind gesture to invite me, but I am aware that it's not practical."

Mr. Kemble looked sad. "I wish there was a way to change your mind."

"It's my wardrobe that one would have to change, Mr. Kemble. But it would take a miracle. Please don't worry about it anymore. Good night!"

"Well, I reserve the right to worry," Kemble said, leaning back in his seat. "Good night, Miss Merriot."

Daisy spent the next few days as she usually did. Life was busy, but she managed to send a few letters. One went to Camellia, who was abed with a nasty cold according to her last letter. Daisy told her that if it persisted, she'd arrange to send some of Tabitha's throat drops. Despite the abundance of apothecaries in London, Daisy secretly believed Tabitha's cures were more reliable. Another letter went to Rose and Poppy, in which Daisy told them about the ball. It was still exciting, even though she herself wouldn't be able to attend.

The routine of life at the Grange was interrupted only by Lady Rutherford fussing about every last detail of Bella's outfit. A seamstress couldn't be found at such short notice, so Daisy used one of the baroness's old fur wraps to trim a floor-length cape for Bella. Daisy was kept busy pressing fabrics and stitching up stockings and running about on the littlest errands.

The mornings grew cooler day by day. The leaves on the oaks had turned and the leaves on the birches fell. It was that perfect season between seasons, when the sky was silver in the morning and gold in the evening. But the afternoons were still mellow and warm, like a second summer, with skies bluer than any June day.

She encountered Tristan later that day, while she was walking through a meadow at the very corner of the

Grange property. He was riding, and seemed to only cross her path by chance, but Daisy suspected that luck was not what brought him to the spot. He brightened when he saw her, and Daisy waited for him, feeling her heart rise.

"Daisy," he called when he was close enough. "I'm happy to see you."

"I'm happy to hear that," she returned, feeling warmth in her belly at the sight of him. "What brings you here?"

"Stormer, obviously," he said with a smile, as he dismounted and walked over to her.

"I meant…" she began.

"I know what you meant, darling Daisy." He took her hand in his. "I was hoping to see you. One would think you've been hiding from me."

"No, never." She avoided telling him that the baroness had ordered her to remain at the Grange. Knowing Tristan, he'd blame himself for Daisy's restrictions. "I've been busy. There are a lot of preparations to make for your event," she said, thinking of how she had to sew some extra pearls onto Bella's gown later.

"Yes, I can't wait to see you there. Don't tell me your costume! I want to be surprised. You know, this is only going to be tolerable with you there, Daisy."

Daisy bit her tongue. So Mr. Kemble hadn't passed on her regrets. Or perhaps he had tried, but Tristan hadn't listened. And she had so hoped that she wouldn't have to refuse his invitation personally. Regardless, there was no way she could appear at a formal event at Lyondale in what she called her best dress. She just couldn't.

She opened her mouth to tell him she couldn't attend, but what came out instead was, "That's…that's most kind of you."

"It's not entirely kindness," Tristan said cryptically, not noticing her discomfort in his own distraction. He glanced back toward Lyondale. "Damn, I wish I could stay with you longer, but I should go back. I had a devil of a time getting out for this short ride. There are too many things to do." He smiled at her again. "There will be fireworks."

"So I heard," she replied, unable to meet his eyes.

His smile faded. "There will be more than one kind, possibly."

"Oh? What?" she asked, curious despite herself.

"That's a secret. And perhaps it won't come to pass."

"You're being very mysterious, your grace."

"I like it better when you say my name." He looked at her with an expression of both heat and longing and it stirred a fire in her belly. "Daisy," he said then, his voice raw. "No matter what happens…"

"Tristan?" she asked, alarmed at his tone. "What's wrong? What's the matter?"

"God, Daisy, there's so much I want to tell you and I don't have the time, but maybe at the ball…"

"About the ball—" she began to say.

"No, don't make me think of it. The fact that you'll be there is the only reason I'm tolerating the notion. Unfortunately, I can't stay. I wouldn't want anyone to get the wrong impression." He gave her a crooked smile, and moved back to Stormer, mounting up before looking around the meadow. "It's pretty here. Is this one of the places you keep as meadow for the livestock?"

"Yes, your grace."

"See? I'm learning! God, I can't wait till this stupid party is over and we can talk about planting schedules again. Did you know you can make any topic riveting, Daisy?"

"I do my best, your grace."

"Tristan, sweetheart. I told you I don't want any *your*

graces from you. Good night!" He rode off.

She felt a smile spread over her face as she listened over and over to the memory of him saying her name.

Daisy felt a little shiver, and shook herself. She was letting her daydreams get quite out of hand again. It didn't matter anyway. She couldn't go to the ball, because she had nothing to wear. "But I *want* to go," she said out loud, and knew it was true.

"I want to go," she said aloud to the gathering night. "I want to go. I want to go to the ball. Please." She wasn't sure who or what she was asking, but she remembered her conversation with Mr. Kemble about the need for a miracle. She looked at the sky and found one of the first faint stars. "I wish for a miracle," she said to it, her voice rising slightly. "Just one evening with *him*. Please let me go to the ball."

Chapter 12

❀ ❧ ❀

THE NEXT MORNING, DAISY ROSE early, because her whole day would be devoted to preparing the baroness and Bella for tonight's event. She pressed the gowns, she stitched the hems, she heated the hair curlers, she tied ribbons, she pulled out stockings, she polished jewelry.

When the ladies stepped out, they'd be marvels—perfect confections of female beauty, dressed in the very latest fashions, bedecked with glittering gems, and glowing with excitement as they traveled to join a rarified world, while Daisy would be left behind to tend the kitchens and clean up the ladies' bedchambers in the aftermath of their preparations.

"It's not fair," Daisy whispered.

She felt the defiance behind the words. She had spent so long repressing the truth that it was shocking to say it out loud. Keeping Daisy away from the ball was *not fair*. The baroness could make any excuse she wanted, but the fact was that she knew Daisy cared for Tristan, both as a friend and as something more. And she was determined to prevent them from seeing each other again.

"I am sorry you can't attend," Bella said once, while Daisy curled her hair into ringlets. "You were invited, after all."

"Perhaps another time," Daisy replied, thinking of how nonsensical a comment that was. How many times did a duke host a ball that *everyone* was invited to? Surely once he settled into his life, probably with Bella at his side as the new duchess, only the true aristocrats would cross the threshold of Lyondale. And Daisy was no longer one of that class.

It isn't fair, she thought again.

When Bella was fully dressed, she did look exactly like a snow princess, ethereal and regal and fair. Her gown was bedecked with pearls, and the fur-trimmed cape draped around her slender shoulders. Bella even had a tiara of icy silver and pearl. Daisy had no idea how the baroness had acquired it, but she shivered to think of the cost. But the final effect was dazzling, and she couldn't deny that Bella would turn every head at the ball. Including the duke's.

"You look beautiful," Daisy told her when she was done helping her dress.

"I suppose," Bella replied, glancing at her reflection in the mirror. She did not appear delighted, but then, she so rarely displayed strong emotion. "I do hope he'll like it," she added in a soft tone, more to herself than Daisy.

Then Daisy hurried to her stepmother's chambers, to see if the baroness needed anything else. But when she arrived there, the lady looked perfect. In her way, Lady Rutherford was just as resplendent in her costume. She was dressed as a peacock, complete with long, showy feathers in her mask and headdress. The aubergine and teal-colored outfit flattered her complexion and she seemed extremely pleased with the result. "The vicar is dressing up as a raven. Won't that be fun? We'll complement each other nicely during a dance. I don't know what the duke will be, but I am sure Bella will look splendid beside him."

"Bella looks splendid all on her own," Daisy noted.

"True, true," the baroness said, smiling at Daisy. "It should be a memorable evening. We shall bring you back a piece of cake."

Cake? Daisy thought. *Bella gets the duke and I get a dessert?* But she nodded and thanked her stepmother for the thought. It was very hard to push against the politeness she'd been taught was so important. She asked, "If you are both ready, shall I tell Jacob to bring out the carriage?"

The baroness glanced at the mantel clock. "Yes, indeed. It is all well and good to arrive fashionably late to society events, but we do not want to miss a single minute tonight!"

So Daisy went downstairs and called for the carriage, and helped the baroness and Bella get in without damaging their outfits. And she watched the carriage drive off, taking them to the one place that Daisy wished she could go.

Tears threatened to fall, but Daisy fought them back. She stood in the doorway of Rutherford Grange, watching until the carriage disappeared entirely. Then she began to turn back into the house.

A new sound stopped her short.

A cart had rumbled up the road from the direction of the village and had just stopped at the gates. A man got out and pulled a large wooden box off the cart. Daisy ran to him.

"Excuse me, sir," she said. "What is this?"

He shrugged. "Don't know, miss. Just delivering it to the place it says. There was a mistake and the package got held up for a day. Hope nothing inside has spoiled." He was already off down the road before she could ask more.

The large box was unmarked, aside from a stamp indicating that it originated in London. She brought it inside to the kitchens, assuming it must be some kind of household necessity she'd forgotten about. Elaine and Jacob gathered to view the opening, drawn by the unexpectedness of it. Daisy opened the inner pasteboard box to expose a layer of undyed muslin. Elaine said, "What's underneath?"

Daisy pulled aside the dull muslin to expose a rainbow. "Oh!"

Daisy took hold of the colors and held them up. The rainbow took shape. It was a dress, far more fabulous than anything she'd seen in years.

"Where did this come from?" she asked, not expecting an answer.

The dress was a bewitching mass of silk, woven in such a way that the color was uncertain. Depending on how one looked at it, the shade ranged from a ruddy orange to a dark, dreamy violet. The colors shouldn't have worked together, but they did. Daisy kept tilting the fabric different ways, mesmerized, trying to see how it was done.

"Miss Daisy!" Elaine said, pulling out another item. "There are wings!"

And indeed, Elaine held a set of wings, made of silk and shaped with fine wire, painted with care to resemble the pattern of an orange and gold and black butterfly.

"That's so beautiful," Daisy murmured, touching the wings. She also found little black dancing slippers with flowers embroidered onto them, and gloves of a silk so thin that they were nearly transparent.

"Daisy!"

She jumped. It was clear her name had been repeated several times. "Yes! What?"

"Aren't you going to try it on?"

"This dress can't be meant for me. There's a mistake."

Elaine held up a card that had been nestled in the muslin. "Miss M. Merriot. One ball gown. Charges paid."

"Yes…it *says* that. But I know it can't be so."

"Sometimes, miss, you must accept what Providence bestows. Someone wants you to attend the masquerade." Elaine held up a mask, designed to cover the top half of the face, again patterned like a butterfly's wings, with cunning antennae of thin wire extending above. The whole effect was like magic.

"I just wish I knew who sent it," she said. "Who is my fairy godmother?"

In her room, she tried the dress on with Elaine's assistance. It fit as if it had truly been made for her. The explanation of fairy magic sounded more plausible by the moment.

Inspired by the shifting colors of the fabric, Daisy unlocked the hidden box where she kept her most precious things, and pulled out the ruby necklace that had once been her mother's. The delicate gold chain was strung with seven rubies, the largest at the center. Daisy had always loved the piece, for she had a faint memory of her mother wearing it on a Christmas Eve long ago.

Daisy fastened the chain around her neck and then examined herself in the mirror.

"Elaine," she said, a little shocked at the reflection. "This dress! It's…"

"Perfect. It looks like it was made just for you!" Elaine put a hand to her mouth to stifle a laugh.

Downstairs, Jacob stared at her with delight. "Oh, it looks like someone wove all the colors out of an autumn morning into the gown, miss," he said, with uncharacteristic poetry.

"It's marvelous!" Elaine agreed. "You'll be the belle of the ball!"

"I'll fetch the cart," Jacob said. "Not exactly riding in style, but it will get you there."

"I suppose that means I'm going after all," said Daisy, feeling faint.

A ball.

A ball hosted by the Duke of Lyon.

A ball hosted by the incredibly compelling Duke of Lyon.

A ball hosted by the incredibly compelling Duke of Lyon who told her he wanted nothing more than to see her there.

She was so excited to truly be going that she couldn't suppress a giggle. Elaine told her she'd be lucky to end up at Lyondale and not at Bedlam.

In the cart, she sat carefully, surrounded by a crop of pumpkins and squash that had already been loaded in anticipation of being taken to the village for sale the next day.

As the cart trundled down the road, she began to have second thoughts. She'd enrage her stepmother simply by attending the ball. She looked down at the mask on the seat next to her. Perhaps there was a way to defer the woman's wrath, at least long enough to enjoy herself for a few hours.

"I'll leave before she can really see me," Daisy said to herself. Then she remembered the baroness had said that everyone was announced as usual, revealing their true names. "But if I give a different name..." Daisy murmured, thinking hard.

Lyondale stood tall and grand on its hill. Every window was lit, and guests were arriving from all over the area. Jacob pulled the cart to the side of the drive quite a distance away, realizing that it would look odd to pull up with a crop of pumpkins and a butterfly. "Can you walk from here, miss?" he asked.

"Certainly," Daisy said, sliding down. "You get back home, Jacob. Thank you so much!"

"Thank you, miss," he returned with feeling. "Just seeing you dressed up like that makes me think of your fine mother. You enjoy yourself tonight, just as you ought."

Concealed behind her mask, Daisy walked through the front doors feeling that she was entering another world.

The wonderful dress evidently transformed Daisy to such a degree that several local people didn't even recognize her, thinking her some aristocratic guest of Lyon's.

"Your name, my lady?" the majordomo asked diffidently when she walked to the doors of the ballroom.

"Announce me as Lady Wildwood."

Boomed out in the man's bass voice, the announcement turned heads, and all eyes turned to Daisy, standing in her finery at the top of the stairs.

Daisy suddenly felt a stab of anxiety. She did not want to draw so much attention. Had she made a mistake? She wanted to slink away into the shadows, but it was too late. Tristan had seen her.

Lord Lyon left off whatever he'd been saying to another guest and headed directly for Daisy.

He looked exactly as handsome as she'd imagined he would. The concept of his costume was a medieval knight, though his main outfit was still very modern. He was dressed in a grey velveteen jacket over a simple white shirt and black pants. The more fanciful parts of his outfit were the mask, which was a silvery leather that evoked a knight's helmet with face shield, and the "broadsword" at his waist, which was wooden but painted silver. Everything was so well-tailored that the lines of his body were unmistakable.

As he came up to her, though, he said nothing. No greeting, not a word about her outfit, and she worried that she had misunderstood something. Was she dressed all wrong?

"Lady Wildwood, is it?" Tristan asked, his lips curving into a smile as he bowed over her hand. His fingers squeezed hers, the silk gloves doing nothing to prevent the heat of his hand from shooting through her. He added in a low tone, "You look so much like another lady I know, Miss Daisy Merriot."

"Please don't tell everyone," she pleaded.

"My God, why would I? This is perfect. Now I can spend the whole evening with you, and leave them all wondering about my mysterious guest. They're going to speculate endlessly."

He offered her an arm and Daisy took it. To be escorted into the heart of a ball by Lord Lyon was more than enough miracle for her. And the evening was just beginning.

There was dancing. There was food. There were drinks and desserts and more dancing. Daisy had no concept of time, but she was sure it must be whirling past. Everyone was polite and attentive to her, doubtless because she was so often by Tristan's side. She didn't quite mean to be, but it always seemed to happen that he was there at the end of a set, sending Daisy's dance partners off to find their next companion. He seemed to materialize just when she decided she was thirsty, and asked her if she wanted a little wine. Even when he was on the other side of the massive room, she would look up from her conversation and find him in her line of sight. It was the dress. It had to be magic. Daisy never could have negotiated the social complexities of a ball without a dress like this to guide her steps.

And everyone was introduced to Lady Wildwood, and no one besides Tristan seemed to guess that she was merely Daisy. Several ladies asked her about her gown in breathless tones. They wanted to know who her London modiste was, and where the fabric had been made. Daisy merely answered that her dress was a gift. Then she would comment on the other woman's attire, praising the clever stitching, or how the fabric flattered her skin, which deflected the conversation admirably.

Only once or twice did she glimpse her stepmother, glaring in her direction. But there was no recognition in her face. She was merely annoyed that someone besides her Bella was occupying the duke's attention. For her part, Bella seemed content enough to dance with the many other gentlemen there who were dazzled by her snow princess costume and her pretty manners. When she wasn't dancing, she sat near Mr. Kemble, who was very cleverly costumed as an old-fashioned wizard in a tall hat and a long, loose robe covered with stars. He even had magic tricks to perform, which allowed him to sit at a table while still looking very proper.

Some children had been permitted to attend the festivities on the strict proviso that they didn't disturb the adult guests. Kemble seemed to have taken charge of the group, along with a few local matrons. His heretofore unknown skill at card tricks made him incredibly popular with the children.

"Where did Mr. Kemble learn that?" Daisy asked Tristan during one set in which he partnered her.

"Oh, he's dabbled in stage magic for years," Tristan replied. "He likes the mystery of it. Lightened the mood on many occasions. Although one had to be careful when he appeared at the card table—your winning hand might disappear."

She laughed. "He didn't!"

"He did. His way of teaching the dangers of gambling." Tristan's expression clouded, but before Daisy could ask what was wrong, he introduced her to someone else and the opportunity passed.

They danced again. Tristan was openly flouting the convention of dancing with a particular lady only once (or twice in rare cases). He danced with Daisy every chance he got, clearly relishing how he could break the rules. Who tells a duke no? For one moment, he held her by the waist. Daisy barely wanted to breathe. She hoped that if she didn't, the moment would go on forever.

But the dance went on, and soon Daisy was swept away into the pattern of the steps, curtsying to some other gentleman for a moment, and then passing on again.

As it ended, she found her hand claimed by Tristan. "You could use refreshment," he said.

She nodded, though it hadn't been a question.

He led her away from the dancing, saying, "The waltz hasn't made it all the way out here, has it?"

"It is still a thing to be discussed rather than danced," she said, laughing. "The local matrons have not approved it yet."

"As a dance, it has advantages," he noted.

"Such as?"

Tristan smiled at her. "I will show you a few steps sometime, and you'll see." His eyes dropped a little, as if he might be thinking about a kiss. She was thinking about a kiss too. She knew that the waltz entailed a rather *close* embrace on the dance floor, and for that reason was highly suspect by morally minded mothers. A close embrace during a dance might well lead to something else…

But she had no more time to muse on that, because Tristan was offering her punch, which she drank down gratefully. It was warm in the room.

"I was just thinking," she said, "how terrifying this night would have been if I didn't already know you."

"Terrifying? A party?"

"A party where one is expected to smile and chatter and dance."

She noticed that they were standing a little apart from everyone else, as if Lyon created a wall around himself. But then why was she able to stand right next to him?

"Go on," he said.

"What was I saying?" she asked.

"You were saying you *knew* me, which I found charming." His gaze drifted over her face and then down to the floor and back. He did seem strangely…entranced.

"Your grace," she whispered, conscious of where they were. "You're staring."

"I am," he said, tilting his head. "But did you know that if you look at the fabric one way, it's this fiery orange, and if you look at it the other way, it's a burgundy or purple, and yet it's neither of those colors… I'm sorry. I don't have words for this sort of thing. How is it done? The colors?"

"I don't know. Magic, perhaps."

"It must be. You look more beautiful than ever."

"It is a lovely dress," she said, happy to be wearing it even if it was only for a night and it might vanish tomorrow.

"No. I mean, it is. But *you* look beautiful. It has nothing to do with the dress. It's your smile, and…everything else. Lord, I'm bad at this, aren't I?"

Daisy flushed. "It sounds good to me."

"I would beg another dance." He glanced at the clock.

"Unfortunately, I have to address the guests now. The time for my plan has come. Will you stand right here?"

Daisy nodded, suddenly very curious.

Lyon walked to the center of the room, and took command of the party without even raising his voice. He thanked everyone for coming, and then moved so smoothly into the real meat of his announcement that he was halfway through before people truly realized the import of what he was saying.

Daisy listened avidly. The recent years of indolence and neglect were over. There would be changes. New practices. New ideas. New orders, and new expectations, inspired by forward-thinking people he'd been discussing the matter with. Daisy realized he was referring to her. People might feel discomfited, he went on. They might not like it. But Lyon was determined to make Lyondale a model of modern agriculture, able to support everyone living there, from the lord on down to the most humble tenants.

He didn't go into too many specifics, but it was obvious that this was not a mere whim. Change *would* happen. And Lord Lyon would be the one changing things. People suddenly understood that the newest Duke of Lyon was not content to mold himself into the shape they expected. He would change the shape of his inheritance to suit him.

Come along with me or get out of my way, his eyes said.

Daisy looked around. She could tell from the stiff postures and pinched faces that some didn't like it. Yet most people were listening. They were wary, but definitely listening.

"I look forward to many years at Lyondale," he concluded. "And better lives for everyone on the estate and in the village of Lyonton. But for now, enjoy the rest of the evening. As a special treat, we've arranged for a fireworks show later tonight. Listen for the announcement of when to gather on the lawn."

Applause broke out as he signaled the end of his speech. Some of the reactions were strained, Daisy noted. But many more were enthusiastic.

"Well?" he said, returning to her side. His face was more relaxed now, and she realized how nervous he'd been the whole evening. "Have I given the whole parish a collective fit?"

"Only the few people still living in the sixteenth century," Daisy responded. "But you're right. It's time to try out new ideas."

"Speaking of new ideas," he said with a wicked light in his eyes. "Lady Wildwood, come upstairs with me."

"Your grace," Daisy breathed. Oh, how she wanted to, and oh how scandalous it would be.

"Please, Daisy," he said, his voice low and urgent. "No one will know. It's a masquerade, and I wager you never told your stepmother you'd be attending."

"I didn't know it myself until an hour before."

"Perfect. Here, you're the mysterious Lady Wildwood—you'll vanish before dawn, leaving nothing but questions. Indulge me."

Chapter 13

❧⟞⟊⟊❧

DAISY TOOK HIS HAND AND allowed him to escort her away from the glitter and din of the party, down the long hallways of his massive home, farther and farther into private territory. Daisy realized that for all she had done with Tristan, she'd never seen where he slept.

The private chambers of the duke turned out to be at the far end of the west wing, facing out to the large meadow and the pond. The rooms were large and lofty, lit by candlelight. A manservant was working within, tidying up. He looked startled at the arrival of the duke. If he was equally startled to notice that the duke was accompanied by a masked woman, he gave no sign.

"Light the fire, then leave us," Tristan ordered abruptly.

The servant nodded and obeyed. He managed to not look toward Lady Wildwood once while he completed his task and made his way to the door. It was as if she were not there at all...except for how the servant made a deliberately wide circle around her.

When the door closed, Tristan moved to turn the key in the lock, and then pulled the key out.

"At last," he sighed. He walked back to Daisy, gently removing her silken butterfly mask. "Now I can see you properly." He leaned forward, taking her mouth for a kiss. It was hungry, demanding, even desperate. Daisy recognized the emotions because she felt them all herself.

"Tristan," she murmured, reaching for him, running her fingers through his hair, reacquainting herself with the feel of his skin beneath her fingers.

"It was torture until you arrived tonight," he said. He pressed his hand against her lower back, drawing her body against his. She let her curves mold themselves to his own muscles, then slid her hands up along the front of his chest, clinging to the jacket as she kissed him back with an unstudied eagerness.

Tris slid his tongue along her lower lip, drawing out a shaky little sigh from Daisy. She closed her eyes to more fully experience the sensation. His attentions left her flushed, her lip wet. Her breaths came quick and soft, her chest swelling every few moments.

"Hell," he muttered, pulling away a fraction.

"What's wrong?"

"I am. I fooled myself into thinking that all I needed was a taste of you to keep me going. To maintain my sanity amid all the chaos right now. But a taste isn't enough." He moved so he could murmur in her ear, "God, Daisy, I want to ruin you."

She sighed. Being ruined shouldn't sound so delicious. "Then please do it."

Tristan's body reacted to that statement in the most primal way, and Daisy felt it through the layers of costumes between them. But then he stepped back, his expression tormented.

"Don't tell me that till you know that's what you really want."

"Of course it is! Haven't I just said so?"

"Yes, but you haven't seen all of me."

They were face-to-face when he began to disrobe, already tugging his shirt out of the waistband of his pants. He straightened up to pull the shirt off.

Daisy swallowed as she beheld him half-naked for the first time. His right arm and the right side of his torso were marked with scarring, but that only highlighted his figure, all muscle and taut skin.

After a moment, Tristan slowly removed the rest of his clothing, allowing her to see him with nothing to obscure his appearance, which was so stunningly, magnificently male that Daisy could hardly breathe. She didn't know that men got so…big when they were aroused. Her heart pattered with a newfound excitement when she saw him like this. *My love*, she thought wildly. *We are alone. And together. As we should be.*

"This is what I look like, Daisy," he said, staring down at her, his expression tense, wary of her judgment. "You can leave this room now, and I'll understand. Is this really how you want to remember things, losing your innocence to a monster?"

He was too focused on his wounds, she knew. It blocked him from seeing the truth. And yes, the scarring was not trivial, but to think that anyone would reject him for that—Daisy couldn't imagine it. What did it matter, when she knew his real worth was that he was kind and compassionate and deeply invested in the lives of those around him?

She stepped closer and cautiously touched the scars along his right side, long jagged lines that were paler than the rest of his skin. "Do they hurt?"

"Sometimes. Not the scars themselves," he clarified. "Underneath, there's still pain, especially at night. But I'm talking about how I look, Daisy."

"You look like you," she said simply. "When you first

spoke to me that day, I couldn't even talk back, I was so entranced. I thought you were the handsomest man I'd ever seen."

He gave a laugh. "Handsome? You're joking." He gestured to the scar on his face, the one that pulled at his right eye and his mouth, giving him that perpetually cynical expression. But Daisy had learned how to read his face, and she didn't see cynicism there at all. She saw fear.

"Tristan, you need to stop worrying about how different you look from however you looked before. No one is perfect. And whenever you touch me, I am ready to be ruined."

He blinked slowly, as if unable to believe her words for a moment. Then he kissed her roughly, and Daisy accepted every kiss and returned it with one just as passionate.

After they paused to catch their breath, his hands dropped to the few buttons and ties of her gown, gently starting to undo them. "You've been so elusive lately."

"My stepmother did her best to keep me away. She forbid me to even attend tonight...but I disobeyed."

"This is a very daring Daisy I've got in my arms. I'm proud of you."

"There's little to be proud of. I spent far too long being obedient and invisible. I have to live my own life too, because no one else is going to live it for me."

"Lady Wildwood," he said with a laugh. "You're certainly growing wild." Tristan helped her out of the gown, and with a few quick moves, her chemise followed, leaving her naked in front of him.

He regarded her with pure pleasure, and gently guided her to the bed, lowering her down onto the softness of the linens. He leaned over, one knee placed between her legs, his hand roaming her body, waking her up in ways she'd never dreamed of before.

"My God, Daisy. I think you might end up ruining me."

"Why should it be ruin? Why can't it just be us enjoying each other?" she whispered, reveling in the touch of his hands along her inner thighs. "All the books I read said it would be enjoyable, Tris, I swear...*oh, yes.*"

Daisy moaned when he found her most sensitive parts, and all she wanted was to feel more of that and feel it with Tristan. Hearing his own breaths coming quick and laced with passion, she smiled.

"What is it?" he asked softly, having noticed her expression.

"I think this is what happiness feels like," she confessed.

There was beat of silence, and then Tristan said, "I think you're right, love."

He proceeded to make her very happy indeed, using his hands and lips to offer several demonstrations that Daisy breathlessly confirmed were much better in real life than in the thin paper pages of the forbidden books.

At her insistence, she reenacted a few illustrations that she'd been particularly intrigued by, and Tristan was more than pleased to allow her to do so, judging by the way he moaned as she stroked and then licked him.

"If you want more books, Daisy, I'll buy them," he panted, his body stretched beneath her as she ran her hands along his torso, very much enjoying the way he felt under her fingertips.

"That's very sweet," she said, "but I think that we won't need them. Just looking at you gives me all sorts of ideas." Was it possible that he grew even harder at her words? Maybe. He certainly felt hard in her hand as she explored that part of him once again.

After they both couldn't stand waiting any longer, Tristan laid Daisy on her back and drew her legs around his hips. He braced himself on his hands, looking down at her with both lust and tenderness, and a little doubt, in his face.

"You're certain?" he asked. "It can be over now. You don't have to take this step."

"I want all of you," she declared, her eyes locked with his. "If I wanted to leave, Tris, I'd have done it already. I'm staying because I want to be with you."

After that, what was there to say? All talk ceased for a short, breathless while as the two of them indulged in an inevitable, inexpressibly sweet joining. Daisy had questions before, but now—just for a moment—all her questions were answered. She belonged with Tristan, and he belonged with her.

There was only the tiniest flash of discomfort, but it was gone in a moment. Tristan went slowly, careful of her, asking if she needed him to hold still to let her adjust.

She wanted to not stop, ever. But he was right and she did need to take a few deep breaths as she learned how to accept his body in hers. He kissed her over and over, telling her that she was everything to him. Daisy had never been anyone's everything, and the thought alone nearly made her swoon.

Despite the newness of her feelings, he knew exactly how to bring her to the peak of pleasure, using his whole body to draw out the experience into a shivering, shimmering dream. When the joy became overwhelming, Daisy grabbed a pillow on the bed to muffle her cry of completion. Tristan growled with satisfaction at a job well done, and then took the pillow from her, stifling his own shout as he withdrew from her and finished on the bedsheets a second later, his breath ragged as he slowly recovered his senses.

"A near thing," he said at last, as if to himself. Then he moved to lie next to her, kissing her deeply. "Never stay away from me so long again, Daisy. In fact, never leave again. I ought to keep you here in this bed forever."

Daisy stared at him with widening eyes, still recovering and not sure what he meant.

He seemed to realize the implication of his words, for he said hastily, "That's not what I meant, Daisy. You're not made to be someone's mistress."

He moved to hold her, his arms big and comforting after the havoc he raised in her body. Daisy sighed, slowly returning to reality. The truth was, she didn't want to leave his bed. If that was the only way she could have him, perhaps she could...no. It was one thing to consider being a man's mistress when she was among strangers. But here, where she knew the whole village and all the neighbors? She'd never live down the shame of it.

As she looked over the room, still recovering from the intensity of their lovemaking, her eye was caught by a smoke-scarred pebble on the nightstand. It was such an odd thing to see there—a homely, lumpy object in this refined space—that Daisy leaned over and picked it up, rolling it in her hands.

"Why do you have this little rock by your bed?" she asked. "Does it mean something?"

"Yes," he said bitterly. "It's my reminder that I can't trust anyone, and that I am God's fool."

Daisy looked at him, alarmed. "What do you mean? That's a horrible thing to say! Can you not trust me?"

He sighed, taking the stone from her. "Of course I can trust you. I just meant that...never mind. I don't want to talk about it. The truth will come out soon enough, probably, unless a miracle occurs. And I do not believe in miracles."

Daisy had experienced a miracle that very day, with the appearance of her magical costume. But she suspected Tristan was in no mood to hear it.

"Come outside with me," he said suddenly. "The fireworks will start soon, and…and I'd prefer to see them with you."

She hesitated, thinking that it would be too easy for someone to see her plainly. But then her eyes lighted on the mask. Of course! She was completely safe, disguised and known only as Lady Wildwood. When else would Daisy ever have the chance to see fireworks burst over the pond at Lyondale, up on the balcony as if she were the lady of the manor…and in a beautiful gown?

Tristan helped her to dress once more, his touch driving her to wish that he'd take the gown off again immediately. But they were soon properly attired again. Daisy's face was concealed behind her mask, while Tristan left his on a table. The idea that he had deceived anyone from knowing his real identity was laughable.

Her heart still unsteady, Daisy let him lead her to the wide balcony that opened from his suite. It was paved with stone tiles and held a few potted plants in the corners, but was otherwise empty. She walked to the stone rail and looked over the pond, where the rest of the guests were gathering along the shore at the direction of the servants.

"They should start any moment," said Tristan. "Jack promised he'd oversee the lighting of them—it was his idea anyway."

Tristan let a long breath out as he stood beside her, resting his hands on the wide stone rail. She looked over and saw his face in profile, anxiety etched in its lines once again.

"Tristan," she began. "Is everything all right?"

He closed his eyes briefly, then straightened up and smiled at her. "Yes. I confess I was nervous about that little speech earlier tonight. I half expected them to throw tomatoes at me and tell me I wasn't a real lord."

"They wouldn't dare. And anyway, you can announce whatever you like."

"Can I?" His lip quirked. "In that case, I should—"

A sizzling, shrieking sound cut him off. They turned and watched the first streak of light soar upward above the water. It burst into a bright orange flaming flower and then dissolved into golden sparks, which fell into the pond like stars.

"Oh, how beautiful!"

Tristan stood stiffly by her side. "Is it?"

"Yes, it is! And here's another!"

A new pinwheel of color dazzled their eyes, then another and another. Vibrant reds, glowing yellows, and vivid silver-whites exploded in the air. The guests cried out and applauded as each one burst above them.

Tristan didn't say anything, but Daisy put her hand on his, which still gripped the railing. She ached to think that such a pretty display would be hateful to him because of his experience in the war.

He finally moved, shifting so that his left hand came up as if to take her own away. "You're holding my scarred hand," he said, in a voice so low, she could hardly hear it.

Alarm ran through her. "I didn't think about that. Did I hurt you?"

Paradoxically, as soon as she started to lift her hand away, he stopped her from doing so. "It's long past hurting. But you wouldn't like to… That is, you shouldn't have to…"

Daisy took a moment to register what he was trying to say. "You think it *bothers* me?" How could he think that mattered to her? She pursed her lips in anger, but then an especially large firework distracted her, drawing her gaze to the pond again. She settled for keeping her hand firmly on his, actually tightening her grip. "After all we've done...how I've seen you and touched you... If you think that any part of you, inside or outside, repels me, your grace, you're...you're a...an idiot!"

He said nothing for a long moment, as an explosion drifted into silver snowflakes on the surface of the pond. Then he said, "I am an idiot."

"No, I should not have said that."

"I'm glad you did. At least a few people need to tell me what's actually happening, instead of what they presume I want to hear."

"I don't want to upset you," she said, feeling the familiar urge to smooth things over, to be the voice of calm.

"You're the party who should be upset. I expect that if not for the allure of the fireworks, you would have slapped me and stormed off."

She looked at him curiously, her pique fading. "Are the fireworks affecting you at all?"

"No. I don't think so. I'm not sure," he said, looking less certain with every moment. "Perhaps I need to think of something else entirely."

Wordlessly, Tristan pulled Daisy close enough so she could feel the lines of his body next to hers. She could step away—he gave her plenty of time to do so. She chose not to.

But she was also sure it was very lovely to be held like that, and to feel his arms enfolding her. He was so warm, especially with the cool autumn air all around. She seemed to smell a tingling, sweet warmth like cider and honey. Except more delicious than that, and somehow surprising despite the fact that she ought to be used to his touch now, after what they'd done only moments ago in the bedroom.

And why did she think she might fly apart when he bent his head to kiss her gently, his tongue grazing her lower lip. It felt meltingly right, and why was she now touching him, with her hands on his chest and now twining around him as if she feared he might let her go to breathe...

Daisy had no idea why people invented fireworks. Why bother, when there was this other thing?

"Tristan," she breathed.

He bent his head closer. "I do love to hear you say my name, my Daisy."

Delicious little shivers coursed down her spine. *His* Daisy.

He smiled and kissed her again. Knowing what his kiss did to her in no way lessened the effect. She sighed with pure happiness when she finally pulled away.

"I must tell you something, sweetheart," he said then. "I'm ashamed to tell you, but you have to know."

Daisy's heart contracted, painful and sudden and horrible. He was going to tell her that he was about to propose to another woman, probably her own stepsister.

"Not long ago," he began to explain, "I received a letter from an old friend, who I count as one of the most good-hearted men I know. I saved his life once, he saved mine once. Well, John wrote and told me that he was in India and had got involved with a mining venture. Diamonds. He wanted me to invest."

Tristan gave her the pebble again, and Daisy stared at it in puzzlement. "Is this a diamond?"

"No, and that's the shame of it. I was a fool, Daisy. I

agreed to put up ten thousand, which I don't have, and the estate can't generate. I was so starstruck by the dream of it, being able to have an income that would allow me freedom, freedom to choose what I wanted to do, and who I wanted to be with…" He touched her face. "But it was for nothing. Too late, I discovered that John was wrong. The stones he thought were diamonds are some other mineral, worth practically nothing. And I've ruined the whole future of Lyondale and everyone who lives here… unless I can find a way to get myself access to a lot of wealth, very quickly."

"A marriage," Daisy said dully.

"Yes." Tristan looked so defeated that she could only put her arms around him, holding him close. "But listen—"

Just then, there was a scream.

Tristan's eyes went wide, and Daisy could see fear in them. She looked below, out to the pond, and saw a woman running after a young boy, one of the children who'd been permitted to come to the festivities, and was now holding a long stick that was fizzing and sparking with lights on one end. The child was shrieking with excitement.

The woman reached the boy, and scolded him for behaving badly. Though Daisy was too far away to hear her, the expressive gestures made her tone quite clear.

"It's fine, it's just the children playing," Daisy said to Tristan, trying to soothe him.

But Tristan had stiffened up, staring at the scene below but apparently seeing something else entirely. In the lurid blaze of a red explosion, Daisy saw his scar in stark relief.

Dear God, he's reliving the past, she thought. Out loud, she said, "Tristan? Tristan? Are you all right?"

He shook his head, raised his hands to cover his face and sank into a crouch. "The roar…" he muttered.

"This was too much, too fast. I'll get help," Daisy told him. "I'll find Mr. Kemble. Or Miss Wallis. Stay still, Tris. I'll be right back. I promise!"

Fear running through her, Daisy ran off the balcony, through the huge bedroom suite, and down the hallway to the grand stairs, glad her mask was already on. She'd forgotten her wings, but that didn't matter. She looked for a footman or a housemaid, but everyone seemed to be gone, probably watching the cursed fireworks.

Daisy ran out the huge front doors, calling for Mr. Kemble, Miss Wallis, any help at all. In her haste, she bumped into a figure dressed in very dark clothing.

"I'm sorry…" she began.

"Watch yourself!" a cross voice said. "Whoever you are!"

All at once, she felt her mask being pulled off, revealing her face to the world.

It was the vicar who stood in front of her, holding the mask in his hands. He was dressed as a black-feathered, beaked raven, and it felt like an omen.

"Why, it's Daisy!" he boomed out. When the vicar gave his sermons, he sometimes used a huge voice to fill the church when he had a particularly dire point to make about sinners. That was the voice he used now.

"What are you doing here?" he continued. "Under a false name too. Lady Wildwood? Explain yourself, girl."

Something cold slid down Daisy's spine, pushing away all the wonderful warmth she'd been wrapped up in since Tristan told her he needed her.

"Give me back my mask, sir," she said, reaching for it. Not that many people had seen this exchange yet. Perhaps the evening could be salvaged.

But he turned and stepped back, not allowing her to regain her precious anonymity.

"This mask?" he said, holding it up and away, far out of Daisy's reach. "Such an extravagant thing! Not to mention the gown. These items cannot be yours. This behavior has no place here. You have no *right* to be here."

"I was invit—"

"You can't presume to think you belong here." His voice was low, but Daisy heard every word, and her face flamed with embarrassment and impotent anger.

"I *do* belong," she began, standing up to face him.

Hornthwaite sneered at her. "So you got a fancy gown for a night! Do you think that changes who you are? You're a spinster living on a pittance. I saw you dancing with Lyon all night. Gave you airs, didn't it? You think he has any honorable interest in a girl with no fortune? Think again. If you were wise, you would leave this place to preserve your own honor, such as it is."

"Lord Lyon has never impugned my honor." But he had taken her innocence.

"So you'll be announcing your engagement any day?" Hornthwaite's lips parted in a thin, cold smile. "Has he asked you to solemnize your…ahem, union?"

Daisy opened her mouth and then closed it. Tristan kissed her senseless, made her into a woman, but he had never even suggested he was intending anything like marriage.

"That's none of your business," she managed. Her voice came out thin and weak.

"Seeing as I'm the vicar of your church, it is in fact my business. Who do you think conducts marriage ceremonies around here? And his lordship has said nothing to me about anything involving a marriage. Not a marriage to the Hon. Miss Bella Merriot, which is what we hope for. And *certainly* not to a ragamuffin like you."

Lady Rutherford rushed up, looking askance at Daisy. "My goodness, it was *you*?" she asked, horror in her tone.

"Please, his grace needs help!" Daisy said, trying to draw the focus away from her to the real problem. "The fireworks—"

"You shouldn't be here," the baroness said, her horror turning to rage. "I made that clear, and you agreed. You lied to me, Daisy!"

Daisy was so upset she couldn't even talk anymore. When Mr. Kemble walked up, Bella on his arm, asking what was the matter, Daisy just shook her head helplessly.

"That necklace," Lady Rutherford said, pointing to Daisy's throat. "It's real rubies! Where did it come from?"

Daisy raised a hand to her chest, to hide the necklace from her acquisitive stepmother's eyes. "It is mine."

"Where did you get it?" the baroness pressed.

"It was my mother's."

"So you say. But I've never seen it."

"As if I'd let you see it!" Daisy burst out. "I hid it, because I noticed so many other things going missing after you got to them. You've been selling them off one by one."

"How dare you!" the baroness practically spat out.

"Now hold on a moment. Where is his grace?" Mr. Kemble asked.

"That's what I've been trying to tell everyone," Daisy burst out. "He's…"

"I'm here." Lyon himself spoke from behind her, his voice distant and cold. "What the hell is going on?"

Daisy tried to say something, anything, but she couldn't.

Hornthwaite raised the butterfly mask in his hands. "Nothing to concern you, your grace. We've discovered that this girl is a thief. A matter the family will deal with."

"What?" The duke looked shocked—perhaps even more shocked than he'd been by the flash and pop of the fireworks.

"Not only did she come here and lie about her identity, everything she's got on is stolen!" the vicar pronounced.

"Stolen?"

"Yes, your grace. The gown, the jewelry, the shoes. The baroness did not purchase them for her, and how does a woman with no money procure such things otherwise?" The vicar let the insinuations in his words linger for the whole crowd to hear. Daisy wanted to die.

Tristan's eyes found Daisy, and she just shook her head. He couldn't possibly think that she stole the gown. Yet who would believe the truth?

Low mutterings began to spread through the crowd, which had now gathered to surround the front steps of Lyondale to watch this new version of fireworks, surely even more of a spectacle.

"This is quite an accusation," Tristan said slowly.

"Where did you get the gown?" Hornthwaite demanded.

Daisy said weakly, "It was a gift."

"From who?"

She paused, then said, "I don't know. It arrived in a box at Rutherford Grange. The box was addressed to me."

"What a fairy story!" The vicar snorted in derision. "You mean to suggest that some benefactor simply sent you an expensive gown through the *post*?"

"That's what happened."

Mr. Kemble took a few steps onto the stairs. "Your grace, I—"

Lyon put up a hand. "I'll ask the questions."

Daisy wanted to sob. *Questions.* So no one believed

her, not even Tristan. And why should they? Unless she could produce her fairy godmother...

All round, people were talking, arguing. Daisy heard her name, she heard comments about the quality of the dresses and the depth of Daisy's personal poverty. And in the center of it all was Tristan. He'd shared a bed with her less than an hour ago, but now he appeared to be acting as judge.

Kemble moved toward Tristan, and they exchanged a few muttered words.

"You are a thief," the vicar spat then, as Daisy backed away from him. "I have it on good authority that you told your stepmother that you had no suitable outfit for this evening. And yet you now appear in something far beyond your means."

"Perhaps she borrowed it from her stepsister," Kemble offered.

But Bella shook her head, looking as bewildered as Daisy. "The gown is not mine. I wish it were!"

"So where did it come from?" the vicar pressed, looming over Daisy. "You stole it. Who knows what else you may have taken over the years, possibly from Rutherford Grange itself!"

"I would never! Rutherford Grange is my home!" Daisy objected.

At the same moment, Mr. Kemble said, "Your accusations are now growing spurious, sir. What proof have you that *anything* has gone missing from Rutherford Grange, let alone that something has been forcibly removed?"

"I know an opportunist when I see one," the vicar continued. "There is a term for a woman who receives costly gifts from unnamed givers."

Bella gave a little gasp of shock, a sound echoed by several other ladies in hearing range. Lady Rutherford looked grim, and faced Daisy with cold eyes. "I believe this discussion should continue in a less public venue."

Daisy shrank from the tirade. She searched for Tristan, and caught his gaze, but saw only coldness there. Not a trace of love or support.

Before Tristan could say anything more, she was running, through the startled crowd, past the outbuildings, past the pond, and out into the fields.

Shouts echoed behind her, and she heard the sounds of footsteps. But she was fueled by fear, and that made her fly. She plunged into the darkness of the night, running through the fallow fields, lost to view. Where she was running to, she didn't know. All that mattered was that she got away from Lyondale, and Tristan, and everyone who wanted to hurt her.

Just then, Daisy's foot struck a rock and her slipper got caught on the jagged edge. Her continued movement ripped the delicate shoe right off her foot, but Daisy could hardly stop to retrieve it, not when she was being pursued. She left the destroyed slipper behind.

Why not? It was fitting. The whole evening was destroyed, her whole life was destroyed, and all because of her desire to pretend to be something she wasn't. She never should have opened the mysterious parcel, and she never should have put on the dress. How could something so beautiful bring such misery?

Chapter 14

❦

MERCIFULLY, THE SOUND OF EXPLOSIONS had stopped. Tristan blinked, trying to remember where he was, because for some period of time, and he could not say how long, he was in two places at once. First, there on the balcony with Daisy, about to tell her something very important, something she needed to hear…and also back in the war, with shouts in the distance and the reverberations of dropped shells and the barrage of cannon fire. It was impossible to sort out, and when he heard a scream and saw Daisy's face lit in a fiery red, his mind just shut down.

He didn't know what to do, or where he was, or even *when* he was. Tristan had had nightmares like this in the early days, in hospital. He hated them more than anything else, more than the pain of the wounds, or the stink of the operating rooms, or the moans of the other soldiers. He couldn't escape the nightmares, which left him feeling helpless and weak. One of the doctors told him that the nightmares would fade, and he should just "man up" until then.

After the doctor left, the soldier in the bed next to him, a man who'd lost a leg above the knee, had muttered, "He's an idiot. He doesn't know what *we* dream. I dream I'm running away, and at least in the nightmares, I've still got legs to run...."

Tristan had nodded, but said nothing. What could be said?

And now, nearly two years later, far away at Lyondale, he was still suffering, still being incapacitated by his old wounds.

He heard Daisy's voice, but then it was gone. Panic filled him, and he tried to follow where he thought she'd gone. He couldn't lose Daisy, not now! Tristan wasn't sure where he was going, but he followed the sounds of voices. Along the way, a few people spoke to him, but he ignored them completely.

Then he saw Daisy. Thank God. But something was wrong, and there was some argument. His mind not fully back to the present, he tried to follow the thread, but only got confused. Something about theft? And Daisy? He couldn't put the ideas together, and kept repeating what others said, and then he shuddered, his brain finally snapping back to where his body was.

He stood on the front steps of Lyondale. The party guests were all gathered around, having been drawn away from the fireworks display to this sudden drama. Hornthwaite gripped Daisy's mask in his hand, pointing at her in a self-righteous but sly fury. Tristan realized all at once that her identity had been revealed, and more than that, she was being denounced as a criminal.

She pleaded with Hornthwaite, who refused to back down. Daisy looked to Tristan for help, but he didn't even know how to react, still half-stunned. Inside, Tristan was furious. Seeing Daisy so hurt by the accusations made him want to *break* things. But his voice and his body were taking too much time to stir.

Then, with a sob, Daisy turned and fled. Beyond the immediate circle of the house, where lanterns blazed, the world was dark, and even in her brightly colored dress, Daisy was soon lost to sight.

A moment passed, and then Tristan ordered someone, *anyone* to find her and bring her back. What was Daisy thinking? Running in the dark, on uneven ground in dancing shoes? She'd trip and hurt herself within a minute.

His anger fueling him, Tristan looked over the crowd, most of them still gawking, not helping to locate Daisy in the slightest. And then there was Hornthwaite, smug and self-righteous, the butterfly mask held like a shield in front of him.

"Well, as the festivities are um, over, I suppose we ought to head home?" Lady Weatherby ventured, sounding as if she would rather be anywhere than here.

Tristan didn't care where she wanted to be.

"No one is leaving," he declared. "I will discover what has just happened if I have to throw every single one of you into the pond to get answers." Any objections people might have had to his manner were silenced in the face of his anger.

With the exception of the servants, who were ordered to fan out and locate Daisy before she hurt herself, the whole group was herded back into the ballroom, though there was no gaiety in the air now. Using all his military bearing and his newfound clout as lord, he separated out those people who were involved from the ordinary party-goers, and quickly determined that nearly everyone was ignorant of the matter, with the exception of Hornthwaite and Lady Rutherford. Hornthwaite was the one who unmasked Daisy, claiming it was an accident, and he was the one who first called her a thief. Lady Rutherford staunchly defended the vicar's claims, adding that many valuable items had gone missing from Rutherford Grange over the years (a fact that Bella hesitantly confirmed).

Tristan didn't believe the accusations for a minute, but it was clear that Daisy's running away made the matter worse. The guests were whispering among themselves, and casting glances Tristan's way, and he heard the name *Lady Wildwood* more than once.

At Jack's suggestion, most of the guests were dismissed to return to their homes. Tristan added that anyone seeing Daisy on the road should report to Lyondale immediately.

"Or to the magistrate!" one of the guests added helpfully.

"No, to me," Tristan snapped. He didn't even know who the magistrate was around here, and he didn't trust anyone else to help Daisy now.

Then Tristan ordered his own carriage brought up, and he and Jack got in to follow Lady Rutherford's coach back to the Grange.

Surely, Daisy would be heading home, and with luck, they'd see her trudging along the road within a few minutes.

"What was the man thinking?" Tristan grumbled, remembering Hornthwaite holding the mask. "Exposing her like that?"

"The identity of Lady Wildwood was the subject of much speculation all evening," Jack told him. "And small wonder. She was the only woman you had eyes for. So much for finding a suitable match tonight."

"I don't want anyone but Daisy."

"That is clear enough," Jack said drily.

Tristan realized what his friend meant. The fact was that he showed far too much attention to a specific woman tonight, and that if anyone did know that he and Daisy were alone together in the house, her reputation would be in tatters.

And of course, there was also the little fact that she was no longer a virgin.

Tristan meant to talk to Daisy on the balcony earlier, to explain to her about the financial straits he was in, and how he intended to find the next heir, and if the man was suitable, Tristan would renounce the title of duke and pass it on so he could be with Daisy.

But then all hell broke loose.

He had to find her, tonight. The road to Rutherford Grange seemed interminable, and Tristan spent every second peering out the carriage window to see if he could glimpse Daisy along the way.

She was well ahead of them, though, even on foot (and not even fully shod, for a servant had quickly located one lost slipper in the fields nearest Lyondale). Jack told him to sit back, and not jump out of the carriage altogether.

"She'll be at the Grange," Jack said. "And you can talk to her there and get this whole theft nonsense sorted. Personally, I think Hornthwaite just likes stirring up trouble."

However, at Rutherford Grange, Daisy was nowhere to be found. Following Lady Rutherford's anemic calls for her stepdaughter to appear, Tristan took over, ordering the servants (how could such a large estate employ so few?) to investigate every single room, outbuilding, and shed on the property. He himself went to the stables, but was told that all the horses—only three!—plus the mule were accounted for. When asked where Daisy might be, the stable boy merely shrugged. "She's always lived at the Grange, sir."

That was true, and Daisy clearly felt it was her home. So where could she be?

After a fruitless search and some very unsatisfying

answers from the servants, Tristan threw himself onto a chair in Lady Rutherford's large but dim drawing room.

Bella was there, offering a drink to Jack, who had been too tired to join the search himself. Bella was still dressed in her snow princess costume, and she looked out of place in the dark, shabby room.

Lady Rutherford sat in front of the fire. Hornthwaite had left shortly after seeing the ladies home, citing the need to return to the vicarage to prepare for the Sunday service, which was three days away.

Daisy's mask was nowhere to be seen.

Tristan refused Bella's offer of a drink, and turned to Lady Rutherford in frustration. "How can you be so calm? Surely you want to know where she is!"

Lady Rutherford sipped her tea and gave a little sniff. "Who knows where the girl has run off. She was always an ungrateful wretch and now it seems quite obvious who was behind the many missing items from the Grange over the years."

"Mama, please!" Bella said, her eyes wide in the dim light of the room. "We don't know that. It must have been servants or something."

"What was she, but a glorified servant with airs beyond her station? You are too sweet, darling," her mother said. "And my goodness, look at the hour. You should retire, or you'll have circles under your eyes tomorrow."

That hardly seemed like the most pressing matter to Tristan, but it was clear that Lady Rutherford didn't have much interest in locating her stepdaughter.

"She is a lone woman, with no more than one dancing slipper to run on, it's near freezing temperatures tonight, and she's dressed like a *butterfly*," Tristan said. He faced the assembled group, asking the same questions he'd asked since she fled. "Where did she go? Why has no one seen her? How could she simply disappear?"

As before, no one had answers.

Jack suggested that there was little more anyone could do tonight. "Let's head back to Lyondale, and arrange for a proper search first thing in the morning. I'm sure the baroness will be willing to lend her servants to the effort."

Lady Rutherford sighed and said that she would. "The girl has to come back sometime. She's got nowhere else to go."

If this was the atmosphere Daisy called home, perhaps it wasn't surprising that she ran away. But where did she go?

In the coach, Tristan told Jack, "I'm going to find her, and we are getting to the bottom of this."

"By *this*, you mean the running away?" Jack asked.

"I mean all of this. The charge of theft, the strange attitude of the baroness, and every other mystery of the Grange. I owe her that. She may never forgive me for what happened tonight, but I'm going to clear her name if it's the last thing I do as duke."

Chapter 15

❧ ⟨ornament⟩ ❧

WHEN DAISY HAD FLED FROM the ball, she ran through the fields, heading roughly south. She'd lost one her dancing slippers almost the moment she entered the gardens, but she couldn't go back for it, not now. Not ever.

She had dashed through the formal gardens and the meadow, then plunged into the farm fields. Her gown snagged on the broken stalks of whatever crop was growing there. Daisy ignored the scrapes from the stubs of the crops and the jabbing from the stones in the dirt. She had to get away from Lyondale, and Tristan, and everyone else there who stared at her with cruel, judging eyes.

At first, all she wanted was to rush home to the kitchen at Rutherford Grange, to the warm hearth and Elaine's motherly embrace. But even before she saw the lights of the great house, she knew she couldn't go there. Now everyone knew that "Lady Wildwood" was plain old Daisy Merriot—thief and interloper. She'd be discovered at home, probably arrested or dragged off for whatever punishment the vicar and her stepmother and the duke dreamed up.

She needed another refuge.

All at once, she remembered Tabitha's cottage, and the old woman's strange exhortation that Daisy must come to her if she ever left the Grange. How prophetic, but how welcome now. The old woman would hide Daisy for a night! And it was unlikely the fine folk of the county would even think of the old woman's place for a day or two, by which point Daisy would be gone.

When Daisy knocked on Tabitha's door, she was exhausted, foot-sore, and in tears. "Tabitha, it's Daisy! I need your help, please let me in!"

Moments later, the door swung open and a thin, bony arm reached out to pull Daisy inside. The door slammed shut behind her.

"What's going on, girl? Are there brigands out there?"

A flame suddenly illuminated the tiny cottage, as Tabitha lit a tallow candle.

"I'm in trouble," Daisy said, her breath coming in great heaves. "I am so sorry, but I had nowhere else to go."

"You poor dear! Sit down, and be easy. No one will find you here."

And before Daisy knew it, she was divested of her once-beautiful but now tattered butterfly gown, wrapped in a woolen blanket by Tabitha's fireplace, her hands around a mug of chamomile tea.

She poured her heart out, explaining about the magic of the gown's appearance and sneaking into the ball under a false name, then dancing with Tristan and slipping away with him to his rooms. She recalled the forbidden liaison with pain in her heart, for even though it had been foolish, she couldn't say she didn't want it. But oh the troubles that followed...

Daisy told Tabitha about the fireworks, which the old lady had heard even at this distance. She explained about Tristan's reaction to the explosions and how she ran for help, only to be unmasked and suddenly accused of theft and worse.

"And the duke now thinks me shallow and mean, I'm sure. Probably like so many other women, trying to trap him into a marriage by being compromised, though I didn't say anything! But people must have seen him and Lady Wildwood leave the ballroom together, and they now know it was me. I can't stay here anymore. Even if I can prove I'm not a thief—and how could I?—I'll be ashamed to show my face. And the baroness will never let me stay at the Grange anymore. It would reflect badly on Bella, to have a ruined woman in the house. Oh, I don't know what to do."

"Sounds to me as though you need a good night's sleep, child," Tabitha said. "You're distraught, and tired, and cold. Let's see what tomorrow brings. I promise you that no one will bother you through the night."

Daisy slept fitfully, expecting to hear fists hammering at the door and the local magistrate yelling for her to come out. But Tabitha's cottage was tucked deep in the woods, and the night was dark, and no one would have reason to think that Daisy chose to flee here.

In the morning, she got up, feeling as if she'd not slept a wink. Outside, the sun shone brightly, but Daisy felt none of the warmth.

"What will I do?" Daisy moaned in despair. "Oh I wish I'd never left my school all those years ago! It's never been the same here since Papa died!"

Then Daisy blinked, the tears clearing from her eyes. School! She remembered Mrs. Bloomfield's offer, made weeks ago (though it seemed like years). She could go to Wildwood Hall!

"But how would I get there?" Daisy asked out loud.

"Get where?" Tabitha asked, looking interested.

"Wildwood Hall, where I was at school. Mrs. Bloomfield once told me she'd offer me a position as a teacher if I wanted to try it. Now I can't do that, obviously. But she'd employ me as maid…"

Tabitha snorted. "Don't fetch your bucket and mop yet, girl. First we've got to get you there. Now give me a moment to think."

"The law will be watching for me," Daisy said, sure she'd be seized the moment she showed her face on the road or in the village. No, she could never go into the village again! How was she to get a ride on the coach? And she had no money!

She touched her mother's necklace. Well, she could sell that, and she'd have a respectable sum. Enough for travel and room and board…

Tabitha told Daisy to stay at the cottage while Tabitha went out to the village and made a few inquiries. She also promised to alert Jacob and Elaine of Daisy's whereabouts, since Daisy hated to worry them.

Later that day, Tabitha returned, flush with news, and more importantly, plans for Daisy's escape.

For someone living in near total isolation, Tabitha had incredible reach when it came to finding little tidbits of information. That plus the servants' network of gossip allowed the old woman to call in a few favors and arrange for Daisy's departure.

The first part was easy. Jacob really did have to deliver the cartload of pumpkins to the village, a task that had been delayed by the widespread hunt for Daisy.

So the next morning, he was eager to complete his journey to the village. And he just so happened to stop at a quiet, concealed spot on the road while Daisy crawled in and hid herself among the mound of squashes.

At the village, Jacob drove the cart into a barn, where Daisy was unloaded along with the pumpkins.

"You take care, miss," he whispered, looking as if he might cry.

As instructed, she hid herself in an empty horse stall until about noon, when another vehicle rode up and stopped. Horses whinnied outside, and a slim woman dressed as a lady's maid entered the barn.

"Last call for London!" the maid announced, a conspiratorial smile on her face.

Daisy peeked out. "You're going to London?"

"Yes and you are to join us. But hurry, please!"

Daisy grabbed her case and came out to the main area of the barn. Thanks to a carefully packed bundle from Elaine delivered the night before, Daisy now wore her most drab clothing—a grey dress and brown cape.

The maid eyed her curiously, then said, "That will do. You look like any other woman in those clothes. Call me Lucy, miss. Now let's get you away from here."

Lucy hustled Daisy into the coach, which had all the curtains pulled to conceal the inside. No markings on the other part indicated who the coach might belong to.

The interior was plush and comfortable. As the driver coaxed the horses to move again, Daisy realized that she was the only passenger besides the maid.

"Who are you?" she asked, perplexed.

"I told you! Lucy. The driver is named Jem. This coach belongs to our mistress, but it needed repairs, so she took another to London and we're following now. Beats riding the mail coach!"

Daisy agreed wholeheartedly, having experienced the cramped, bumpy, and bone-jarring ride in the mail coaches. But she said, "Your mistress won't be upset with you for taking me along?"

"Certainly not! My lady would insist, if she knew. And of course we'll tell her when we do get to London.

You may stay at the house should you not find a connection to your final destination."

"Oh, I couldn't possibly impose further."

"Nonsense. Miss Tabitha requested that we help, and that is what we'll do."

"How do you know Tabitha?"

"Well, I never met her personally," Lucy said. "But let us say that we have mutual friends, who are deeply loyal, if a tad disreputable."

Daisy found the explanation quite mysterious, but it seemed that Lucy wasn't about to give more details. And in any case, Daisy ought not to look a gift horse (or coach) in the mouth. She needed to get away from Lyondale and the Grange, and this was how she could do it.

Lucy asked no questions about Daisy's predicament beyond wondering if Jem should be looking over his shoulder.

"No one would dream I'd be in a coach, especially not one this excellent," Daisy said. "I'm nobody."

"You look like somebody to me, Miss Daisy. Do you like lamb? I've got a lamb pie in the hamper here. And some cheese. And some apples…"

And so it was that Daisy arrived in London well-fed and well-rested, and given a place to sleep at a lovely house on Quince Street. In the city the next day, she was able to arrange for another hired coach to take her to Wildwood Hall. This one was the standard quality coach, and held four other passengers. But the ride was shorter, and Daisy was standing at the gates of Wildwood Hall just as the sun was setting.

Chapter 16

❧ ❧

BACK IN GLOUCESTERSHIRE, THE SEARCH for Daisy Merriot went on, though it was increasingly clear that she was no longer in the area, having been spirited away somehow, by someone, for how was it possible that a young lady dressed as a butterfly could just disappear?

On the morning after the ball, Tristan was optimistic that Daisy would be found shortly, and that he could sort out any misunderstanding.

The second morning, his mood could be more accurately described as frantic.

The third morning, despair set in.

And finally, Tristan had reverted to his most terrible mood, the bitter rage that he lived in after his injury. He growled at nearly everyone he saw, wondering why not a single one of them could bring him news of Daisy.

It made no sense. If she had hurt herself on her flight back to the Grange, she would have been found. The fields and roads and paths between the two estates had been searched over and over again in the days following the ball.

If she prevailed upon a neighbor to host her, someone at that house would have passed the news onto the duke, whether a servant or the neighbors themselves.

And if she tried to leave the area via public conveyance, she would have been spotted on the coaches for hire that passed through Lyonton.

But she remained missing, and the manner of her disappearance only became more puzzling the longer people searched for her.

One day, a week after the initial search began, Tristan did not get out of bed. What was the point? Daisy was gone.

A maid entered to open the curtains and light the fire, but she didn't dare disturb the master. A footman came in a bit later, bearing Tristan's customary tray of coffee and several newspapers. And then his valet entered, asking if Tristan expected to rise before noon.

"No," Tristan growled. Then, "What time is it?"

"Ten minutes to noon, sir."

"Damn it."

"Yes, sir."

"No news?" He didn't have to ask that, knowing that if there had been news of Daisy, good or bad, people would be knocking down his door.

"Nothing concerning Miss Merriot, sir. You do have a package postmarked from Calcutta. Arrived this morning on the London post coach."

"A package?" Tristan couldn't think what it would be. Perhaps it was a cobra, to put him out of his misery.

"I'll leave it by your coffee, your grace. Do ring should you want to dress for dinner." The valet left, with that silent swiftness only the very best servants mastered.

It was the aroma of coffee, rather than the promise of news, that got Tristan out of bed. But once he had a cup in him, he felt up to opening the package and finding out just what more horrible news John Cater had for him.

A letter was attached to the package, and Tris opened

that first.

Dear T—

Where to begin? I suspect you'll not even read this, after what you received from me at first. I have three letters from you, and I regret that I did not answer them at once, but you will, I hope, understand why I waited, once you learn all that happened.

The bare fact of the matter is that my partner, Mr. Rait, turned out to be a bounder of the worst sort. He switched stones on me! He slipped some rubbish into the package meant for you, and he switched another stone that I sent for an appraisal from a reputable Hyderabad firm that I wanted to work with on cutting. Apparently, after using the ten thousand from your generous loan, his plan was to make the venture seemed doomed, buy us both out for a pittance and then own the whole diamond mine himself!

And it does produce diamonds, my friend, I can confirm that at last. When the firm sent me the report that my beautiful diamond was a mere chunk of quartz, you can imagine my horror. Well, you don't have to imagine it, for you would have felt the same if you sent your sample to an appraiser, as I assume you did. I got sick to my stomach and nearly threw myself into the nearest pit, and I've got plenty of pits to choose from now, as workers are digging like mad. I couldn't believe the news and thank God, I had another little stash from our initial foray into the caves that I kept separate, and I sent those to the appraiser to put them to the test. And wouldn't you know, they were the genuine article, lovely diamonds worth their weight and more.

On the advice of the firm, I hired a man to investigate Mr. Rait, and it was discovered that the cad had pulled tricks like this before, though not on such a scale and never involving the money of the British aristocracy. As soon as I said a duke was involved, the law here snapped to. My partner was arrested trying to board a ship, his luggage full of our diamonds. He was a much wanted man, known to be a snake by those he's wronged. And it seems that the prisons in India are not for the faint of heart, for he tried to bribe the judge with a few diamonds to be let off. The judge took the diamonds, and sent him to the prison anyway. Such is justice for the wicked.

This means that you are now owner of half the mine, instead of a third. And the mine is already producing quality stones. I have sold some already, and I directed the bank to alert the London branch of the running total of our account there. I believe that you will soon find it easy to repay your loan far earlier than would be expected. And there's much more profit to come.

I include a collection of some of the first stones to be extracted by our miners. The large one will have to be cut of course, but I am confident that it will go some way in making up my debt to you, for you must have thought me a liar and cheat, when in fact I was merely an idiot and a coward. I beg you to forgive me. I am sailing to London early in the new year, and I will call on you when I arrive in the country, in hopes you will receive me.

I urge you to contact the bank in London to verify the deposits, and to contact your appraiser to verify the included stones, not least because you will wish to insure them...

Tristan read the letter twice before the words sunk in, and a third time before he opened the accompanying package.

When he did, a clutch of stones gleamed out at him. They were rough, uncut pieces. But there was a special weight to them, an electricity in the surface. Tristan picked up the largest one, which he could grip in his closed fist. He then read the neatly written report folded into the package, which stated that the stones within were gem-quality diamonds, estimated to be worth over one hundred pounds per carat, once cut.

Tristan didn't know whether to laugh or cry. He held real wealth in his hands now, after fearing that he'd be ruined. But what was the point of having such wealth when he had no idea where Daisy was, or if she was even alive?

"Jack won't believe this," he muttered. Thinking of his friend, Tristan rang for his valet. Twenty minutes later, he was dressed and striding down the hall to the study where Jack spent most of his time.

"Read this," Tristan ordered, shoving the letter in Jack's lap.

Jack dutifully read it, his eyebrows rising with each sentence. At the end, he put the letter down. "My God," he said, shaking his head. "What a roundabout way to come out on top. At least there's one problem solved."

"But the less important one. I'm losing my mind, Jack. Where the hell could she have gone? Is she lying in the woods somewhere…" He couldn't even finish the sentence.

"Not near here, with all the dogs set out to search for her," Jack noted with his usual calm. "Personally, I think she must have found some shelter and is hiding there. The servants from all the houses around here have been… *furtive* isn't really the right word, but if you ask me, even if one of them knew something, it wouldn't be passed on to us, lest the authorities get wind of it. Somehow, Miss Merriot has allies in low places, and they'll keep silent, so long as they think it's safer for her if they do."

"But if she got hurt, or lost…"

"Lost? This is her home. Well, it used to be, before the baroness showed up."

"What does that mean?" Tristan blinked at the new thread in the conversation. Jack clearly had something on his mind. "She told us both what happened after her father died. It's odd and not fair to her, but she made the best of it."

Jack said, "I know what she told us, and what others said. But the explanation never held water. So I did some investigating on my own."

"How could you do anything when you can barely walk around the gardens?"

Jack pulled a letter from his jacket pocket. "There are other ways to get information. Over the past several weeks, I've been making inquiries of a few solicitors' firms in London, and learned some very interesting things about the late baron's last will and testament."

"Time for that later," Tristan said, though his curiosity was piqued. "What's more important is to find Daisy as soon as possible. It's impossible to vanish into thin air!"

A knock at the door startled them both. The butler said, "Apologies, your grace, but you have a visitor. Miss Bella says she has some information about Miss Daisy Merriot."

"My God, man, then send her in!" Tristan ordered.

Moments later, a very nervous Bella stood before the two men. She scarcely lifted her eyes, and never looked at Tristan directly. She chanced only tiny glances toward Jack, the less imposing figure.

She curtsied. "Your grace. Mr. Kemble."

"Please sit," Tristan said, pointing to the seat at right angles to where Jack had risen to greet the lady. "We are told you know something about Miss Daisy."

"Yes, sirs." Her normally quiet voice was scarcely more than a whisper. "I believe I may, *may* know where she is."

Tristan leaned forward. "Then tell us."

"When she was younger, Daisy attended a school called the Bloomfield Academy for Young Ladies of Quality."

"Yes, she mentioned that," Tristan said, remembering Daisy's affectionate account of her days there, though he didn't understand the relevance.

"The school was at an estate called Wildwood Hall," she added.

"Wildwood," Tristan echoed. That was the name Daisy had used for the masquerade. "You think she might have gone back there, years later?"

Bella rummaged through her lacy reticule and produced a folded letter. "She maintained steady correspondence with several of her schoolmates and with Mrs. Bloomfield, who owns the school. This letter is from Mrs. Bloomfield, from a few months ago, and it contains an offer of employment."

"She left her home at Rutherford Grange to become a…a schoolteacher?" Tristan asked, befuddled.

The young lady's expression grew morose. "I have come to realize—too late—that Rutherford Grange was less of a home than it should have been, while Wildwood Hall was more so than ordinary people would think. I believe that following the vicar's very…harsh words, Daisy took a lifeline offered to her, fleeing the gossip here to take a position at the school. I can only hope she reached her destination."

"May I?" Jack asked, gesturing to the letter.

Bella handed it over and he perused it silently. "How did you come into possession of this?" he asked Bella.

"I stole it from her bedroom," the girl replied, her tone matter-of-fact, but her cheeks pink with shame. "When it became clear that she had truly gone missing, I thought I might find a clue among her letters."

"Very enterprising, my lady," Jack said, with a trace of a smile.

"It was necessary," she replied, without looking at either of them. "The servants won't say anything, and Mama hopes that Daisy never comes back—" She broke off, having said more than she intended to.

"Your mother does not care for Miss Daisy, does she?"

Bella winced. "I can't understand why, because everyone loves Daisy so. But Mama has such...*opinions* sometimes."

That was an understatement, Tristan thought. He asked, "And what is your opinion?"

"She is my sister by marriage," Bella said, blinking in surprise at being asked her opinion on anything. "I have nothing but good thoughts for her, and a wish that she may be safe and well, wherever she is." Then the young lady's voice trembled. "But I fear she is neither safe nor well! No one has seen her since the ball, and she was all alone, at night, in the cold...I would have perished before dawn had it been me. Daisy is ever so much stronger, but why can no one find her?"

Jack reached out to offer the letter back to Bella. She took it, but he kept his hand over hers. "We will find her," he promised.

Tristan nodded once, as his confidence returned. "Wildwood Hall is the clue we needed. I will inquire personally, and God willing, this Mrs. Bloomfield will have good news for us all."

And if she did not...Tristan had no idea what he would do.

Chapter 17

❧ ❧❧

AT WILDWOOD HALL, DAISY HAD finished teaching French lessons for the day, and helping the younger students with their reading as well. It was a tenet of Bloomfield's Academy for Young Ladies of Quality that everyone had a duty to serve to the best of her ability. Daisy took that tenet to heart perhaps more than any other, for she loved to see people smile when their burdens were lightened even for a little while. It soothed her own aching heart.

For just over a week now, Daisy had been employed as an instructor, primarily for the younger girls. She was grateful to have any position. She would have worked as a maid. Mrs. Bloomfield merely laughed at that notion, telling Daisy that teaching little girls to be young ladies was quite grueling enough.

"You'll have your hands full," Mrs. Bloomfield said. Which was true. Daisy worked as hard as possible, not just to prove herself to Mrs. Bloomfield, but also to try to forget why she was at Wildwood Hall in the first place.

That was a more difficult task, for whenever she closed her eyes, she saw Tristan. And every time she heard a footstep or an approaching voice, she worried it was someone come to find her and haul her back for questioning.

At dinner one night, when the instructors who lived at the school all gathered for blessedly grown-up conversation, Daisy asked what she ought to do next. She was well aware that she could not remain at the school forever.

"You could go to London," suggested Mrs. Cannon, a gray-haired woman who taught mathematics, Latin, and Greek to the older girls. "Find a position as governess. But London is a terrible place." She shuddered at the thought of living in the city.

"It's not a terrible place," Mrs. Bloomfield said with a chuckle. "And some of Daisy's good friends live there, so she'd not be without company. But the life of a governess is perhaps not fulfilling enough for a young lady like Daisy, who has other interests and skills."

"Not to mention that a letter of reference will be hard to come by," Mrs. Cannon muttered.

"Really, dear," Mrs. Bloomfield said, "it would be best if you returned to your home to sort this mess out. We know you're innocent of any charges of theft—the whole idea is ludicrous—but the longer you stay away, the more difficult it will be to settle the matter."

Daisy looked down at her plate, where most of her meal remained uneaten. "I know that would be the right thing to do, but I'm not brave enough to trust that I'll get a fair hearing. My stepmother seemed to believe it, and the vicar is very influential, and the duke said nothing to support me..." That hurt worse than anything. Though Daisy had kept the full extent of her relationship with Tristan to herself, Mrs. Bloomfield certainly understood that she had fallen in love with him, and was worse off for it.

"You need someone who knows the law to defend you," Mrs. Cannon said.

"And where would she locate a man willing to take that case on, against a baroness and a duke and the whole shire?" Mrs. Bloomfield frowned. "I wish I had funds to pay for such a person, but I'm afraid..."

"Oh, no!" Daisy put her fork down, rather more forcefully than she intended. "You have been so kind to take me in. You mustn't spend a penny more on me. I promise I will decide what to do soon...just not yet."

"You may stay here as long as needed," Mrs. Bloomfield said, patting her hand. "But remember, the world rarely waits until a person is ready for it."

Daisy nodded. How true. She didn't feel prepared for a single thing that happened to her lately, whether it was meeting Tristan in the woods one day, or being showered with a mysterious gift, to being accused of theft in front of the whole county...

But at least Wildwood Hall was a haven. Daisy was so grateful to be there, among the young students and the familiar rooms and the books in the library that she'd read years before. One day, the youngest class decided to play hide and seek. The weather had turned cold, so no one could hide in the gardens, like Daisy had done when she played it. But the many corners and tucked away closets of the Hall provided many hiding spots, and squeals echoed through the building as girls found each other.

It was a fun game...as long as one did not mind being found. Daisy briefly imagined playing such a game at Lyondale, perhaps with a little girl who had her blonde hair and Tristan's eyes.

The thought swept her back to the night they'd lain together, and how she'd been so overcome with passion that she threw all her good sense to the wind just to be with him. Was she possibly pregnant now? After only one time? Daisy knew it was possible, though unlikely. Tristan had taken care to avoid the outcome. And even if she were, would she ever approach Tristan and tell him? A duke would probably not welcome news of a bastard, though she guessed that Tristan would support the child. But Daisy was not at all sure she'd want him to know. In fact, she wasn't sure of anything, except that she ached for Tristan, and would give just about anything to hear him say her name again. Or to kiss her and tell her that everything would be fine, and that their troubles were over. And then he'd sweep her into his arms and kiss her...

"Miss Merriot?"

"Yes!" Daisy's attention snapped back to the present moment. "What is it, Joanna?"

"The headmistress would like to see you in her office," the younger girl said, eyes round at the thought of going to such an august place. "She didn't say why."

"Ah, must be a new student coming to Wildwood. I'm to give the tours now." Daisy put her book away and rose to her feet, gently running her palms across her skirt to flatten out any wrinkles. Since she had very little clothing to her name now, she treated everything she did own with utmost care.

She took a quick glance at the mirror to be sure her hair was in place, and that the younger students had not left paint on her nose. All she saw was her own plain face, her cheeks a little pinker than proper for a lady.

When she reached the office door, Daisy knocked politely. "It's Daisy, Mrs. Bloomfield."

"Come in, come in."

Daisy entered and sat on the polished walnut chair across the vast desk. She was in no fear that she'd done anything wrong, but she could not think why she'd been summoned.

"Daisy, you have a visitor."

Mrs. Bloomfield turned in her seat to indicate a figure standing by the window. Daisy hadn't noticed anyone until now, but her heart dropped to her stomach when she saw Tristan in the light.

"Miss Merriot," he said, very formally. "I was hoping we could speak."

"Your g-grace," she stammered out. "I did not expect…"

"No you wouldn't, considering that you didn't tell anyone where you went, and I've got a lot questions about how you managed it." As he spoke, he approached her, and Daisy instinctively leaned back, expecting censure.

But Tristan stopped short a few feet away and bent his head down in supplication. "But none of that really matters now. What matters is that you hear me out."

"Hear *you* out?" she echoed, confused. Wasn't she the one in trouble?

"Perhaps you two would like to take a stroll around the grounds," Mrs. Bloomfield suggested. "Meet me back here in a half hour so we may discuss the next steps." Her meaning was clear—Tristan could talk to Daisy in relative privacy, but no misbehavior would be tolerated.

Tristan was still wearing his coat, so Daisy murmured that she'd fetch her cape before they went outside.

The gardens of Wildwood Hall were quiet, the plants dried and brown, the trees bare. Winter hovered, about to sweep in any day now. Daisy walked down the brick paths, unable to say a word. At last, Tristan said, "You have no idea what it's been like since you left. Never has a person vanished so completely. I thought you were dead."

"How did you find me?"

"Miss Bella remembered the school and suggested

you might have come here."

"So you rode out here on a whim?"

"I'd ride over the whole island to find you," he said simply, and Daisy's heart pounded at the emotion in his words.

"I was scared," she admitted.

"Understandable, but my God, Daisy, you scared the hell out of me by disappearing like that."

"My apologies, your grace. It was not my intent to worry anyone."

He stopped and took her by the shoulders to make her face him. "No, I'm the one who needs to apologize. I should have defended you at that moment, but I didn't. I failed you, Daisy. It was a mistake."

Daisy felt wounded. Was he going to apologize for the time they made love? "Don't apologize for that, your grace. I encouraged you by going with you to your room."

"I'm not going to apologize for *that*, Daisy." He held her hands, as if afraid she'd vanish if he let her get too far away.

"Then what?"

"For not being there where you needed me. For being so…useless in the one moment I should have been defending you. Forgive me."

She felt a bit stunned, so all she said was, "I never blamed you for that. You were suffering. It wasn't your fault. Tristan, it's not up to you to defend me."

"It is," he said. "And I promise that I'll set everything right."

"How can you do that? The law will take its course…"

He shook his head, pushing her words aside. "Daisy, listen. It is very important that you return to Lyondale."

"I'd rather not," Daisy said. Hornthwaite and the baroness might well be assembling witnesses against her at that very hour. "I don't think I am wanted there."

"*I* want you there, and I will not let anything happen to you, Daisy. Please trust me."

Daisy's stomach was in knots, and she wanted so badly to believe Tristan. But a part of her held back. "I don't know."

"How can I convince you?" Tristan suddenly bent his head, gathered her close, and kissed her. Daisy protested for half a second before her body melted in response to his touch. She raised her hands to his chest, feeling the rise and fall as his breathing quickened. Her eyes closed as she reveled in the touch of his lips on hers. This was what she wanted, Tristan and her together, entwined, forever.

But she broke off, whispering, "We can't do this here."

"Then come back to Lyondale," he countered. "I will set things right, my love. I've been working and Jack's been working, and others too. We will get to the truth, but I need you there. Please. I swear I'll never betray your trust again."

The look in his eyes undid her, and she would have promised him anything in that moment. She took a deep breath, then nodded. "Very well, I will return."

But what would she walk into when she arrived?

Chapter 18

❧ ⟡ ❧

A FEW DAYS LATER, DAISY indeed returned to Lyondale,
just as she promised. Unwilling to allow Daisy to go
alone (or with an unmarried man as escort), Mrs. Bloomfield insisted on taking Daisy home herself. She left the
school under the charge of the dour-looking Mrs. Cannon,
who would ensure that the pupils behaved perfectly.

The duke had offered for them to stay at Lyondale,
which would have been technically acceptable as both
Mrs. Bloomfield and Miss Wallis would be there. But
Daisy didn't want even a breath of scandal to come near
Tristan, so she wrote to Lady Weatherby, who responded
with surprising speed, insisting that Daisy and her chaperone simply *must* stay with the Weatherbys as long as
they liked, adding that Lady Caroline would be especially
delighted for the company, and also it was such good
news that Daisy wasn't dead.

On a cold and blustery November day, Daisy rode up
to Lyondale, accompanied by Mrs. Bloomfield and the
Weatherbys. The ladies entered the great house and were
immediately ushered inward all the way to the ballroom.

But on this day, the massive and imposing ballroom
was not set up for festivities. Rather, rows of chairs were
arranged to create a makeshift court. And in a large, well-

cushioned chair at one end, the local magistrate sat in state, looking around as though wondering how he got there.

Others were present as well. Lady Rutherford and the Hon. Bella Merriot sat in the front row of chairs. Next to Lady Rutherford was the vicar, dressed in ecclesiastical black. Local gentry had come, and everyone turned to watch Daisy as she entered and took her seat, thankfully surrounded by Mrs. Bloomfield and the Weatherbys.

Tristan stood up, silencing all conversation. He turned to the magistrate and said, "Sir, I must first thank you for coming here to adjudicate this matter. It is my hope that for all concerned it can be settled here today, without the need for a full, formal inquiry."

"Well, it is most irregular," the magistrate said, frowning a little. "But for the Duke of Lyon..." He left the rest unsaid. Of course the law would bow to the desires of the highest-ranked gentleman around.

"Then we shall begin," Tristan said. "There are a few matters to address today, and I have asked all of you to attend to assure the world that it was handled in a fair and prompt fashion."

Several of the guests sat up straighter, flattered that the duke would request this of them.

Tristan continued without allowing anyone to interrupt. "The first matter is an accusation of theft. Let us hear from the man who made the accusation: Mr. Hornthwaite. Sir, please rise and come over to this table, which shall serve as our witness stand."

The man at first demurred, citing his position in the church as a reason why he should not be questioned. But the crowd was anxious, eager to hear the root of this gossip, and it was clear the duke would prevail. So the vicar walked up and took his place, perhaps viewing it as a sort of pulpit for him to use as he liked.

Tristan began simply enough. "Now then, you are the vicar in Lyonton, at the church with no steeple. You are also the man who accused Miss Daisy Merriot of stealing items for a costume ball, among other things."

"I did, as God would have wanted me to," Hornthwaite said stiffly.

"If you made such an accusation, you must have evidence to back it up," Tristan said.

Hornthwaite sniffed. "I know well Miss Daisy's financial situation, your grace. Everyone around here does. The idea that this woman—"

"This lady," Tristan corrected.

"This *lady* could afford a new dress of such quality is laughable."

"Miss Daisy did not claim to purchase it. She has said it was a gift. Yet you accused her of theft. So now I hope to see evidence of that statement, beyond your assumptions."

"I have not formally accused her of anything."

"No, you merely announced it to an indiscriminate number of people in a very public environment, and then permitted the charge to spread, leaving her to be judged by hastily formed opinions, and perhaps abusing people's implicit trust of a clergyman. Your sermon the following Sunday was on the subject of the sin of thievery, was it not?"

Hornthwaite looked quite smug, but he said, "It's an eternally germane topic."

"I'll ask again, here in the presence of our esteemed magistrate," Tristan said, his voice icy. "Do you have evidence?"

"Not as such," the vicar ground out.

"Not. As. Such," Tristan repeated, biting off each

word. "So you must have, I assume, faith."

"I do," Hornthwaite said, straightening up.

"In other words, God is on your side."

"I should hope so."

"So you would stake your living on your intuition."

"Excuse me, your grace?" he asked, faltering.

"You have been afforded a living as the vicar of the church in Lyonton. Is that not right? You were installed before I inherited the title, of course. I believe the Dukes of Lyon have traditionally been quite influential in choosing the curate here. But you have your living now."

"Yes," Hornthwaite said, unsure of where this was going.

"So you will stake it on this…matter of truth."

"I don't understand."

"It's simple. If you can produce positive evidence of theft on the part of Miss Margaret Merriot, then you'll have the satisfaction of seeing her go to gaol—and her stepsister embarrassed, the other servants likely shamed as well. An odd aspiration for a vicar, to see others made miserable, but I suppose you can point to some passage in the Bible to uphold your view."

"And if I don't do it?" Hornthwaite asked, clearly nervous now.

"Well, if you don't—or if someone produces evidence that the dress was purchased for or gifted to Daisy Merriot—you'll resign. Our local vicar must be a man who can be trusted. There must be no hint that a liar could have care of the whole parish. I recall some passage about bearing false witness. Sort of an important point, it was. A commandment, in fact."

Hornthwaite knew he was being lured into a trap, but he couldn't think of an escape. "That is clear in the Scripture, yes."

"Excellent. We are all on the same page. Now, let us proceed. Mr. Kemble has taken on the role of legal counsel for Miss Daisy Merriot. Do you wish to avail yourself of a solicitor, Mr. Hornthwaite? Or will the angels defend you?"

"I shall speak for myself, your grace. And the young lady can pray for all the help she likes. The angels will ignore her."

"This is most unfair!" Daisy burst out.

"Keep silent, Miss Merriot," Tristan ordered, his tone forbidding. "Mr. Hornthwaite, you may return to your seat."

Then Kemble stood up, taking over. "Your grace, I believe this matter will be easily resolved. If the footman—yes, John, you there—please bring in the person who has been waiting in the small parlor."

Daisy looked around the room, puzzled. Who was missing from this assembly? Who could Kemble possibly want to interview?

Then a familiar figure entered through the large double doors. She was dressed smartly in a green gown, and had snapping brown eyes that missed nothing in the room.

"Poppy!" she whispered.

Her schoolmate strolled up the aisle and her gaze locked with Daisy's for just an instant, but in that instant she felt all the warmth and rage and righteous indignation of a furious friend.

Poppy walked to the makeshift witness stand by the magistrate, and looked over the assembled guests as if *she* were the one who invited *them* in.

Kemble began his interview. "Your name is Poppy St. George, and you reside in London, is that correct?"

"That is true, sir."

"And do you know Miss Daisy Merriot?"

"Very well, for we were at school together at Bloomfield Academy. Our headmistress, in the first row there, can confirm it." She pointed out Mrs. Bloomfield with a smile.

"You are friends then."

"Dear friends."

"Tell me about your family, Miss St. George."

"My stepfather is in trade, sir. He deals in fabrics."

"Fabrics, you say. And is there anything about your family's business that might be relevant to today's matter?"

Poppy, having obviously expected this question, said, "Very much so, for the costume made in our shop is the very one Daisy wore to the ball."

"Are you saying that *you* sent the ball gown to Miss Daisy?" Mr. Kemble asked, with the false surprise of a lawyer who asks a question to which he already knows the answer, but can't wait for the rest of the courtroom to hear it for the first time.

"I did."

"Poppy!" Daisy burst out. "Why did you? And why did you not say anything?"

"I wanted to make a game of it," Poppy told her directly. "I never dreamed it would turn out as it has!"

"Details, please, Miss St. George. Why did this ball gown get made?" Kemble asked.

"My stepfather was eager to import some new fabrics, very modish ones that might advance his standing among the various buyers, who are always looking for the next fashion. The dusk pattern, as we called it, was very intriguing, but we had to make sure a seamstress could work with it. Thus a gown was sewn start to finish, and I had the notion of a butterfly coming out and spreading its wings for the first time, and so that is what we created. As it happens, the measurements of our mannequin are identical to that of Miss Daisy Merriot, a fact I was well aware of. So when we had a finished gown and costume elements, I thought, why not send it to Daisy and let her find out for us how it wears? You see, I'd just had a letter from her discussing a ball that she would have liked to attend, but of course she had no suitable outfit, her wardrobe being quite modest ever since the death of her father." She glanced over at Lady Rutherford with disdain.

"So you mailed the whole package to Miss Daisy at Rutherford Grange."

"Yes. My plan was to let her know in a fortnight or so that I had sent it, and to inquire of her opinion of the gown. However, events did not fall out that way."

"Indeed not."

Daisy nodded in silent agreement.

"But the necklace!" Hornthwaite interjected.

"Ah, yes," Mr. Kemble said. He walked to his table and picked up a piece of paper. "I knew the vicar was most concerned about the ruby necklace Miss Daisy was wearing with the costume. So I inquired at the firm that insured the previous baron's valuables. They have kindly sent along a list of items, and you'll see, sir," he said as he handed the sheet to the magistrate, "the description for item seventeen is that of the ruby necklace I hold here, which Miss Daisy lent to me for today's proceedings. As indicated, it was first purchased for her late mother, and remained at Rutherford Grange ever since, so there is an impeccable path from original owner to now."

The magistrate read the description and peered at the necklace, then nodded slowly. "They are one and the same. And I understand that Lady Rutherford herself announced on the night in question that she had never seen the necklace before. So Miss Daisy Merriot clearly could not have stolen it from *her*."

The baroness pursed her lips, obviously annoyed to have her own words used in such a way. Daisy began to feel a spark of hope. Perhaps she would get out of this unscathed.

"Well, that seems to clear things up in regard to the accusation of theft," said Tristan, clapping his hands once to get everyone's attention. "Do you have other accusations to make, Hornthwaite?"

The vicar swallowed. "No."

"No…" Tristan prompted.

"No, your grace."

"I'm so glad to hear it. Now, if you'll just make a short announcement to the good people gathered here, we can conclude this whole business."

"Conclude?" Hornthwaite asked hopefully. "What do you wish me to say?"

"You're the orator, not me. Just a short speech, man. Explain how wrong you were, how you regret defaming the reputation of Daisy Merriot…that sort of thing."

"And then I can leave?"

Tristan nodded, and swept a hand outward to indicate that it was time.

Hornthwaite looked nervously over the crowd. They'd all heard everything, so his apology was a mere formality. For a man used to speaking every Sunday, his speech now was quiet. Tristan urged him to speak up more than once.

When Hornthwaite finished, he heaved a sigh of relief, though the looks of mingled shame and contempt on the faces of the others would likely haunt him for years.

Tristan held up a hand to stop anyone from leaving or speaking. "Thank you, all, for hearing Mr. Hornthwaite's words. I think we can agree that he's been brave through-out, from the first accusation to the revelation of his remarkable mistake." Tristan offered a hand for Hornthwaite to shake. "Well done."

"Thank you, your grace," Hornthwaite said, bewildered.

"That's all then. You'll want to return to the vicarage, I expect." Tristan paused for a fraction of a second, then delivered his final blow. "You better be moved out by the end of the month. I wish you the best of luck in finding a new position. Anyone who is interested in offering you a living should of course feel free to speak to me personally. I'll be happy to explain the situation. That will be all."

Hornthwaite paled, but said nothing.

Some others present were not so restrained.

"We *can't* be without a vicar, your grace."

"The search will take months!"

Lord Lyon smiled wider. "Not to worry. I have a candidate in mind. A military chaplain with a respectable, if humble, background. With luck, he'll consent to take the position." Then he turned back to Hornthwaite, looked him over with utterly aristocratic disdain, and said, "Why are you still here?"

Hornthwaite cast one look at Daisy, a look filled with hatred, and then looked to Lady Rutherford, who seemed to find the fan in her lap absolutely fascinating.

After a moment of deadly awkward silence, he hurried from the room.

"And now for the next matter at hand," Tristan said. "Mr. Kemble, will you proceed?"

"Thank you, your grace. I wish to address the theft that occurred at Rutherford Grange."

The spectators greeted this statement with obvious confusion. One man even said, "Didn't we just hear the end of that?"

Kemble shook his head. "I do not refer to the false

accusation made by Mr. Hornthwaite. I refer to a previous theft, carried out several years ago."

"I don't understand," Daisy said.

"You will, Miss Merriot," the duke said quietly.

"Shortly after the death of William Merriot, Baron Rutherford, his second wife stated publicly that not only would she remain as baroness, not dowager, but that the title would even pass to her own daughter, Bella Merriot, who was born Bella Dunley, as that was the name of Lady Rutherford's first husband. The baron's daughter, Margaret, his only blood offspring, would inherit nothing—neither the title nor any part of the baron's considerable holdings."

"This is all well known," Lady Rutherford said. "What need to bring it up now, after poor Daisy has already endured such a trying day?" She stood up. "We shall take our leave. Bella, walk with Daisy."

"Everyone will remain exactly where they are," Tristan declared. "Lady Rutherford, sit down."

Eyes wide, she sank into her chair once again.

"Kemble, continue."

"I was curious about the apparent details of the baron's will," Mr. Kemble said. "So I investigated the matter, seeking assistance from several colleagues in London. In particular, I wished to see a copy of the will. However, I discovered that no such document existed in the pertinent records. In fact, a very different will had been filed only a few weeks before his death."

"So Papa did make a new will at the end?" Daisy asked.

Kemble pulled a document from his leather case. "He did, and it's very clear that his only blood relation, his daughter, Margaret, was his sole heir to both the title and the estate. He made provision for his second wife to live at the estate for the rest of her life, if she chose. And he designated a thousand pounds a year to her, instead of the five hundred previously allotted. But that is all. She has no more claim to the title of baroness. She is the dowager baroness, and her daughter is Miss Bella Merriot, nee Dunley."

"Mama, tell them it cannot be true!" Bella said, her voice small and frozen in the vast room. "You're a lady. You'd never do such a thing. It would be *wrong*."

Lady Rutherford refused to look at her, and did not answer.

"However," Kemble went on. "For some reason the new will did not get filed properly. Why that is, we'll never know. Possibly it was mere oversight, or possibly someone was paid to make the mistake. I do not accuse the dowager baroness on this point." Kemble's nonaccusation hung in the air, more damning than if he'd yelled it from the rooftops.

Kemble pulled out another document, and he went on, "I do make *this* accusation. The woman calling herself Lady Rutherford produced a forged document written expressly to benefit herself and her own daughter at Margaret Merriot's expense."

"But that's impossible!" This comment came from a horrified Lord Dallmire in the audience. "Any such will must be signed and witnessed! Who would have put their names to any document that they could not be sure was genuine?"

"Excellent question," Lady Rutherford said, high color in her cheeks. "Of course the will was signed and witnessed. Lord Fothergill did us the honor. The baron, rest his soul, and I visited the Fothergill estate to take care of the matter."

"He passed away later that same year," one of the

townspeople noted. "He was very ill for a long time. There is no way to question him, either to confirm or deny what happened."

"True, he is no longer alive, and thus cannot give evidence here today. But the current Lord Fothergill is here."

A young man sitting in the third row stood up, and Daisy recognized him as the heir, the grandson of the man in question.

"Your grace," he said bowing. "Should I take my seat at the witness stand?" He seemed to regard the whole interlude as a slightly odd diversion. He was happy to help, but he clearly didn't think he had much to add.

"Yes, my lord," Tristan said. "If you would, please answer the questions this man asks."

Kemble then showed the young lord the document in question, asking if he could confirm the signature and date.

"The signature is…well, I can't rightly say. My grandfather's health affected his writing as well, and his signature may have been very shaky."

"And the date?" Mr. Kemble asked, not at all perturbed by this lack of confidence.

"It says 28 June," the man said. "No, that must be incorrect! By late May, my grandfather had taken to his bed. His visitors were very few, owing to his weakened state. He certainly would not have been able to sign a document at the end of June. He could not even sit up in bed, and he was scarcely aware of his surroundings. He lapsed into a coma and passed away not long after."

"You are mistaken, young man!" Lady Rutherford nearly shouted.

"With respect, ma'am, I am not. I spent every day at home that summer. A visit from the Baron Rutherford and you would have been an occasion I and the servants surely would have remembered. No such visit ever occurred."

The noose was tightening, and Lady Rutherford clearly knew it. One by one, her excuses failed. Bit by bit, her carefully constructed lies fell apart. She looked around the room for friendly faces, and found none. Even her daughter sat silent and shocked.

"This is all nonsense," Lady Rutherford shouted (even though Lady Rutherford *never* shouted). "Lies and deceit! I will not bear it. I will return to my home until reason shall prevail. Good day, my lords. Bella, come along, girl."

Bella Merriot's expression was ashen, but she rose on shaking limbs and wordlessly followed her mother.

Daisy watched them go, her mind overwhelmed by what had just occurred.

"My goodness, Lady Margaret," Lady Weatherby said, relishing the new mode of address. "What a scandal. And you must be so upset."

"I don't know what I am," Daisy said slowly.

"You're a baroness, first and foremost," the magistrate said, clearly shaken at the results of the makeshift trial. "To think that woman tried such a thing!"

"Monstrous," Lord Dallmire declared.

Daisy could see how the titled guests closed ranks around her, horrified by this transgression more than any other. If one person's title could be successfully stolen, why, any of them could be at risk. The rightful baroness must be supported at all costs!

And the rightful baroness was Daisy.

She was still trying to understand everything, not least that when the other observers came up to her and addressed her as *my lady* and *Lady Rutherford*, they were referring to *her*, Daisy, and no one else.

Then Poppy stepped up, and Daisy flung her arms

about her old schoolmate. "Oh, Poppy," she gasped. "It was you! You sent the dress!"

"And started quite the circus!" Poppy added. "I am glad it has ended well, but my goodness, you must have had a time."

"You've no idea," said Daisy. "But I shall tell you every last detail. How long are you here? Where are you staying? I'm at Lady Weatherby's now, and I'm sure she'll be glad to have you."

But Poppy shook her head. "I have a room at Rampant House on the main street of Lyonton. Mr. Kemble arranged it all when he contacted me and asked me to come and give evidence for you. However, I'm afraid I must leave first thing tomorrow morning, for Rose needs me in London. She was glad for me to come, of course, but it is difficult for her without a full-time companion."

"Oh, of course," Daisy said, disappointed but understanding. "You'll both have to come and visit me soon though."

"As if I could keep Rose away, after she hears what occurred—"

Interrupting the girls' talk, the duke raised his voice once more, commanding the attention of the room. "Attention, everyone! Thank you for coming, but I'm quite done with you now."

The stunned guests filed out of the ballroom, whispering among themselves. Rumors would rage through the whole area by teatime.

Daisy slipped out of the room when Tristan turned away to speak to Kemble. She didn't intend to leave—not exactly—but the thought of actually speaking to him as though nothing had happened was inconceivable. She remembered the very first time she saw him, his eyes studying her with such interest. She had felt so shy then, and she felt the same shyness returning. She needed a moment alone. So she left.

Or rather, she tried to leave. Daisy passed through the front doors and had got about twenty steps when she heard Tristan calling her name.

She turned. "I shouldn't be here." She didn't mean to say that—she had no idea what to say—but that was what came out. She took a few more steps away from Lyondale.

Tristan was distraught at the words. "You can't mean to run away, *again*."

"No," Daisy said, stopping. She looked everywhere but at him. "I don't know what I mean to do."

"Come back inside. It's getting cold. And I need to talk to you. With you, I mean."

"About what?"

"About everything."

"No, we needn't talk about anything, Tristan," she said, thinking that he'd been through far too much today to discuss a topic as fraught as their relationship. "Please understand that I'm not upset at you. I know you are my true friend, no matter what happened."

Tristan's unhappy sigh clouded the air. "Friend? That's how you think of me?"

Daisy looked down at the ground, her emotions fluttering nervously in her chest. "I…I'm not certain how to think of you."

"How about as a suitor?" he asked. "I thought I made my interest fairly plain. Or have you forgotten our night already?"

"I have forgotten nothing," she said, with a slow flush.

"Because I meant it." Tristan took her hand. "Please come back inside."

She let him hold her hand, but didn't step back toward

the house. "You never believed that I was a thief?"

He actually laughed. "Not for a moment. Your person-ality is defined by what you give, not what you take. It's one of the reasons I love you."

Daisy looked up, surprise taking her breath away for a second.

He didn't wait for her to recover. "On the balcony that night," he said, "I intended to ask you what you wanted me to do, after telling you about the whole mess with the diamond mines. I needed to know your mind, so I could offer you marriage, or—"

"You never mentioned marriage before, not even after we…" She stopped, suddenly shy.

"I was wrong," he said bluntly. "I was worried that I'd lost my financial independence, and only a strategic mar-riage would save me. And you had talked about how much you were needed at the Grange, how it was your home. And I didn't understand till too late how you were being used there, and how you took it upon yourself to hold the place together while your stepmother was squan-dering the fortune that wasn't even hers."

"So now you can make a strategic marriage," she said, feeling devastated. "To me. For I'm an heiress, and titled again." Was that all that mattered?

"What? No, Daisy. That's not it at all. Did I not tell you? The diamond mine is real! I mean, it is producing real diamonds, and I have nothing to fear about losing all my money to repay that loan. I am wealthy on my own now. Daisy," he said, taking her hands in his, "I'm not asking you to save Lyondale with your inheritance. I want you to marry me because I love you."

She found her voice. "Love?"

"Yes. It's not required for a marriage, from what I can see, but I would prefer it in mine. And I think I could eventually persuade you to love me as well."

"Oh, Tristan. It's too late for that."

He looked stricken. "Too late?"

"I already fell in love with you. Ages ago." Daisy couldn't stop from smiling as she said it.

"Oh," he said, his relief obvious. "Then you should definitely marry me."

"Is that...proper?"

A slow smile spread across his face. "Considering all the things I want to do with you, yes. Marriage would be a proper and very necessary step."

Daisy's cheeks burned at the intimation. "Tristan," she whispered. "You can't *say* things like that."

"You'll be surprised by the things I'll say when we're alone, love." Tristan held her closer, enjoying her reaction. "Remember, I'm only a lord through an accident of succession. Whereas you're a born lady and a baroness and the talk of the shire. And your family name is just as good as mine, for those who care about such things. You belong with me. And Lyondale needs a family in it."

"A family?"

"Naturally. Everyone should come. Elaine, Jacob. Bring the chickens. I don't care. Just so I have you."

Daisy smiled at the image. She paused, then said, "Yes."

His arm tightened around her, as though he wasn't quite sure what she said. "What?"

"Yes. I'd be delighted to marry you. Following a proper courtship, that is. And following an actual proposal." She frowned, thinking. "I think everything may have got a bit jumbled up, although I did enjoy some parts very much."

"Then let's address the first matter. I can court you?"

She nodded decisively. "Yes."

He gave her a delighted smile. "Excellent. Now, can I kiss you, to seal the bargain?"

"Out here?"

"No one's watching," he said, his voice teasing and challenging.

She tilted her head up. "Then do it, before I change my mind."

At the touch of his lips on hers, Daisy knew she would never change her mind about Tristan Brooks, the very surprising Duke of Lyon. She did love him, and she grew dizzy at the thought of marrying him, so she could be with him every day.

When the kiss ended, she heard voices, and turned to see *everyone* watching: maids and footmen and the majordomo and Poppy and Mrs. Bloomfield and the Weatherbys and Mr. Kemble, whose pleased smile she could see even from this distance.

But she was too happy to be embarrassed. Instead, she put her arms around Tristan and whispered, "We've been caught. You are thoroughly compromised, and you're stuck with me now."

He just grinned and said, "Good. That was what I hoped for." He put his arm around her and led her back inside. "Come, love. We have plans to make."

Chapter 19

❀ ❁ ❀

NEEDLESS TO SAY, LIFE CHANGED immediately for Daisy, who was now formally Lady Margaret once again, just as she'd been expected to be when she was younger. Lady Weatherby, who had become quite motherly toward her, insisted that Daisy must rest after the ordeal. So she went back to the Weatherbys' home and sat with Mrs. Bloomfield as she tried to digest all that she'd learned that day.

"Papa always meant for me to be his heir," Daisy said wonderingly. "He expected me to become baroness and take on Rutherford Grange and run it as he did."

"You did run it," Mrs. Bloomfield reminded her. "You acted as owner and estate manager and scullery maid, doing whatever was needed to keep things operating well. I'm sure your father would be very proud…after he got done being furious at your stepmother for cheating you."

"I still can't believe she really did that. Papa was going to take care of her! A thousand pounds a year, plus a home for life. And of course she could have married again, and Bella is going to make a splendid match no matter what. Or *was* going to."

"Perhaps your stepmother feared you'd take her funds away…just as she did to you. People always seem to think that others are like them. Good-hearted people think everyone is good-hearted. Greedy people think everyone is greedy."

"I shall tell her that she may stay at the Grange if she likes, when we go back tomorrow."

Mrs. Bloomfield frowned. "You'd let her stay, after what she did?"

"Well, it was Papa's intention to give her a home. And I may soon find myself moving to Lyondale." Daisy smiled, recalling Tristan's kiss after he requested the right to court her. When he escorted her to the carriage, he whispered that their courtship would be proper, but not a day longer than necessary.

"Yes, you and your duke do seem cozy together," Mrs. Bloomfield said. "Your mother was never able to sit you down and tell you the sort of thing mothers tell their daughters when it comes to courtship and marriage…and the night of the wedding. Shall I take some time soon to do that with you?"

"Um…it would not be strictly…new information at this point," Daisy whispered, blushing furiously.

Her sometime teacher raised an elegant eyebrow. "I see," she replied. "Well, no doubt that fact will hasten your suitor's proposal."

"I do hope so."

Mrs. Bloomfield chuckled. "Oh, to be young again. Now you rest, dear. Lady Weatherby and I shall deal with any callers. I thought we should have Poppy to dinner tonight, so she doesn't have to dine alone at an inn. And tomorrow morning we'll go to Rutherford Grange and settle things with the dowager baroness."

The next morning, Tristan came to Lady Weatherby's in his own coach. Daisy and Mrs. Bloomfield climbed in, and the driver started down the road that led to Rutherford Grange.

"Are you ready to go home, my lady?" Tristan asked her.

Daisy nodded. "It will be good to see the Grange again, and see Elaine and Jacob and the others. And to speak to Lady Ru—my stepmother, that is. I have many questions for her."

"And you'll have reinforcements should you need them," Tristan assured her, leaning across the coach to take her hand for a moment, "though you are a force all on your own."

"Well spoken, your grace," Mrs. Bloomfield said, with a smile at Daisy.

When the coach arrived at the Grange, the place was strangely quiet. But the moment Daisy stepped out of the carriage, the servants and local farmers seemed to pop up like mushrooms. Everyone bowed or curtsied to *Lady Margaret*...except for Elaine, who enfolded her in a hug and sobbed with joy to see her.

"Stop now, wife," Jacob muttered, though he was trying not to laugh. "You're spilling your tears all over our rightful baroness."

"Oh, I'm just so relieved to see you again, child! And so happy to hear that right will be done and the true heiress will be in charge of the Grange, just as it ought to be."

"I do hope that everything will go smoothly," Daisy said. "But first we must speak with my stepmother."

"I've been in the kitchens all morning," Elaine said. "Where's the girl who sees to the upstairs? Eliza, come here!"

A slender housemaid with dark hair and a worried expression hurried up to Daisy and Tristan. "I'm here, my lady, your grace."

"We are here to speak with the dowager," Tristan said.

"And I am not in a mood to wait. Show us to her immediately."

"I cannot do that, your grace," the servant said nervously.

"Whatever she may have ordered you to do," Tristan said, more kindly, "ignore it. I will see to it that you suffer no punishments for disobeying her."

"Oh, sir, that is not what I meant." Eliza looked tormented. "You must understand, I cannot show you to her ladyship because her ladyship is not here!"

"What?"

"She is gone, as are a few trunks and the carriage and the pair of chestnuts. The chestnuts were our best horses."

Tristan scowled, and Daisy knew why. She hadn't dreamed that the woman would be so cowardly as to flee.

"We must locate the vicar," Mrs. Bloomfield said suddenly. "Though it may be too late."

"Blast, you're right!"

Tristan ordered one of the men nearby to ride to the village immediately. But Daisy already had a sinking feeling that Hornthwaite would be gone as well.

But then she decided that she could only do what was in her own power to do. So that very day, she set about making Rutherford Grange a proper home once more. She and Tristan had discussed the fate of the Grange, and agreed that the two estates could be more effectively managed as one for the time being, with Daisy offering discreet supervision to a new manager. Tristan, rather brilliantly, suggested that the house itself could serve as a school...until such a time when one of Tristan and Daisy's heirs would take possession of it, just as a tier would eventually take on Lyondale for their own. This vision of the future was so dazzling that Daisy had nearly wept with joy.

The maids showed great zeal in packing the dowager's things out of her suite and moving Daisy's few items in. They cleaned the room and fluffed pillows and lit a huge fire in the fireplace to air the room out.

Daisy walked through each room with Eliza, who wrote down every little thing that Daisy wanted to be attended to.

"We'll need more staff, my lady. The baroness—not you, *her*—let so many go over the years."

"I shall correct that," Daisy said. "The Grange deserves to shine again. Let it be known in the village that I want to hire several servants. Maids, footmen, stablehands, others too. They can come tomorrow morning and I'll interview them."

"You, your ladyship? That's a job for the housekeeper."

"Ah, but we don't have a housekeeper yet!"

"Elaine should be housekeeper," Eliza said. "She does it all anyway."

"So she does! I'll ask her if she'll accept the position."

They came to Bella's room. With a sigh, Daisy pushed the door open. She was sad that she couldn't have at least spoken to Bella one last time. She had seemed truly shocked at her mother's actions.

"Who's there?" someone asked. "Is it morning? I didn't sleep all night."

Daisy went still at hearing a voice from the darkened room.

"*Bella?*" she asked. "They left you?"

"Left me?" Bella sat up in bed, awake all at once. "Who left? What's happened?"

Daisy explained it to her while Eliza ran to fetch a tray of toast and strong tea. Bella was completely unaware of her mother's plans, and horrified to hear that she had been abandoned without a word.

"She's gone?" Bella kept repeating at intervals, staring at nothing while she hugged her knees. "Is she going to send for me? What am I to do?"

As the day went on, it was discovered that both Mr. Hornthwaite and the dowager were indeed long gone, along with the rest of the church funds, and several remaining valuable items from the Grange. The duke sent riders along all the roads in search of them, and notified the magistrate of the situation. Daisy wasn't sure she even wanted them found, though.

As Daisy and a few other servants suspected, the dowager had been selling off items to fund the creation of her and Bella's wardrobe, as part of her plan to marry Bella off to the highest titled gentleman she could find. It was further discovered that the dowager and the vicar had been lovers for years, a fact which Daisy hoped she could magically forget as soon as possible.

That chapter in her life was better off closed forever.

The new chapter was much fancier than she'd been used to. Within a few days, she found herself with a lady's maid hired from nearby, who managed to retool the old baroness's abandoned wardrobe into several lovely items for Daisy. Bella showed no interest in acquiring a lady's maid of her own, or in visitors, or in anything. Daisy was growing worried about her continuing melancholy. Her shock was understandable, but Bella seemed to be bracing for yet another blow.

There was only one more task Daisy had to do, which was to visit Tabitha and tell her all that happened. She managed to slip away one afternoon and stroll through the quiet woods. A few birds called in the upper branches, and a squirrel pursued her suspiciously, but other than that, Daisy was alone.

To think that she'd once feared being lonely while walking through these same woods not long ago! Now she had all the company she could manage, and the most desired suitor in England visiting her every day. She sang under her breath, utterly pleased with the way things turned out.

Then she saw Tabitha's cottage, and hurried toward it, calling her friend's name.

The old lady opened the door and leaned out. "What's this? Thought we spirited you away from here, girl."

"You did, but I'm back, and oh, Tabitha, everything is grand!"

"Hmpf," Tabitha said, shaking her head. "Told you it would be."

"Everything has changed top to bottom. I have so much to tell you..." And Daisy told Tabitha every last detail, from hiding in the pumpkin cart to returning to Wildwood Hall, to coming back for the impromptu trial that revealed far more than Daisy ever dreamed.

"Well, good thing he took the left turning, as I told him," Tabitha murmured under her breath. "No point in arranging all the pieces when the pieces get notions of their own."

"What?" Daisy asked, confused. She wondered if the old woman was not as sharp as she used to be.

"Nothing, child. I'm just so happy to hear of your good fortune."

"That reminds me. I'd like you to share my luck. Won't you consider coming to live closer to Lyondale, or the Grange? I worry about you living all alone in the woods here. Half the time, folks can't even find your house! Tristan told me he sent men to look for you after I'd run away, and no one remembered where you lived! Isn't that odd?"

"Oh, very odd. But that's how I like it, child." Tabitha laughed. "I'll stay here, and quite happily. But a visit from little Daisy will always be welcome."

"I should hope so!" Daisy said. Being a lady would never keep her from the friends who had helped her when she had nothing.

By the time the sun was setting, Daisy had to return to the Grange. Her stomach rumbled when she got closer to home, and by long habit, she headed toward the kitchen door.

"Oh, no, my lady!" Elaine called, seeing her approach. "You use the front like a proper baroness!"

Smiling, Daisy obeyed, veering to the grand front entrance. Elaine and Jacob wouldn't even allow her to pick up a dusting cloth at Rutherford Grange anymore.

In fact, she was bowed and curtseyed to by literally everyone who came into view, from the stable boys to the villagers to the visiting gentry (who visited *constantly*). Daisy had to keep asking Elaine to bake more cakes for tea, and for more dishes to be made up for the ever-expanding dinners.

Bella never joined Daisy in visiting with guests. She haunted the Grange, lost and lonely and bereft. Every day that passed brought no word from her mother, and the girl was obviously torn in pieces about it. Daisy reflected that the erstwhile Lady Rutherford had used Bella for her own ends, Bella had truly loved her mother, and now she was suffering for it.

Daisy spent the visiting hours on her own, receiving yet more guests, including a young gentleman who seemed quite taken with Lady Caroline, who was there with her mother. Lady Weatherby commented that Bella was missed, and Daisy concurred, saying that nothing she could do seemed to get through.

"Then try again, dear. Miss Bella is probably very frightened."

So after she bid her guests goodbye, she went in search of Bella once more. She found Bella in a small sitting room. She held an embroidery project on her lap, but she was staring out the window at the lifeless late autumn landscape.

"Bella, you know that you are welcome to receive guests with me. Lady Weatherby was asking after you—I think she fears you'll make yourself ill with melancholy. You should join us tomorrow. It's warmer there than in here, if nothing else."

Bella sat in the chair, her manner stilted and chill, the mortification plain on her face. "I cannot," she declared, in a tiny voice. "Now that it is known what Mama did to you...to us...she stole your legacy, Daisy, I mean, my Lady Margaret..."

"Call me Daisy."

"How can I call you anything?" Bella asked morosely. "I am ashamed to even be in the same county as you. You must hate me. *He* must hate me. Oh, Lord, I'll never be able to look him in the eyes again."

"The duke has a very forgiving nature," Daisy said.

"Not the duke." Bella waved one hand, the first gesture she'd made, the first sign she was human and not a doll. "I refer to Mr. Kemble."

"Mr. Kemble?"

"He's so kind and so intelligent. He talked to me, really *talked* to me, and didn't go on about my pretty face or my blue eyes. I know my eyes are blue! But Mr. Kemble asked me what I thought about things and it was wonderful...but I must be like the lowliest fly to him now."

"Wait. You have feelings for Mr. *Kemble*?"

"Oh, Daisy, I'm afraid I love him." Bella looked at her

with gigantic eyes, ripe with tears. "Mama would never approve, so I said nothing. But every time I could be near him…" She sighed wistfully.

"My goodness, Bella! Does he know?"

"I pray not! Better that I can disappear before there is a chance that we cross paths again. Not that it is likely. For I now find myself quite outside society. I'll be shunned. No more invitations for me. No one will want to associate with the dowry-less daughter of a disgraced widow. They'll all think I'm looking to steal a title for myself."

"Do you desire a title?"

Bella shook her head firmly. "I thought I did, but I know now that it was Mama's wish for me. She was always talking of it to me, telling me that it was what I wanted. But I never wanted that. *She* did."

"Oh, Bella. I am so sorry for you. You must be overwhelmed."

"I will endure it," Bella said stoically. "I do have one request, if you can grant it."

"What?"

"Allow me to stay here for another week or so? Just until I can make arrangements…"

"Arrangements for what?"

"I…I don't know." Bella looked stricken. She was a gently bred young lady who only ever planned on becoming a gentleman's wife. She had no skills and no connections, and no ability to make her way in the world. "What do you advise, Daisy?"

"I advise that you stay here for now, and if I marry the duke before you decide what to do, you should come live with us at Lyondale. We have been sisters by our parents' marriage, but we will be sisters in spirit now. You should not be punished for your mother's misdeeds. Tristan will agree with me—you will always have a home where I call home."

"I don't deserve it," Bella whispered.

"We can argue about that later," Daisy said. "Now come. Dry your cheeks off before your tears roll down and stain that pretty silk dress. And I think that you should not run away before seeing Mr. Kemble one more time, for I suspect that he may have something to say to you as well!"

In fact, Daisy was sure of it, for love seemed to be in the air.

Epilogue

❀ ⚬Ɡ⚬ ❀

Dear Rosalind and Poppy,

My darlings, you'll be getting a formal invitation very soon, but I cannot wait to share my news. I shall be married in the new year, and I beg you—out of love and our childhood bonds—to attend, despite the likely January weather. As an incentive, I will tell you that Camellia has already agreed, Heather lives only in the next county, and even Mrs. Bloomfield is coming, as the school will be closed for several weeks while the roof is being repaired. Remember that mighty oak in the front lawn? She wrote recently and told me it finally fell during a windstorm just before Christmas. Thank goodness all the girls had left to be with their families by then!

You will stay at Lyondale, the home of the Duke of Lyon, who is my fiancé...

Daisy loved writing that part, and she finished the letter swiftly to get it to the post.

As planned, the wedding took place shortly after the beginning of the new year. The very proper Lady Margaret refused to be married in a steeple-less church, so Lord Lyon directed a storm of both money and effort to see the building repaired as quickly as possible.

Naturally, the new vicar conducted the ceremony. Mr. Langdon was a grey-haired, severe-looking but gentle man who'd served as chaplain in Tristan's army company, and he'd accepted the duke's invitation to serve as the Lyonton vicar. He was already proving to be a good choice.

The ceremony was attended by, well, everyone who could manage to cram into the space. The bride wore a lovely dress in a pale blue, carrying a bouquet of white flowers that had been grown under glass, for it was now the dead of winter. She also wore a necklace of diamonds—real diamonds—from the mine Tristan invested in, the mine now producing an astonishing number of quality stones every week, the result of workers who were well-compensated for their effort. The proceeds were astronomical, and a few new accountants had been hired at Tristan's London bank to handle the flood of incoming business. Tristan had given her the necklace that morning, and Daisy had merely stared at it for a while, watching the stones sparkle and flash in the sunlight. The center stone was larger than the rest, and tinted an unusual pale yellow, setting off the whole necklace. Tristan told her that the jeweler who made it had already named it: the Duchess diamond.

"It will be in our family for generations, if I have my way," Tristan said.

At the wedding, Daisy was flanked by her maids of honor, her four school friends from Wildwood, who also carried flowers and wore smiles as big as the sun. Miss Bella Merriot watched from the family pew, sitting next to Mrs. Bloomfield.

Daisy and Tristan exchanged their vows, and then he kissed her as if he'd never got the chance before. Beneath the sensations of love and joy, Daisy reflected that there was something to be said for kissing where others could see—now she was irrevocably tied to Tristan. Her wildest dream had come true.

After the ceremony, everyone in the village was invited to celebrate at Lyondale, which had thrown open its doors once more to provide food and music and amusement to anyone who entered.

Daisy took a few moments to escape the well wishes of her neighbors to gather in a small room with her school friends.

There they were, loyal and steadfast and delighted at Daisy's good fortune. Dark-haired Rose and blonde-locked Poppy sat together on a long couch, while the more bookish Camellia stood in front of the bookcase, scanning the many titles, and Heather peered out the windows at the snowy fields beyond.

Heather turned at Daisy's entrance, and rushed up to her. "My word, Daisy, I mean your grace, you're like a fairy-tale princess in that gown, and with that necklace. You surely don't need that old pasteboard crown now!"

"I wish I could see your jewels, Daisy," Rose added wistfully. "I remember Mama wearing her diamond ring, and it sparkled so in the sunlight."

"Well, multiply that memory a thousand times, and you'll get a sense of Daisy's necklace," Poppy told her, giggling. "But of course it's not nearly so sparkly as Daisy's smile. I do believe she is in love with her duke!"

"Very much so," Daisy admitted, without a trace of embarrassment.

Camellia shut the book she was holding. "I think that it's not quite fashionable to be in love with one's husband, at least among society."

Poppy rolled her eyes. "What nonsense. That's just because so few members of society marry for love."

"Well, *I'm* going to marry for love," Heather declared.

"I'm not going to marry at all," Poppy countered. "That is, until Rose gets married."

The girl on the couch sighed, saying, "That will never happen. Who marries a blind girl?"

"A man with good sense," Camellia said quickly. "For she wouldn't ever think him ugly!"

The girls all laughed, but as the chatter continued onto other topics, Daisy felt a little sad. She wanted all her friends to be as blissfully content as she was. She hoped that they would find their matches soon, because they were all deserving of love. In fact, everyone was deserving of love, even her horrid stepmother, who was evidently in love with the ex-vicar Hornthwaite. She hoped that even they were happy together...somewhere *very* far away.

There was another couple that looked to be quite content. Bella stood next to Jack Kemble the whole day, doting on his every word as the villagers came up to him and congratulated him on his efforts to clear Daisy's name. Only when the old baroness was mentioned did Bella look away, and Jack hurriedly changed the subject to something more pleasant. He still sat in a chair most of the day, but he looked far better than he had when he arrived at Lyondale, and Dr. Stelton declared he would be fit and healthy by April...which was not coincidentally when he and Bella planned to get married and move to London, where Jack was going to set up a law practice.

Lord Lyon rarely left his wife's side the whole day, though he did sneak her away from the crowd of well-wishers for a moment.

He led her upstairs and out to the balcony.

"It's too cold to stay out here, Tristan," Daisy said.

He put his arms around her. "You can't possibly think

I'd let you get chilly, your grace."

She laughed. "I won't get used to that."

"That's what I thought, when they started calling me your grace." He bent to kiss her lightly, then said, "It's amazing though, what one can get used to."

"I will get used to you kissing me," Daisy whispered. "Though you really ought to learn to do so when we're alone."

"We are alone," he said. "As you say, no one's outside in the cold. So can I kiss you again?"

Daisy didn't take much convincing. Tristan kissed her again. A distant round of shouts and teasing applause suggested that they weren't alone after all, but Daisy kissed him back all the same. The lesson about waiting until they were alone could be discussed later.

Much later.

ABOUT THE AUTHOR

Elizabeth Cole is a romance writer with a penchant for history. Her stories draw upon her deep affection for the British Isles, action movies, medieval fantasies, and even science fiction. She now lives in a small house in a big city with a cat, a snake, and a rather charming gentleman. When not writing, she is usually curled in a corner reading...or watching costume dramas or things that explode. And yes, she believes in love at first sight.